※ ※ ※ ※ ※ ※ ※ ※ ※ ※ ※ ※ ※ ※ ※ ※ ※ ※ ※

HARLEQUIN HEARTWARMING

Aimée Thurlo

Homespun Christmas

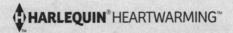

Recycling programs
for this product may
not exist in your area.

ISBN-13: 978-0-373-36648-4

HOMESPUN CHRISTMAS

Copyright © 2013 by Aimée and David Thurlo

Printed in U.S.A.

www.Harlequin.com

AIMÉE THURLO

Aimée Thurlo is an internationally known bestselling author of mystery and romantic suspense novels. She's the winner of a Career Achievement Award from *RT Book Reviews,* a New Mexico Book Award in contemporary fiction and a Willa Cather Award in the same category.

Aimée was born in Havana, Cuba, and lives with her husband of forty-three years in Corrales, New Mexico, in a rural neighborhood filled with horses, alpacas, camels and other assorted livestock. Her husband, David, was raised on the Navajo Indian Nation. His background and cultural knowledge inspire many of her stories.

Dedication

With special thanks to Sydney Abernathy
for her help. You're a terrific assistant!

Acknowledgments

To Michele Kiser, who helped me by sharing
her knowledge of Churro Sheep.
Also to State Senator Steve Komadina, M.D.,
who allowed me to get to know his camels and
learn about their wool. You guys were terrific!

CHAPTER ONE

INDEPENDENCE, NEW MEXICO, was buzzing with the news. The bad boy was back in town.

Joshua Nez had captured the hearts of half the girls in high school. She hadn't been immune, even though they'd run in different circles. Myka Solis smiled, thinking of those carefree days. She'd been head cheerleader, the quarterback's girlfriend, and a straight-A student. Joshua had been trouble with a capital *T.*

Although her parents hadn't approved of Joshua, living next door to each other had made avoiding him almost impossible. She'd soon learned that just being around Joshua added a high voltage charge to everything. He'd followed no one's rules except his own.

Sophie Boyer, her neighbor from across the street, called out to her as she hurried up the driveway.

"I understand he's coming in with a rental van," she said, catching her breath.

No need to ask who she meant.

Like Myka, Sophie was dark haired, petite and twenty-eight years old.

"Makes sense," Myka said. "He'll have to sort through his dad's things and pack up everything he doesn't want to keep. Considering Adam had a lot of stuff, that's going to be a tough job. I thought I'd offer to help."

Sophie smiled.

"No, don't go there, Sophie. It's just the right thing to do. From what I've heard, Navajos don't like being around the personal possessions of someone who has passed on. I figured I could help him box the stuff he doesn't want and give it to the church."

"Yeah, a number of people around here could use the donations," Sophie said, nodding somberly. "You and I are the lucky ones, despite the fact that my only job is nursing Mom. At least you have your online business while you take care of your parents' home."

Sophie's mother, Millie Boyer, had just turned sixty-seven. She'd broken her hip after a fall last winter and Sophie came home from Albuquerque. As her mom's primary caregiver, Sophie was paid a small sum by the state, and between that and her mother's social security, they got by.

Myka suspected there was a lot more to Sophie's story, but she hadn't pried. For now, the details of Sophie's life in the city remained a mystery.

"Did you get a chance to talk to Joshua at Adam's—I was going to say graveside service, but it was a burial, right?"

Myka nodded. "When his grandfather died years ago, Joshua told me burials take place as quickly as possible. It's like the belongings of the deceased, a lot of Navajos believe it's dangerous to be around the body, too."

"How come?"

"Something about the person's ghost, I think," Myka said, bunching the edge of her shirt and tugging nervously at it. Seeing Sophie glance down and taking note of it, she stopped instantly.

"I'm sorry, Myka. I shouldn't have brought it up. I'm sure this brings back all kinds of memories for you. Losing your husband so young…"

"Tanner's been gone two years." Myka took a deep, shaky breath. "It doesn't hurt as much as it used to, but I try to avoid things that remind me so directly…of what happened."

"I understand," her neighbor said softly.

Once again, there was that haunting undertone in Sophie's voice. Myka suspected that life hadn't been particularly kind to Sophie, either.

"Everything is so different these days," Sophie added. "An entire generation is disappearing. Mom warned me that things were going downhill here, but I didn't realize the magnitude of it until I saw the town for myself."

Their town, Independence, was dying, and too many of their residents had left already. For the past half century, theirs had been a company town. Independence Vehicle Accessories, IVA, hadn't been the only domestic supplier of steering wheels and other vehicle interior "hardware" in the nation—far from it—but the plant's employees had taken special pride in their work. Then, eighteen months ago, the economy took a nose dive, and IVA shut down.

Eventually the auto industry had been bailed out, but unfortunately for the residents of Independence, IVA's jobs had been outsourced overseas. Now the ties that had made them such a strong, vibrant community were slowly and systematically breaking down.

"By the way, whatever happened to Adam's dog, Bear?" Sophie asked, cutting into her thoughts.

"He took off the same day Adam died, though that couldn't have been the reason he left—Adam was in the hospital at the time. I've put out food and water, but it hasn't been touched, except by the birds and stray cats," Myka said. "I promised Adam I'd take care of Bear. He was my responsibility."

"He'll come back. Same way he just showed up one day," Sophie reassured her.

Myka hoped so. "The two sure hit it off instantly. Adam said that Bear chose his owners, not the other way around."

"Do you think Josh will adopt the dog—if he comes back?"

Myka smiled. "I don't think he even knows about Bear, but I hope so. He's close to two hundred pounds, though, so it's a commitment." The mastiff and pit bull mix was really incredibly gentle.

"If Josh doesn't want him, what'll happen?"

"I was hoping he'd move in with me."

"Josh or Bear?" Sophie gave her a wicked smile.

"The dog," Myka said, laughing.

"I'll keep an eye out for the big guy." Sophie took a step toward her house. "I better go check on Mom. She's having one of her bad days. Thank heavens for her knitting."

"The sweaters she's been making for my shop are just gorgeous. Once I post the photo online, I usually have a buyer within a day or two."

"Her skill and your homespun yarns make an unbeatable combination," Sophie said. "I'm doing my part by tweeting about your site every chance I get, too."

"Thanks!"

As Sophie left, Myka glanced down the street for maybe the tenth time that day. Bertie from the post office had said that Joshua would be back this morning, and she always knew the latest. Joshua had come home last week to bury his father, but he'd returned to San Francisco almost immediately afterward to finish moving out of his apartment. This time, supposedly, he was coming home to stay—at least for a while.

Joshua's blue pickup was still parked over in his dad's driveway.

She looked over at the simple, well-maintained wood-framed house next door. It would be good to see Joshua again, at the home where he'd grown up. He'd be a reminder of the old days when her biggest worries had been her grade point average and keeping Tanner from getting past first base.

That all seemed like an eternity ago, long before her perfect life had shattered into a million pieces.

Sitting on her stool beside her low wheel, she picked up where she'd left off spinning the wool into yarn, working automatically, drawing out the fleece to the desired thickness and tension.

A strong gust swept across the porch, carrying a cloud of dust and sand. The wail of the wind through the trees, like that of a crying child, added to the sense of desolation. If the downward spiral continued, in another six months Independence would be nothing more than a ghost town.

The yellow van driving slowly up the street gave her a reason to smile. Maybe that was Joshua at last.

Seconds later, the van slowed at the end of the street, turned, then came to a stop in front of her house.

Joshua climbed out. He was a handsome man, around six foot one with a broad chest and a leggy stride. Today, he was wearing a black windbreaker, a dark blue T-shirt and jeans.

Myka stood up, stepped off the porch and went down the flagstone walk to meet him, reminding herself to remain casual and not walk too fast.

He strode toward her, a ghost of a smile on his lips. "Myka, I'm glad to see you again. I didn't get the chance to talk to you when we laid Dad to rest. You were there, then you were gone."

His dark eyes shimmered with mystery and the scar that cut across his left eyebrow made him look even more masculine. "You had others waiting for you and I didn't want to intrude."

"You wouldn't have been intruding," he said. "So what brings you back to the old neighborhood? Did you move back in with your parents?" He glanced at the mailbox.

"For now, kind of," she said. "After Dad retired, my parents took to the road in their RV and asked me to look after the place. I jumped at the chance. Betty, Tanner's sister, is living at our old house in town."

"So you came back to heal in a place that held only good memories," he said with a nod. "Makes sense."

"It felt strange at first, with Mom and Dad gone, but your dad was a terrific neighbor. I really miss him."

"He never mentioned he wasn't well. If he had, I would have come home sooner." Joshua rubbed the back of his neck with one hand.

"He didn't think it was serious. He only went in for some tests. He expected to be back home after a few days. His death was a shock to all of us."

Joshua glanced at his dad's house, then at her. "I'd heard about Tanner's accident at the plant. Getting taken by surprise with news like that…I know how it feels," he said and gave her an impromptu hug.

The second she felt his strong arms around her, Myka's pulse began to race. That flicker of life took her by surprise. Unsettled by her reaction, she stepped back.

She stared at the ground for a moment, breathed deeply and looked back up at him. "At least Tanner was spared having to see what has happened to the community. Independence is in trouble."

He acknowledged the real estate signs lining the street. "I've seen things like this on the news, but it's different when it hits home."

"IVA held the town together. Luxury—

American Style." Myka took another deep breath. "Now that IVA's gone, the only way we're going to survive is by reinventing ourselves."

He smiled. "So you're still an optimist?"

She shrugged. "What else can you do?"

"You'll be staying here, then?"

"I'll try to stick it out," she said, "but right now Independence feels like a home with all the children gone. I keep hoping a new industry will move in. The plant is just sitting there, the buildings empty."

"I passed by on the way in," he said with a nod.

Her sheep began to gather along the north end of the pasture, which stopped at the front corner of the house. Here, the semi-rural neighborhood was still zoned for certain livestock. Joshua smiled and went over to the fence. They readily let him pet them. His touch was gentle and calmed the sheep even as they clustered around.

This was a side of Joshua few ever got to see, particularly back in the day.

"I feel as if I've stepped back in time," he said. "You still have your *Churro* sheep. More head than ever, too, if I remember correctly."

"You bet. They've allowed me to fend off

the bill collectors. I spin and dye the wool and then sell the yarn on the internet through my store, Myka's Wooly Dreams."

"Now that's the Myka I remember. You always had a knack for turning a bad situation around."

"Life doesn't give us much of a choice sometimes," Myka said softly. "So what are your plans?"

"I don't know," he answered. "Not yet anyway. I need time to figure out my next move. I had to close my architectural firm. My partners and I couldn't make it work. The downturn in housing hit our company hard. We hung on as long as we could, but in the end, we all knew what had to be done."

"Yes, I'm sorry, I had heard about that. Every time Bertie visits her daughter Andrea in San Francisco she brings back the latest news." She felt helpless and didn't know what else to say about his career, so she changed the topic. "I gather you and Andrea remained good friends."

He nodded. "She and I would get together for lunch when we could and catch up. It was good to see a familiar face from time to time."

"And now, here we are," Myka said.

"Looks like I'll be fixing up Dad's house

and putting it on the market." He stared straight out at the for sale signs and didn't so much as blink. "If you hear of anyone who might be interested, let me know."

"It's really a buyer's market right now," she warned, even though she knew she didn't have to.

"I'll do what I can to spruce up the place and see how it goes."

Life's hard knocks appeared to have toughened him and that only added to the raw masculinity that was so much a part of Joshua.

She tore her gaze from his and walked back to her porch. She climbed the three steps.

"That's one of my nicest memories of home—you spinning yarn out on the porch," he said, walking to the porch rail.

"This is when I'm happiest. But my days here are numbered unless something more lucrative comes along. I'm a good bookkeeper—one of the last people IVA let go. Despite that, I haven't been able to find anything in the area, not even over in Painted Canyon, and they've got that big mining operation just north of the city."

"If I was still in business, I would have offered you a job," he said.

"Running your own company was your

dream even before college. It must have been tough walking away."

Joshua looked out across the valley. "It was, and starting over is going to be even tougher. After you've had your own company and called the shots, it's harder to work for someone else."

She stood beside him with the porch rail between them. "We each got what we wanted, but we just couldn't hold on to it."

"Myka, I'm sorry life's been so rough on you," he said, brushing his knuckles across her cheek.

His unexpected touch startled her. As she saw herself reflected in his gaze, she stepped back. She didn't want pity.

"If you need anything, don't hesitate to ask," she blurted. "Sometimes just talking to someone can make things easier."

"Thanks," he said. "It was good seeing you here today, Myka, but I better get busy."

"Before you leave, I need to tell you about Bear," she said, and explained about his father's missing pet.

He shook his head. "This is the first time I've heard about Dad having a pet. I hope he's okay, but I can't keep a dog. I don't know how long I'll be staying, or even where I'll be living six months from now."

"Then if it's okay with you, I'd like to keep him. Will you let me know if he comes back or if you see him? You can't miss a dog that big. He's really a sweetheart, so don't let his appearance or his bark put you off."

"It was Dad's house. If he comes back and thinks I'm an intruder…"

"He won't bite," she said quickly. Then she added, "He might sit on you, though. He did that to Daniel Medeiros once. Just knocked him to the ground and kept him there until Adam came home. He's not dangerous, but I should warn you, he does drool a lot."

Joshua stared at her.

She laughed. "Don't worry about it. A dog his size doesn't sneak up on anyone. When he's running, he sounds more like a pony than a dog, and you can hear him breathing ten feet away. If you see him, just call me— your dad kept my number beside the phone in the living room. Oh, and Bear can be bribed. Carry some dog treats with you. Your dad has a jar of them in the kitchen."

"So now I'm a dog trainer?"

"Guess so," she said. "Welcome home, Joshua."

He laughed.

"If you need any help sorting, carrying or moving stuff, let me know," she said, pointing to the van. "I figure you'll want to haul a lot of your father's things away."

"The van's full of stuff from my apartment in San Francisco. As far as Dad's things, Dan's coming over later and we'll handle it."

They walked back to the van together, and after he got inside and started the engine, he glanced at her through the open window. "Remember that blue sweater you made for me right before I left for college?"

She smiled. "Yeah. It was my first attempt at making something wearable."

"I've still got it, and it's as warm as ever." Without waiting for her to answer, he drove forward, then backed into the next driveway down.

She watched him as he propped open the front door of the house, then began to carry in boxes from the van. Although she could tell by the way he lifted them they were heavy, he walked with unwavering purpose.

Life might have knocked Joshua down, but something told her he'd soon be on his feet, stronger than ever.

AN HOUR LATER, Myka walked to the three-sided loafing shed in the backyard where she kept the grain. All ten sheep came to the fence, used to the routine.

After scooping grain into the feeders, she noticed a white butterfly perched on the edge of the welded pipe fence. It adapted to the breeze and, against all odds, remained where it was.

She wasn't sure how long she'd stood there, watching, when a woman's voice called her name. Myka turned her head and saw Liza Jenner standing at the corral gate. She waved and walked over to greet her friend.

In her early fifties, Liza was one of the town's most experienced weavers. "Do you have any more of that spice-colored yarn left, Myka? The Spinning Wheels are meeting at my place tonight and we're out of it for our Blankets for Warriors service project."

"Come on. I've got some skeins in a box inside," Myka said, unlocking the gate and letting Liza into the yard. "Has your daughter heard anything yet from that company in Las Cruces?"

"Yeah… She didn't get the job. Unofficially, she was told they don't like to hire anyone who's been out of work that long. Have you ever heard of anything so crazy?"

Myka shook her head. "When Robyn worked in IVA's public relations department, everyone loved her. That's why she got such glowing recommendations. I can't believe the trouble she's having landing a job."

"She took this last rejection really hard, but our get-together tonight will cheer her up," Liza said. "You coming?"

"I'll be there." She looked back at the butterfly. If such a fragile creature could adapt to summer heat and strong winds, why couldn't they be just as adaptable? "You know what this town's problem is? We're stuck in a holding pattern, clinging to our memories of what used to be—but that's not good enough anymore."

"You have something in mind?" Liza said as they walked toward the house.

"Yes. Tonight, instead of just talking about the projects we're working on, let's do something different. Ask everyone to bring a friend or their spouse and we'll brainstorm on how to breathe life back into Independence. We dream up new colors, patterns and designs all the time. Why don't we put some of that creativity to work and see what we can come up with for our town?"

"I'll get busy making calls."

She'd ask Joshua to come, too. It would be good for him to get away from all the memories the house still held.

Liza left five minutes later, and Myka finished taking care of the sheep.

Her mind was racing. Spur-of-the-moment ideas didn't always pan out, but they had to try *something*. Endless waiting for the economy to turn around just wasn't working. For the town's sake, they had to find a new direction, and more important, a reason to hope.

CHAPTER TWO

JOSHUA STOOD ON his back porch, ignoring the dust that was blowing in the afternoon breeze and watching Myka, her hair swirling and falling in soft waves around her shoulders, tend her sheep. The girl he'd known since third grade had grown up and was more beautiful than ever.

He couldn't remember a time he hadn't been drawn to Myka, the good girl who always had something nice to say, and who'd stuck up for him when others tried to put him down. She was a natural leader, never quite falling in step with the rest of the girls, yet seemingly unaware of her own influence.

The fact that she'd eventually married Tanner was no surprise—they'd been a couple most of the way through high school. What *did* surprise him was Myka's loyalty to this dying town. Why was she still here? What was she waiting for?

He wasn't a betting man, but from the

looks of it, he'd say that the odds were definitely against the place.

"You gonna stand out here all day?" Daniel asked, coming out of the house.

"Nah. Just needed some air."

"And clouds of blowing dust from this unswept porch? City boy, all that carbon monoxide must have jellied your brains."

He laughed, and they went back inside together. Daniel Medeiros, his best friend from high school and the town's remaining grocer, had volunteered to help him clear out his father's house. It was a good thing, too. The task was harder than he'd thought. Everything here was a memory wrapped in wishes, most of them never fulfilled.

His father had always dreamed of better things, making detailed sketches of the barn they'd someday build, and the workshop inside, with the benches and storeroom. Yet the money and time for his dad's projects had never materialized as he spent his life laboring at his backbreaking job as IVA's head custodian.

Joshua hadn't made it any easier on the man. He'd constantly gotten into fights after school and around town. A group of guys, knowing his dad was a janitor—and a Navajo to boot—had hounded him since elementary school.

Knowing which buttons to push, they'd counted on getting a reaction from Joshua and had rarely been disappointed. Eventually, he won enough fights to earn respect, and that had somewhat toned down his defensiveness.

After high school he'd left to pursue his own goals, and somewhere along the way his dad's time on earth had run out. Adam Nez's dreams were just another footnote in the history of a man who'd done his best with what he had.

"We should donate most of your dad's clothing and furnishings to Reverend Anders," Daniel said, jarring him back to reality. "These days, he's got a long list of people who need a hand."

"Sure. That's fine."

"Help me load the boxes into my truck and I'll take the stuff over there now."

"After that, let me buy you dinner," Joshua suggested.

Daniel laughed. "Hey, if you don't mind, I'd rather buy the groceries at my store, then cook something on your dad's old grill after the wind dies down—like the good ole days."

"No problem," Josh said, then thought

about it a moment. "Business is okay for you, right? I mean, everyone needs to eat, and you're the only full service grocer left."

His friend shrugged. "I'm selling a lot more chicken and hamburger than steaks these days, and too many people are asking for credit. I'd give it to them if I could, but I've got to pay my suppliers, too."

"You thinking of leaving?"

"I'd need to sell the business first, and that's not going to happen. Not only are there no buyers, but the place has been in my family for generations." He jammed his hands into the pockets of his windbreaker.

"It's hard to walk away from things that matter," Joshua said quietly. "When I look around here…" He shook his head.

"What might have been, huh?" Daniel asked, following Joshua's line of sight as he gazed through the window at Myka's place. "You always had a thing for her, didn't you? But she was Tanner's girl."

"She and I have both gone through some tough times these past few years."

"Which is why maybe you should back off. She's a widow just trying to survive. Don't complicate her life."

"I don't have any designs on Myka, Dan.

I'm here to wrap up this part of my life then go on to whatever's next."

"So how long, exactly, are you planning to stick around?"

"No idea." His pride wouldn't let him admit it, but until he found a job, he couldn't even afford cheap rent. He'd sunk every dime he'd had into trying to save the firm. When that had run out, he'd used his personal credit, just as his partners had, trying to stem the tide.

"So, dinner?" Daniel repeated. "After I drop this off at the church, I'll stop at the store and pick up the food. You can grill us a couple of steaks and microwave some potatoes."

Joshua pulled out his credit card and handed it to Daniel. "Just put whatever you bring on this."

"There was a time when I would have argued with you...."

"No, this is on my tab. It's a thank-you Wish I could do more."

"No need, buddy." Daniel headed out to his truck. "Give me about an hour."

Joshua watched him leave. That card was his only credit these days. It had to last until he was back on his feet again, and he had no idea how long that would take.

He'd sent out a lot of résumés and his application for a license in New Mexico, but he'd yet to get an interview in or out of state. He guessed that some employers didn't want to hire a guy who'd failed to hang on to his own company. No matter, he'd figure something out. Joshua knew he was a good architect. All he needed was the chance to prove himself.

He walked around the house for a while, remembering old times, like reading on the sofa while his father snoozed in his recliner, supposedly watching the baseball game. But memories belonged in the past.

This place had been fine for his dad, but it would never be enough for him. He still wanted it all—success, and more importantly, the kind of respect it commanded. For him, it wasn't about money, it was about recognition for his work and achieving the American Dream.

No one in his family had even come close to that elusive brass ring, but someday he'd claim it. As far as he was concerned, it was meant to be.

JOSHUA EASED HIMSELF onto the back porch bench beside Daniel and took a long pull of a cold one.

"I know you're planning to fix up the house, but be careful not to waste your money," Daniel said, chewing on his after-dinner toothpick, staring at the grazing sheep across the way. "Houses are on sale around here for practically nothing and still no one's buying. We may go down the same road as Soledad."

"The base shut down there, right?" Joshua asked, wondering what he'd do if he couldn't sell the house. This was going to be seed money to start up a new business. Finances could get tough in a hurry and he was living on a shoestring as it was. A businessman with lousy credit didn't have much of a future. Even potential employers might shy away.

"Yeah. It's all gone. Used to be a nice little town, too. Now, without the Air Force test facilities, it's nothing more than empty homes, a natural gas field and a pumping station. Not more than fifty people left. That could happen here, too."

"Well, I need to keep busy," Joshua said, knowing that he couldn't afford to sit around and wait for things to happen. "I figure I'll start by cleaning the place from the ground up and giving it a fresh coat of paint. Like you suggested—sweat equity."

"Is it tough for you? I mean, being here at the house without your dad around?"

Joshua shrugged. "It's not the memories that bother me most. It's the feeling that I'm back to square one. I never thought I'd return empty-handed."

"Maybe you took a wrong turn somewhere and destiny wants you to start over—here. Ever consider that?"

"You sound like Grandma Medeiros," Joshua said. Daniel's grandmother.

"Her words exactly." He reached for his jacket and fished out the keys to his truck. "I'd better get going. I've got to help her close up the store."

Joshua set his beer on the side table. "Your grandma's still working? She's got to be… what? Close to eighty, if I figure it right."

"Seventy-seven, and she still works a forty-hour week to supplement her social security. I can't get her to slow down. I swear she's got more energy than I do."

Joshua walked Daniel to his truck, which was parked behind the rental in the driveway. "Feel free to come by anytime, Dan. It was good to shoot the bull with you again."

After his old friend drove off, Joshua wandered to the woodworking shed he and his dad had built—a concession to the workshop/ garage that remained a faded drawing in his dad's file cabinet.

Memories crowded in around him as he looked up at his own first project, a small sign that hung over the doorway. He'd used a woodburning set to carve out the words Adam and Joshua Nez in a piece of scrap pine.

He stepped inside and turned on the shop light. As a cloud of dust settled, his gaze fell on the yellowed designs tacked to the wall. The one in the corner was his own scale drawing for a treadle spinning wheel he'd worked at in secret for nearly six months. He'd wanted to give it to Myka for graduation, but he'd run out of materials and it had remained unfinished by the time he'd left for college.

He glanced around for the wheel, wondering if his dad had kept it. Adam almost never threw things like that out, so chances were it was still here someplace, maybe taken apart and stored in a box. Perhaps now, with everything in the world just a mouse click away, he could get the flyer assembly and bearings he needed on the internet.

Out of curiosity, he decided to look inside

the big storage cabinets first, but to open them, he'd need to find the keys to the padlocks. All he'd found so far was the key to the shed itself.

He was rummaging through the workbench drawers when he heard a soft knock behind him.

Myka stood there, holding something. "I don't mean to intrude, Josh. I know you're busy."

"Come in. It's been a long time since I've set foot inside this workshop, and I'm trying to remember where everything is."

"Your dad said you spent the night here once."

"Yeah, I fell asleep waiting for some varnish to dry," he said, chuckling. He'd been working on her spinning wheel.

She looked up at the spinning wheel design tacked to the wall. "Cool. Was that one of your dad's projects?"

"Something like that," he said but didn't elaborate. She was standing in the place where he'd first fantasized about kissing her.

"Life was so much simpler when we were kids, wasn't it?" she mused. "I sometimes wish we could turn back time."

"I can't say I do. I don't care much for the

kid I used to be," he said, admiring the way she looked in the glow of the overhead light.

"Any sign of Bear yet?" she asked.

"The only animals I've spotted are lizards and a bunch of daddy longlegs spiders on Dad's shelves," he said. "I kept Bear's dog bed and dishes, though. You'll need those if he shows up again."

"Thanks. I just wish he'd come back."

"He found his way here once before," he said.

"That sounds like something your dad would say."

He nodded. "Navajo teach that everything is connected and forms a pattern. We all have a place within that, the dog included."

She avoided his gaze, stepping outside. "He can jump the fence or dig under, so if it's okay, I'll be walking around the back of your property from time to time looking for Bear."

"You don't need permission, Myka. You're always welcome."

"Thanks." She reached into her pocket. "There's something I should return to you. Your dad gave me his extra set of house and truck keys when you went off to college." She tossed them to him through the open door.

He caught them with one hand. As he did,

he saw the inscribed cedar stick attached to the key ring. "I made this for Dad in eighth grade shop. I didn't realize he still had it."

"You were his son. He was proud of you. You could have chosen a career as a sheep-herder and he would have bragged about you to his friends."

"I just wish—" He stopped and turned away, staring at the drawings on the wall. She was too easy to talk to.

"I know it's hard for you to be here, Joshua. I think what you really need is a distraction. I've got the perfect idea."

CHAPTER THREE

MYKA HAD JUST finished getting dressed for the meeting when she heard a knock on the door. Thinking it would be Joshua, she finished dabbing on some lipstick and answered it.

Tanner's sister, Betty, stood at the threshold with her daughter, six-year-old Evelyn, beside her.

"Aunt Myka! You look so pretty," Evie said, reaching up to give her a hug.

Myka bent down to hold her close. "Thanks, sweetie." Evie was such a terrific kid. With golden locks and the face of an angel, she could charm her way into anyone's heart.

"I hope you don't mind my dropping by unannounced, Myka. I know about the meeting tonight, but I was out running errands and I needed to ask you a favor."

Betty, her sister-in-law, was a stunning blonde with vibrant blue eyes. "Need me to babysit this week?" Myka asked, guessing at the request.

"No, but I can't tell you how much I appreciate your help. You've been a real lifesaver. Shameless that I am, I need to ask you a different favor."

"Come in and have a seat."

"Aunt Myka, do you have any cookies?"

"Evie!" Betty said.

Myka laughed. "They're in the cookie jar in the kitchen. Take as many as you like."

"No, just two, do you hear me Evelyn?" Betty said.

"Three! Mom, please?"

"They're small," Myka said softly. "And I bake a supply of chocolate chip cookies mostly for her. Come on, let me spoil her."

Betty smiled. "Okay, three," she told Evie.

As Evie hurried off, Betty focused on Myka once again. "I have a question for you about the inn."

"You don't have to clear anything with me, Betty. I may own a third of it, but it's your baby."

"I know that restoring the place sounds nuts, Myka, but all the inn needs is some TLC to start attracting paying guests again. Come hunting season, we'll have lots of people looking for lodging or a base camp. I want to be ready, but I've run into a snag." She lowered her voice and in a barely audible whisper, added, "Tony's out of prison."

Betty's husband had almost destroyed her, physically and mentally. He'd been convicted of assault and battery against a former employer. "Is he still refusing to give you a divorce?"

"Yeah, and I don't want him to find out about the inn."

Myka's face hardened. "*You* inherited a stake in the inn, not him. He has no legal claim whatsoever."

"Legalities won't matter to him, and the fear of prison obviously hasn't stopped him in the past. If he decides I'm trying to cheat him, he'll make trouble, and he can do a lot of damage when he's angry."

"Did you know he was trouble back in high school?"

"I guess, but whenever I was with Tony, I felt…invincible. Being Tony's girl meant no one ever gave me a hard time."

"It's hard to believe how wrong things went," Myka said.

"After Evie was born everything fell apart. He lost his job and started drinking when he couldn't find another. His rages..." She shuddered.

"Will's still staying with you, right?" Myka asked. Tanner and Betty's older brother was also the town's police chief.

She nodded. "I've filed a restraining order against Tony, so he'll go back to prison if he comes within three hundred feet of me. But he still scares me."

"Will's a trained officer and almost Tony's size. You shouldn't worry."

Evie ran back into the room and offered Betty a cookie. "These are great, Mommy. Myka makes the best chocolate chip cookies ever."

Betty smiled as she took the cookie.

"Can I watch TV?"

Betty looked at Myka, who nodded. "Go ahead, it won't bother us," Myka said.

Betty waited until Evie's favorite cartoons popped on screen, then she changed the subject.

"How's Josh doing? I heard he's back in town."

"He's fine, I guess," Myka said. "He wants to sell his dad's house, but I warned him about the real estate market these days."

"I'm going to ask him to look at my renovation plans for the inn. I'd like to knock out some walls, and since he's an architect, I thought he might tell me where it's safe to do that," Betty said. "I don't think we should mention that Will's part owner, though."

"You think Josh still carries a grudge? He and Will had fought over Sophie back in high school. That was a lifetime ago."

Betty laughed. "No, not at all, but Josh and Will have always been like oil and water. They've already had a run-in."

"What happened?"

"Josh missed a stop sign as he was coming into town."

"Let me guess. The one on Orchard Lane that's buried by the house-high tumbleweeds?"

Betty nodded. "The town doesn't have a weed and litter crew anymore. Heck, if the rest of us didn't know the stop sign was there, we'd miss it, too."

"Did Will give him a ticket?"

"Yeah. All he said was that Josh was pushing his buttons." Betty rolled her eyes, then glanced over at her daughter. Seeing Evie engrossed in the show, she continued in a low voice. "I think the real problem is that he doesn't want Josh back in town."

"That's none of his business. Why does he care?"

"Will may not actually say it, but he thinks it's his duty to look out for you, his little brother's widow. He's convinced Josh has always had a thing for you."

"No, that's not true. Besides, I choose my own friends. Your brother needs to butt out."

"I agree. Getting back to Joshua, I haven't seen him in ages. Can we go over there and say hi?" Betty asked.

"No need. He's coming over in a few minutes."

"Ah. You two going on a date?"

Myka shook her head, but before she could elaborate, Betty added, "Too bad."

"Joshua Nez isn't right for me, Betty. The most we'll ever be is friends." Hearing a knock on the door, Myka stood. "That must be him now. Come on in, Josh."

Joshua came in a moment later, wearing a lightweight sports jacket, dress slacks and an open-necked shirt. Myka bit back a sigh. No matter what he wore, he was always eye candy. Although he looked professional, there was an unmistakable ruggedness about him. *Untamed*—that word fit him the best.

Seeing Betty, Josh smiled. "It's been a long

time," he said, and shook her hand. Looking down at her daughter, who'd come over, he smiled. "And who's this?"

"I'm Evie," the girl said.

"Pleasure, Evie." Joshua shook hands with her, too, and she beamed.

Evie looked back at Betty. "Is it okay if I go outside to play with Teddy Bear?"

Myka looked at Joshua. "She means Bear."

Joshua raised his eyebrows. "From what you've told me, that dog is way too big to play with a kid Evie's size."

"He's like a big teddy bear," Evie said. "And he's my friend. Can I go get him, please?"

Myka crouched in front of Evie. "Bear's not around right now, sweetie," she said gently. "When Mr. Nez went to heaven, Bear wanted to be by himself for a while."

"Oh, okay," she said. Then, after a heart-beat, "Can I have another cookie?"

"One more and that's it," Betty said.

Myka smiled. "I love the way kids do that. No disappointment lingers for long. They can switch gears in an instant."

"I envy her that, too," Betty said softly, then focused on Josh. "I'm glad you're here, Josh. I wanted to ask you a favor. Would you drop by the Blue Spruce Inn on Main Street tomorrow morning? I'll trade you breakfast—all homemade—for your opinion on my renovating ideas. We have a tight budget, so I have to make sure I don't make any costly mistakes."

"Who's we?" he said, picking up on that immediately.

Betty winced. "Myka, Will and I are partners."

"It's mostly Betty's thing," Myka said quickly. "Will and I chip in with the property taxes and help out with other expenses when we can."

"Wait a sec. I'm missing something. You're spending money to fix up an inn here in Independence?" he asked.

Betty nodded. "It'll be more of a B and B. A lot of people come into this part of the state during hunting and skiing season, and on summer vacation. It'll be a seasonal business, but I think we'll be able to make it work."

"I'll be glad to stop by tomorrow and take a look," Joshua said, "but I should warn you. One of your partners may not appreciate my input."

"That'll be Will's problem, then. Myka and I would really appreciate your expertise," Betty said.

Hearing the grandfather clock chime, Myka

gasped. "Oh, no! We have to go right now, Josh. The meeting is at Liza's house and we'll be late."

"Wait—you're going to a crafter's meeting?" Betty asked, looking at Josh. "There aren't any woodworkers there, I don't think. It's mostly the knitting, crocheting and weaving crowd."

"Tonight will be different," Myka said. "We're going to do some serious brainstorming and try to come up with ideas on how to help Independence. The more input, the better. Why don't you come, Betty?"

"I wish I could, but I have to get Evie home, then it's dinner, bath and bed. Let me know what happens."

Myka saw Betty and Evie to the door, then came back for her purse.

"What's Betty's story?" Joshua asked, after she'd left. "That was Tony's kid, right?"

Myka nodded. "Betty's had some rough times, thanks to Tony, but she and her daughter will be okay now that they're back home," she said, unwilling to add any more details. "Ready to go?"

WHEN THEY ARRIVED, people were in the den hovering around a table covered with inexpensive snacks—everything from pretzels to chips, salsa and iced tea.

The gathering, normally consisting of ten or twelve, was nearly double that size. Many familiar faces were present, mostly the husbands and adult children of the regulars. Liza's sofa and two easy chairs had been supplemented by several dining room chairs and a dozen metal folding chairs borrowed from the Independence Methodist Church.

As Myka stepped into the room, Liza caught her eye then went around to the TV, the focal point of the family room.

"Time to get started, everyone," she announced.

As a hush descended, Myka moved to stand beside Liza. "I'm glad to see you all here. Most of you know Joshua Nez," she said and motioned to where he stood. "I've asked him to join us because he's an architect and he comes up with new ideas all the time. Joshua's also a native of Independence and knows our community."

Several shout-out welcomes to Joshua went around the room, then Myka continued. "We're all having a tough time getting by these days. Individually, none of us are in the position to help the community. What we need to do is pull together. A lot of you already know that I've got my own small internet business," she said, and saw people nod. "Business is good, so I've been thinking of expanding my inventory to include a variety of crafts. I don't have the cash to buy your pieces, but I could take them on consignment. Almost everything I've listed over the past months has sold within a week or less. Something like this could help everyone's bottom line and, ultimately, the town's economy."

Robyn, Liza's daughter, stood up next. She had a stately five-foot-eight frame that always commanded attention, as did her beautiful black hair and blue eyes. "Myka, what you're proposing wouldn't even make a dent in the town's economy," she said in a quiet, nonjudgmental voice.

"I'm not saying it's a cure-all, or that we'd be rich, but we need to start somewhere. Extra money in our pockets could mean all the difference in the world to Mabel's Coffee Shop, for example, or Shorty's Burgers," Myka said.

"I think it's a good idea," Daniel's grandmother, Elise Medeiros, added.

"Thank you, Grandma," Myka replied, then glanced around the room. "We have something to offer the world. Our crafts are based on Rio Grande traditions, and there's always a market for beautiful, handcrafted things."

"The consignment store idea is good, but we'd each have to work pretty quickly to keep things rolling," Bertie said. "We have to think this through. Once we start making stuff to sell, it'll no longer be just our hobby—what we do to relax or take our mind off our troubles."

"Which means we'd be sucking all the fun out of it," said Fran Brown, a town councillor. "Then, if we start depending on it, and it dries up…"

She didn't have to finish the sentence. They'd all been shocked when IVA had shut its doors. Myka glanced around as a heavy silence fell over the room.

"Anytime you try something new, especially in business, there's a risk," Joshua said. "But from what I've seen of the town, doing nothing is no longer an option."

"Time's working against us, but let's take a few more days to think about this," Myka said. "Maybe someone else can come up with a better idea by the time we meet again."

After more discussion, the gathering finally disbanded. Myka and Joshua stayed behind, answering questions and trying to help the others overcome their reluctance.

Finally ready to call it a night, she and Joshua went to the door.

"You've planted the seed, Myka. That's all you can do," Liza said.

Joshua walked beside her as they headed back to his truck. "I wanted to brainstorm, but I did most of the talking and ended up scaring them," Myka said.

"Not everyone can greet change with open arms. Some of the people there tonight have lived their entire lives in Independence, and they want things to go back to the way they were."

"The old days aren't coming back," Myka said softly.

"I know, but they'll have to accept it before they can move on and take action."

As they crossed the street to where he'd parked, she felt the warmth of his body close to hers. It was a welcome awareness, one that contrasted sharply with the familiar ice-cold blasts of fear and sorrow she'd lived with these past few years.

He held the door open for her. "Give them

time, Myka," Joshua advised. "Their backs are to the wall and they're scared."

They were driving down the street at a leisurely pace when they heard a siren behind them and saw the flashing lights of a police cruiser.

Joshua cursed and pulled over, turning off the engine.

Seeing Will behind them in the side mirror, Myka tried not to cringe. He was the last person she'd wanted to run into tonight.

"There was no stop sign back there, right?" Joshua asked.

"No. Just stay cool." A moment later, her brother-in-law came up to the driver's side window. Seeing Myka on the passenger side, he glared at her.

"What's the problem, Will?" Joshua asked.

"I was going to ask the same thing," Will said. "Did you have car trouble, Myka?"

She tried to keep her temper in check. After Tanner's death, Will had been there for her—day or night. She knew he meant well, but this time he was going too far. "My car's fine. Joshua's next door now, so we decided to ride to the Spinning Wheels' meeting together."

He scowled at Joshua. "You taking up crochet?"

"*I* asked him to come," she said, and explained, though she knew she didn't have to. "You would have been welcome, too. Your welded sculptures, like that rearing horse you made out of scrap metal, are just stunning. They're too large to ship easily, so it's not a good match for my online business, but everyone would have valued your input."

He expelled his breath in a hiss. "So far your online company's doing okay, but I still think it's dangerous for you to do business on the internet. There are too many crazies out there looking for trouble."

"I really haven't had any problems, not big ones anyway," she said. "I'm very careful about protecting myself and my privacy."

He looked at Joshua. "You never cared much for Independence, so why were you there?"

"To help brainstorm. I have a house to sell, and to do that, Independence will need to get back on its feet."

"Had to go to college to figure that one out, did you?" Will snapped, then said "Myka, can I talk to you privately?"

She bristled at his tone of voice. Nodding

to Will, she glanced at Joshua and added, "I'll be back in a minute."

Moments later, Myka stood with Will beside his cruiser. "Will Solis, why are you acting like such a horse's butt, pulling Joshua over for no reason at all?" she demanded, keeping her voice low. "One of the reasons I asked him along tonight is because I know what it's like to get a house in order after someone you love passes on. His dad died less than two weeks ago. Cut him some slack, and me, too. And on top of that, mind your own business."

"Myka, you mean well, but—"

"Will, back off. Joshua's got some real tough days ahead, getting his father's things packed and sifting through a million memories. On top of that, he'll have to deal with regrets—all those things he might have said or done if he'd known his dad was going to die…"

"You're identifying too much with what he's going through, Myka. He didn't lose a spouse—you did."

She swallowed hard. "Maybe you're right, Will, but here's what I think. This isn't really about Joshua. It's about you guarding what was Tanner's—in this case, me—because you think he'd expect that of you."

"There's truth there, Myka, but Nez is still bad news," Will said quietly. "People don't change. He may have lived here most of his life, but he never really belonged. From what I hear he couldn't run a business out in San Francisco, either. He's a loser. Do yourself a favor and steer clear of him."

"You're really high and mighty tonight, aren't you? Instead of playing bully cop and judging Joshua for who you think he was, why don't you show a little objectivity for once and get to know him?" Myka stopped for a moment, realizing she was getting louder by the word.

"Look who's getting…" Will began.

"I'm not finished yet, Will," Myka whispered harshly. "Joshua is stopping by the B and B tomorrow. Betty asked him for advice on some renovations, and he agreed to help in exchange for breakfast. Come by, keep an open mind and leave your attitude in the squad car. Hear what he has to say. This isn't high school anymore, Will, and you're not the same kid you were back then, either. Grow up on the inside, too."

His face turned red, then he took a deep

breath. "All right, okay, I'll give him a chance, but don't expect miracles. I see things for what they are, not the way I'd like them to be."

"Fair enough. Just take off the blinders."

"I want you to do something for me, too, Myka. Don't trust Joshua, you hear?"

"Trust is something I can figure out on my own. You're reading way too much into this. To me, he's just an old friend and neighbor going through a rough time. Back off and think before you get in someone's face again."

By the time Myka returned to Josh's truck, she found that his mood had soured considerably.

Once Will drove off, Joshua put the truck in gear and pulled out. "I don't know why he's got a problem with me. I haven't seen him in years."

"You got into a lot of trouble back then, though you were usually provoked. I'm not apologizing for him, but with his brother gone, Will's looking out for family," Myka said. "He's rough around the edges, sure, and he tends to go overboard sometimes. Hopefully he won't act like such a jackass next time you meet."

"I promised Betty I'd take a look at the

inn, but I may have spoken too soon, considering Will's attitude. I won't take his bull, cop or not."

"I'll be there, and I can stop his nonsense without having to throw a punch. What if I buy you a cup of Mabel's coffee, then we'll both cross the street to the Blue Spruce Inn? Betty can cook breakfast burritos that are second to none, but her coffee's just awful."

"Mabel's was my favorite haunt. I'm glad to hear it's still there. Even when I was broke, I'd stand out on the sidewalk so I could enjoy the scent of fresh coffee and those incredible tiny doughnuts."

"She only serves coffee these days but, yeah, Mabel's is still there and her coffee's better than ever. Money's tight for everyone, but we all consider her signature blends a guilty pleasure."

"Okay, then. You're on. What time do I pick you up tomorrow?" he asked.

"How about we get an early start? Seven too early, city boy?" she teased.

He laughed. "By that time, I'd already battled traffic and was sitting at my desk."

It didn't take long for them to get home. As he parked in Myka's driveway, she spotted movement by the juniper hedge. "Bear!"

She bolted out of the pickup and ran toward the dog, calling his name, but the animal vanished back into the dark.

"Are you sure that was him?" Joshua asked, catching up a heartbeat later. "It could've been a coyote."

"Coyotes aren't that big, and there aren't many left around here these days," she said, still trying to peer into the darkness.

"Bear!" she called again, but there was no response.

"If that was him, then it's clear he stuck around. He'll probably come back when he's ready. All the activity around Dad's house might have made him nervous, not to mention Dad's absence. Once things settle down, I'm sure he'll be back." He walked her to her door. "Myka, one last thing…thanks."

"For what?" she asked. The only thing she'd done was lose his father's pet.

"For being Dad's friend when I wasn't around," he said and gave her a quick hug.

His arms were strong and his chest rock solid. It felt good to lay her head against his shoulder and feel the beat of his heart. As his warmth enfolded her, her pulse quickened.

Realizing the danger, she stepped back. "No thanks are needed," she said. "Do you mind if we postpone getting coffee till around eight tomorrow? That'll give me time to feed my sheep and see if I can spot any sign of Bear."

"I'm a lousy tracker, never was much of a hunter either, but I'd be more than happy to help any way I can."

She laughed. "Thanks, but no. He's more likely to approach me if I'm alone. Tonight, I made the mistake of running after him, and that probably scared him even more. Let's meet back here a little before eight, and then we'll head out, okay?"

"Sounds like a plan."

THE FOLLOWING MORNING Joshua waited while Myka searched for his father's dog. It took her forty minutes to return home, and her expression told him she hadn't made any progress.

"Don't let it get to you, Myka," he said, meeting her in the driveway. "You've done your best. The next move belongs to Bear."

She nodded silently. "Let me get my purse and we'll go."

Five minutes later they arrived at Mabel's place on Main Street. As they stepped through the front doors, Joshua looked around. The coffee shop was a lot smaller than he remembered, but a rich aroma still filled the air and brought back pleasant memories. Even the best coffee houses in San Francisco hadn't been able to rival Mabel's premium blend— at least to his taste.

After placing their order, they went to one of the small, circular wooden tables scattered around the room.

Joshua smiled as Mabel brought him a large hazelnut coffee topped with whipped cream and hazelnut sprinkles. As he stood to say hello, she gave him a big hug, welcoming him back to town.

Still standing, he took a sip of his coffee and sighed happily. "Mabel, you've outdone yourself. This is incredible."

"Coming from a well-traveled city boy, that's quite a compliment," she said, then with a mischievous smile, she added, "or was it that you didn't expect the old lady's coffee to be as good as you remembered?"

He laughed. "No way. You're still the standard."

Mabel, a tall, stately looking sixty-year-old, beamed. "Good answer. That might earn you a second cup at half price. Now take your seat again and enjoy."

As she walked off, Myka smiled. "Mabel's

something else, isn't she? Did I ever tell you that a Seattle coffee chain wanted to buy the secret to her special blend, but she turned them down? She said she liked offering the people of Independence something that would always say 'home' to them."

As Josh looked around he saw the chairs were starting to fill up. "I'm glad to see she still does a steady business. I can't imagine Independence without Mabel's."

"I'm hoping that eventually Betty will cut a deal and serve Mabel's coffee over there. Her own..." She cringed. "Motor oil would probably taste better. Just don't tell her I said so."

He laughed. "So is that what it takes to be a silent partner?"

She shrugged. "I've got my hands full processing wool, selling my yarn and managing my online store. Betty needed something positive to focus on, too, besides her daughter, and that's where the Blue Spruce comes in." She paused, then added, "Will uses his welding in much the same way."

"Being the Independence police chief isn't enough for him?"

Myka took a moment before answering, measuring her words carefully. She wanted Joshua to understand, but she didn't want to violate any confidences. "Will knows better than most what's happening around here. He was a cop in Albuquerque for four years, then returned home after Sheriff Mercer died because he felt needed here. He wants to spend the rest of his life in Independence, but things have continued changing, and not for the better. Now, we've got a part-time mayor, and the town can only support a three-officer police department, which includes one volunteer."

"There used to be a dozen officers—plus IVA security," Joshua recalled. "Who's the backup now?"

"Will. He's on call full-time and he gave up a pay increase to keep at least one officer active 24/7. When we lost our fire marshal, he took on that job, too, pro bono, so everyone's insurance rates wouldn't skyrocket. He works ten or twelve hours a day, sometimes more," she added.

"I didn't know that."

"Few people do. Will's stretched pretty thin, and he's doing his best to protect what's left of the community. He's on edge, so go easy on him."

He nodded slowly. "You have nothing to worry about. The kid you knew who got into fights at the drop of a hat finally grew up. That's not who I am anymore."

"Good." She finished the last of her coffee. "Now let's go to the Blue Spruce and see what Betty has in mind for the inn."

CHAPTER FOUR

AS THEY STEPPED onto the sidewalk, Myka and Josh immediately felt the pleasant warmth of the sun rising off the asphalt. This was Main Street, downtown Independence, the oldest part of the community. There were about twenty shops lining the narrow street, which had been laid out when cars and horse-drawn wagons competed for space. It was easy to imagine what the town had looked like a hundred years ago.

Almost all of the multistoried buildings were made of brick and stone and had their roots in the mining boom of the early 1900s. They'd been upgraded many times, and during prosperous years the businesses here had flourished.

Farther down the street were single-story, flat-roofed adobe structures. Those had been built in the Southwest style associated with the Pueblo tribes and early Spanish influence.

But the adobe buildings were in the worst shape, since regular maintenance was costly.

Myka stopped in front of the inn and took a moment to admire the red roses etched on the glass transom above the entrance. They spoke of the grandeur and elegance of days gone by and stood in stark contrast to the chipped mortar and flaking paint which exposed the wood trim.

Joshua opened the door and gestured for Myka to precede him. The Blue Spruce was in transition. Metal scrapers and a steamer that would eventually take off the old wallpaper were resting on the floor where sections of the baseboard had already been removed.

Among all the chaos one thing stood out—the wonderful scent of fresh baking. "Betty, did you make your special honey bread?" Myka called out.

"Yep, I sure did." Betty stepped out from an alcove, then waved them over. A heavy wooden dining table with coordinating chairs faced glass doors leading into a courtyard full of big leafed plants and small wooden tables. "I want to entice you guys to stay, and I didn't think the torn up foyer with peeling wallpaper would do it. So come on. Let's have breakfast here in the garden alcove and then we'll get to work."

Betty wheeled in a serving cart with glasses of freshly squeezed orange juice, thick slices of homemade bread, butter and jelly and plates filled with scrambled eggs cooked with a touch of New Mexico green chile.

The meal was delicious and they took their time, discussing the various possibilities for the dining room and Betty's decorating ideas.

Twenty minutes later, after helping Betty clear the table, Joshua thanked her. "I can be bribed like this anytime, Betty!"

"Ready to get to work, then?"

"You bet. Why don't you tell me what you envision for the inn as a whole? Start with the big changes you'd like made, then add the details as you think of them."

"When the Blue Spruce was built, the rooms were small, to squeeze in as many guests as possible. I want to knock down some walls to create several larger spaces that flow into each other and are family friendly. That's why I'd like to tear out a large portion of those two walls, for starters," she said, pointing to the dining area. "In their place, I'd like archways that provide a better view of the courtyard and welcome the guests to wander about."

"Okay," he said, then took a closer look at the rooms and ceiling above, inspecting the position of joints, adjoining rooms and doorways. "From what I can see here, you'd be taking out a big section of this load-bearing wall. There are ways to do that safely by creating supporting structures, but we need to check the blueprints. Do you have them?"

"No, those were filed with County and lost decades ago in a fire."

"Using imaging tools, we can look inside the walls without resorting to major work, but it might be necessary to cut a few holes to check out the condition of the existing framework. For now, let's talk some more about the kind of renovation you want to do here," Joshua said.

Betty took them around the front rooms, explaining her plans. "I want the place to have a homey, Southwest cowboy feel. Forget the upper-class drawing room that we have now. Open space with plenty of light is a must."

"I can tell that parts of this building were added on, and that complicates things," Joshua said.

They heard footsteps, and Will appeared from around the corner. "You trying to talk up the price?" His voice boomed in the small room.

Joshua turned around, and to Myka's surprise, didn't react. "I'm just here to offer free professional advice."

Will's eyebrows went up. "Betty, I thought you were going to pay him."

"I've already been compensated," Josh said. "My payment came in the form of the best breakfast I've had in a long time."

"You can count on a full spread every morning you come by, if you agree to help me out," Betty said.

"Deal," Joshua answered. "Relax, Chief. I miss my work and I'm a darned good architect."

"Best one in town," Will muttered.

"Will, can I have a word?" Myka led him to the alcove, out of hearing range. "Listen to me, and listen good, Will," she said in a harsh whisper. "I'm not going to stand around while you continue to make a fool of yourself. Joshua's here and he's helping. You're here, and all you're doing is causing trouble. That sum it up for you?"

"Myka, face reality. Do you really think he won't want something in return?" Will scoffed, not bothering to keep his voice down. "I did a little checking up on Nez and he's broke. He lost his business. His only assets are his pickup and his father's house, and you know how much property around here is selling for these days, if it sells at all."

"Be careful how you measure someone's value, Will. You don't own a house, you drive the town's car, and you're forced to work ten hour days or more to pay the bills," she argued back.

"At least I have a job," Will replied. "And the town needs me."

Joshua came over and joined them. "If you don't want my help with the renovation, just say the word and I'm out of here, Will. Your call."

Betty came in and glared at Will. "Just so you know, I was getting ready to knock out a load-bearing wall."

"Picture it, Will. The second floor could have become a permanent addition to the first. That what you want?" Myka said.

Will's face turned red, but he held Joshua's gaze for several seconds, then nodded. "Okay.

It's clear we can use your help, but no favors. We need an architect—you need the money. Set your fee."

"All right. After I get your design ideas, Betty, I'll inspect the building and draw up plans that'll include several options on how to expand the rooms safely." He ignored Will completely while he quoted her a very low flat fee, then added, "Plus a loaf of that bread you made, say once a week for the next month?"

Betty shook Joshua's hand. "You've got a deal. I'll boost the bread offer through December, too."

"So Betty and I vote yes, Will," Myka said.

"All right then," he said. "If things go well, you can use us as references for future jobs."

"I'll take you up on that," Joshua said.

"So what's next?" Betty asked Josh.

"I'll need to look upstairs, then crawl into the attic and check the roof structure."

"Come on. I'll take you," Betty said.

"I'm on duty. I have to get back to work," Will said.

"Go ahead, Will. We'll handle things here." Myka smiled. "Don't worry."

"That's not going to happen. You, Evie,

Betty and Mom are all the family I've got left. I worry." He turned and walked away.

Betty found a flashlight and led Joshua upstairs. Myka followed and watched Joshua work. His gaze took in everything as he concentrated. A shiver ran up her spine. To have him look at her like that… She sighed softly.

The last stop was a hallway access point to the attic. Joshua climbed up the ladder, then spent several minutes overhead before finally coming back down.

"What's the verdict?" Myka asked as Joshua pushed the folding ladder into place and closed the access panel.

"From what I've seen, the inn's had at least two additions over the years, but the work was well thought out and it's in good condition. Before you knock out any walls, I suggest hiring an electrician to check out the wiring and help you decide how to reroute what's there."

"I've been trying to find an electrician, but Harry Westin moved away last month," Betty said.

"Harry's shop is closed, but his daughter Molly took over his business part-time," Myka said. "She's a teacher at Independence

Elementary, but she's also a licensed electrician. She works after hours and on weekends."

"So, Joshua, how soon do you think you'll have those plans ready?" Betty asked.

"In a day or two I can tell you which walls in the guest rooms can be taken out or fitted with passageways. The downstairs portion will require a bit more work. I'll have to do some calculations and take measurements. We'll also need to discuss design options within your budget before I draw up the specs, and that'll have to wait until my New Mexico license comes through. Will ten days be okay for everything?"

"Sure. Take longer if you need to. I've got a ton of work to do first—everything from removing wallpaper to refinishing exterior trim. After that, I'll tackle the big jobs like knocking down walls," she said. "Grandma passed on five months ago, but she let things slide here after IVA closed down. Seeing Independence die a slow death and watching Mom go downhill every day took its toll. Her heart was broken."

"Early onset Alzheimer's," Myka said, answering Joshua's unspoken question about Betty's mom.

"What about your dad?" Joshua asked.

"Dad passed on three years ago, before IVA closed. He couldn't cope with what was happening to Mom. One day his heart just stopped beating," Betty said. "Mom lives in a private nursing home over in Painted Canyon. She doesn't know us anymore, but we visit once a week. Last time I took Evie to see her, she thought Evie was me," Betty added.

"I'm sorry," Joshua said. "That's got to be tough."

"You accept it and go on. What else can you do?" Betty said. "When Grandma left the place to the three of us, Will figured we'd close it down till we could find a buyer, but I couldn't let go. I love this place. I always have. I used to do my homework here after school and I helped at all the big Christmas parties Granddad used to host. You should have seen it back then! Only the North Pole had better decorations."

"Maybe it'll be that way again, once the inn reopens."

"I sure hope so," she said with a wistful smile.

As the phone rang and Betty went to answer it, Joshua asked Myka, "You ready to go?"

"I think I'll stick around. I can catch a ride home later," she said, "but let me walk you to the door."

They stopped in the entryway, and Joshua glanced back into the room. "Now I understand why Betty's so invested in this place. The inn is part of her personal history."

"The Blue Spruce is also her and Evie's future. It's a good place for them."

He brushed his knuckles against her face in a gentle caress. "Myka, it may be too late for Independence, but not for you. Think of your future. You still have your whole life ahead of you."

His touch sent warmth all through her. A fleeting touch, the tenderness of a caress, those had been missing from her life for so long she'd forgotten what a sweet thrill they could bring.

"You put on a brave face for everyone but keep the real you out of reach," he said, his voice quiet.

The way his eyes held hers was mesmerizing, but the spell broke instantly when something clanged onto the tile floor back in the kitchen.

As Myka turned toward the sound, she saw the photo of Tanner, Will and Betty that hung behind the front desk.

"I better get to work," she said. "I promised Betty I'd help her put a coat of varnish on one of the armoires upstairs."

"See you later then," Joshua said.

As Joshua left, Betty walked over to join her.

"Pants warm?" she asked.

"Huh?" Myka turned around and looked directly at her.

"Liar, liar, pants on fire. We're not varnishing anything today."

Myka gave her a thin smile. "Oh, that."

"What are you worried about, Myka?" she asked. "What people will think if you spend time with a man? Tanner's gone. I loved my brother dearly, but he's not coming back."

"I know, but…"

"There are no 'buts' about this…except maybe Joshua's exceptional one," she said with a mischievous grin.

Myka choked.

"What? I've got eyes. You thought I didn't notice?" she asked, laughing.

"*I* hadn't."

"Baloney," Betty said.

Myka grinned. "Okay, maybe."

"Will's being a jerk, but he's right, you know. Joshua has a thing for you. It dates all the way back to elementary school."

"Why on earth would you think that? Because he's nice to me? By that definition, he has a thing for everyone."

"No, it's in the way he looks at you—when you're not looking."

"Betty, we're just old friends."

Betty shook her head. "It goes beyond that."

"You're wrong, but even if we were both wild about each other—and we're *not*—it couldn't go anywhere. Sooner or later he'll leave Independence, and I belong here."

Myka swallowed hard and continued. "Joshua's a heartbreak waiting to happen, and life's hurt me enough. I don't want any more pain."

"Maybe you're right. Josh is destined for city life, and you can't change a man."

Myka heard the pain laced through Betty's words. Reaching out, she gave her a hug.

"You and I bend, but we never break. That's what makes us who we are."

A few hours later, Myka left the inn and headed home. It was a pleasant afternoon, and the mile-long walk back would do her good. She needed time to think. She and Betty were both strong women, but being around Joshua had reminded her that even the strongest among them needed gentleness, too.

CHAPTER FIVE

THE NEXT TWO WEEKS went by in a blur, and September turned into October. Myka was busy packaging yarn and craft orders when she heard a knock at her door. Thinking it was the delivery man, she taped shut the box she was working on, then hurried over, balancing two large boxes in one hand. As she pulled the door open, the boxes shifted and went crashing to the floor.

Myka bent down to retrieve them, her gaze falling on the pair of dusty boots directly in front of her. She looked up the leggy frame and saw Joshua smiling down at her.

"Did you do that so you could check me out?"

Her eyes widened. "No, I—" Seeing his teasing grin, she laughed. "Sorry. Haven't seen you dressed so casually in years. Come on in."

"We live next door to each other, but I haven't been within fifty feet of you since that day at the inn," he said, stepping into the room and shutting the door behind him.

He looked past her and saw the living room filled with open boxes waiting to be sealed, labels balanced on top of each. "Business is good, I see."

"Yeah, it is. I've been thinking of adding more sheep to my herd so I can keep up with the demand for yarn. I thought I was set for the rest of the year, but at this rate..."

Just then, there was another knock on the door. When Myka opened it, she found Liza Jenner standing there with a smile on her face. "Things look busy today!"

"I'm getting some shipments together. Millie Boyer made two beautiful cloaks that sold an hour after I'd listed them. Would you like to see?"

Liza started to answer, then hesitated, glancing at Joshua. "I don't mean to interrupt. I didn't know you had company."

"Nah, it's not company, it's just Joshua," Myka said.

Joshua laughed.

Myka opened one of the larger packing boxes and pulled up a plastic bag containing a folded cream-colored poncho knitted in an intricate cable design. "This one's in a style reminiscent of the seventies. I can't believe how quickly it sold. I put the photo and description up, and by the time I made a pot of tea, someone had already clicked on Buy Now."

"I'm not surprised," Liza said. "It's beautiful! Look at the workmanship."

Myka reached into a second box and pulled out another clear plastic bag containing a wine-colored cloak. The rich color was eye-catching and it was knitted in an elegant rib and lace pattern. "This is my favorite."

"Wow, no wonder it sold right away."

"People are shopping more with Christmas around the corner. Can you believe it's already October?" Myka asked, gently placing the cloak back inside the box. "So what brings you here, Liza? Just visiting?"

"I wanted to see if you'd be interested in selling my rugs on your site. I'm trying to raise some cash, but don't mention it to Robyn, okay? I told her she could live at home for as long as she needs, but stretching out my pension makes it tougher to get by."

"Do you have anything ready to go? If you do, I might be able to add the listing this afternoon."

Liza reached into her tote bag and brought

out two photos of a latch rug. "It's my own design."

The rug featured a beautiful piñon jay nestled in the branches of an evergreen. The colors were brilliant and from what she could see in the close-up shot, the workmanship was intricate, showing attention to even the minutest detail.

"I'd be happy to put this up, but I better warn you. I haven't tried to sell anything like this before. I can't guarantee results."

"I know, but will you try?"

"Sure. Bring the rug by, and let me know what price you'd like to charge."

"What percentage will you take of the sale?"

"It's a first offering favor. I'm not charging."

"That's really unfair to you, Myka. You take the photos, write the copy and pay for your space online. What's it called, the…"

"Domain," Myka said.

"So how about this?" Liza said and quoted Myka a price and the percentage she thought Myka should take. "I think that's a fair commission for you, isn't it?"

"Very," Myka said. "You've got yourself a deal."

After Liza left, Myka realized that Joshua had grown quiet.

"Is something wrong?" she asked.

"I was just thinking that you should consider approaching the others singly, not as a group. They might find it less intimidating if it's one friend to another."

"That's a good idea," she said.

Hearing an odd noise outside, followed by the sound of sheep bleating, Myka glanced out the window. "Bear!"

Josh was beside her instantly. "Is he harassing the sheep?"

"No, not at all. If anything, he guards them." She opened the back door.

"Where is he?"

"On the far side of the pen." She went outside and called the dog's name. Although she didn't try to go after him this time, he once again disappeared through the trees.

"It was Bear this time, no mistake?" he asked.

She nodded. "It was him. The sheep sound different—frantic—when they're scared. The sound you heard was a greeting." She wiped a tear away quickly, but he saw the gesture.

"Why are you so worried? The dog's got

food and water in two places and the weather's still in the low fifties at night," he said.

"You don't understand. This is about keeping my word to your dad. He *trusted* me, and I've got to find a way to make things right." Her voice tightened, and she swallowed back the lump in her throat.

"Sometimes things just go wrong. No one's perfect."

"This isn't about perfection. It's about being able to look at myself in the mirror at the end of the day," she whispered.

"Do you know what I see when I look at you?" he asked, taking her hand.

She shook her head and waited, almost holding her breath.

"I see a woman who's done her best for everyone, and who never hesitates to lend a helping hand."

She smiled. "I appreciate you saying that, but that's not what I'm going to see until I find Bear."

"I wouldn't expect anything less from you," he said, then kissed her on the forehead. "My dad was very lucky to have a friend like you."

The tenderness in Joshua's gaze took her breath away. Her heart ached to feel his arms around her, to feel safe and protected again.

Almost as if he'd read her mind, he pulled her to him. She didn't resist. It was too tempting, and even if it was only for a moment, she needed to feel wanted for who she was, flaws and all.

His lips brushed hers then, slowly. As his kiss deepened, a sweet fire coursed all through her. It was pure heaven, and she lost herself for one brief moment.

Drawing away at last to take a breath and force herself to think clearly, she stepped back. "We shouldn't…"

"No, probably not, but we both needed that," he said. "You and I are connected. We know what it's like to have our dreams taken away."

A connection. That's what she'd felt, but what had given her so much comfort also made her vulnerable. "Maybe that's true, but it can't happen again."

"The problem is that we both want it to."

His words were open and honest. They stated a fact but made no demands. "We're both too fragile, Joshua. You're trying to find a new direction, and I'm fighting to hold on to my life in Independence. We're on different paths right now. I need to stay here and keep what I have, what I need. You want to leave and find something new, bigger, better."

"Is that so bad? Living in the past has never worked for me. It never will," he argued.

"You see? How can we have a relationship when we can't even agree on what we want beyond today? We can't afford to get close to each other, not now, maybe not ever."

"I guess you're right," he said, looking away.

They walked around the yard looking for Bear, but there was no sign of him and his tracks disappeared where he'd crossed the road.

Myka checked her watch. "The delivery van will be here soon. I've got to finish getting the boxes ready to mail."

They went back inside, and Josh helped her by sealing boxes with packing tape and sticking on the prepared labels.

After the packages were picked up, she glanced at the grandfather clock and drew in a sharp breath. "Where did this morning go? I've got a class here in another hour. I didn't realize it was already past one."

"You never told me you were teaching classes," he said.

"I'm not. The Women's Guild meets at two

the first Friday of every month, and we try to teach each other a new skill. I've been learning about *colcha* embroidery, wool-on-wool work, but I've got a long way to go before I turn out anything decent," she said. "Not that it matters. That's not the goal of our group."

"What is?"

"Strengthening our sense of community. There are only a half dozen members left—the others have moved away—so these meetings are more important than ever. It's our way of lifting each other's spirits." She walked him to the door.

"I'll catch up with you later," he said, and headed out.

AN HOUR LATER, as Daniel got something to drink from the fridge, Joshua turned on the light and walked down the hall of his father's house. He stubbed the toe of his boot against a bookcase that was too large for such a narrow space. It was filled with regional history books, most of them University of New Mexico Press titles.

Josh preferred open spaces—that was why much of his architectural resource materials were on DVDs and other digital storage devices. His dad, on the other hand, had been old school, down to his choice of furnishings. All the rooms were cramped and overflowing with large wooden furniture pieces, most of them handmade.

He stepped inside the spare bedroom. This had become his father's library, a testament to his passion for history.

Daniel followed him, handing Josh a Coke, and looking around. "I only glanced in here before, but now I see what you mean," he said, and looked at the open maps on the futon. "You can't just give this away or throw it out. You'll have to go through everything. Collectors might have use for this stuff, or maybe some university professors."

"Yeah," Joshua said. "No way around it. Some of those maps of Independence go back to the late 1800s. I have no idea where Dad got them, or if they're originals or copies, but they might have historical value."

"You could check online, or take them to the librarian over in Painted Canyon."

"What happened to the Independence Library?"

"It closed six months after the plant shut down. IVA had always funded the library utilities and the librarian's salary in exchange for tax benefits. Once IVA left, the librarian had to be let go. Volunteers filled the gap for a while, but they'd cut services so much that people stopped coming in."

"What happened to the building and the collection?"

"The books are still there, but the building's closed," he said. "You could ask the mayor for the keys if you want to poke though the books and reference materials."

Joshua nodded, lost in thought. "Speaking of the mayor, any idea what Dad's connection was to Mayor Allen?"

"I didn't know there was one," Daniel said.

"Something was going on. I found a lot of emails back and forth between them. I haven't had a chance to read through them yet, but I got the impression that Dad was working for him, some kind of local research, I think."

"Wish I could tell you more, but this is the first I've heard of it," Daniel said, casually straddling one of the chairs. "Your dad would come into the store once a week or so, and he and Grandma would go into the office and talk over coffee. You might ask her if she knows what was going on. She knows everyone's secrets."

Josh smiled. "That's because it's so easy to talk to her."

Daniel nodded, then sat for a while, looking around the room at the books, the carved wooden animals on the windowsill and, basically, everywhere but at Josh.

"Okay, Daniel, you finally gonna tell me what's on your mind? You don't generally walk away from your work like this in the middle of the day."

Daniel expelled his breath in a hiss. "Yeah, okay, you got me. I need a favor, actually."

"Whatever you need, consider it done."

"It's about Betty…" He paused, looked down at a stack of old newspapers for a minute, then continued. "She was really antsy at the store the other day, looking behind her, clenching her fists and jumping at the slightest sound. She's afraid of something, and if she's in trouble, I want to help."

"If she's in trouble, Will's bound to know and he'll handle it. He watches over the women in his family. Too much, at least with Myka."

"Will may be in the dark about this. Betty tries to protect him, too. I remember back in June when she got into a hassle at Jerry's Hardware over an unpaid bill. Jerry was giving her a hard time, so I stepped in and calmed things down. On the way out she made me promise not to tell Will. She didn't want him to know she was short on cash, and she thought it would only add to his stress."

"Will's a proud, angry man and if he ever finds out you kept this from him, he's going to be pissed."

"Tough. I did what I had to do. No regrets."

Joshua didn't want to argue the point, but his gut told him that Daniel had made a big mistake not telling Will.

"I'm doing some work for Betty, so I'll keep my eyes open and try to figure out what's got her on edge," Joshua said, then gave Daniel a long look. "Sounds to me like you still have a thing for her."

"Not anymore. I'm just a friend." Daniel met his gaze. "Like you and Myka."

Joshua nodded slowly.

IT WAS CLOSE TO five and, alone again, Myka sat at the kitchen table and finished a peanut butter and apricot jam sandwich.

She was just about to fix herself a second one when Sophie knocked on the back door, opening it partially in the process.

"Okay to come in?" she asked.

"Of course."

"I wasn't sure if Joshua had come back or not, now that everyone's gone."

"He left around one. I think Daniel's over at his place right now."

"So what's going on between you two? Give me all the juicy details," she said in a conspiratorial tone.

Myka chuckled. "There's nothing going on."

Sophie shook her head. "I saw you two outside earlier, and you were kissing. Looked kinda romantic to me."

Myka sighed. She should have known. In Independence, everyone knew everyone else's business—especially when they lived next door to each other.

"Don't worry, I won't tell anyone, but I had to come over and tell you that I approve wholeheartedly."

Myka laughed. "You do, do you?"

"Myka, girl, you need something more in your life than your sheep, yarns and managing an online store. You deserve it. Have fun and stop overthinking things."

"You know that Joshua will be leaving as soon as he can, right?"

"Yeah, sure, but so what? He's here now."

Myka shook her head. "Flings aren't for me."

"You want marriage?"

"What? No! That's not what I meant."

"So why not enjoy the moments you have together like you did today? Later on, when you find someone new, you'll have a baseline for comparisons."

"Come on, Soph," she said, laughing. "It's not like I'm buying laundry detergent."

Sophie winked. "True, but a little comparison shopping never hurts," she said, then added, "plus, it's fun."

"Forget it," Myka said. "Changing the subject, would you like a sandwich? I'm still hungry."

"Nah, you go ahead. I have to go back home. I just came by to warn you. Bertie heard that Mayor Allen will have more bad news for us at the town hall meeting tonight. Word is, if enrollment continues to decline at our elementary school, the state department of education will shut it down. That would mean bussing the kids thirty miles to a school in Painted Canyon."

"It all goes back to what I've been saying. We've got to find ways of creating work here so families won't have to move away," Myka said.

"Grandma Medeiros was at the post office when Bertie told Fran what was going on. Grandma M. suggested that we all take a closer look at selling our crafts through your online store. She said that if we turned it into a cooperative, like an internet farmer's market, it might slow the exodus."

"That's not far from what I'd proposed, but we'd need to be a lot more organized. We'd operate from one website and share expenses and profits proportionately, not just supplying items on consignment."

"If that's what you all decide to do, I can help with the details," a familiar voice said from the other side of the screen door.

Myka spun around in her chair and saw Joshua standing there. "You scared me half to death!" she said, holding her hand over her heart.

Sophie's eyes were like saucers, and she was breathing hard. "Me, too, guy. Wear a bell next time."

He smiled. "Sorry, ladies," he said, coming in. "I just stopped by to ask if you knew any local history buffs. Dad had quite a collection of books and documents. I'd like to give them away to someone who'd appreciate them," he said. "There's a lot of information on Silas Brooks in particular."

"Find out anything about that will he supposedly revised? I know he left his mansion to the town, but what about all the other properties?" Sophie asked.

Joshua was going to comment when they heard a car pulling up outside, then another. Myka went to the front window. "What's going on? There are four cars out there, including Grandma Medeiros. She never leaves the market except during lunch."

Joshua stood behind her. "More cars are coming down the street in this direction." He watched as people climbed out of their vehicles and came up the walk. "Something's going on. They look like women on a mission."

"Maybe this has to do with the cooperative Grandma Medeiros suggested," Myka said. "Stick around, Joshua, okay? My experience is limited to a small online store, but you've run a business with real flesh-and-blood employees."

Before he could answer, they heard footsteps on the porch. "Here we go," Myka said.

She opened the door to four women she'd known most of her life, then stepped onto the porch and waited for the others who were still arriving. "Come in, everyone," she said. "Just move the boxes aside and find places to sit."

Five minutes later, a dozen women were seated in her living room. The packing materials and boxes that had been on the sofa and chairs were stacked neatly against the wall.

"Have you heard about the problem with the elementary school?" Molly Westin asked from her perch atop the arm of the crowded sofa.

"Yes, I have," Myka said. She and Joshua were now the only ones standing—him in the kitchen doorway.

"That's not the worst of it," Grandma Medeiros said. "Some of the big energy companies have sent their geologists nosing around here. If they find enough oil or gas beneath the ground to start drilling, that could be the end of our town. The ones who can will sell out in a hurry, taking the money and leaving behind those of us who aren't lucky enough to cash out. Twenty years from now, maybe sooner, when there's nothing left underground, all we'll have are abandoned wells, pumps and buildings."

"Have any of these companies actually found something to interest them here?" Myka asked.

"Not yet, but even if they don't, we're all going downhill fast," Grandma said. "Unless we find a way to save this community, we might as well go home and start packing."

Myka looked at the faces of the women crowded into her living room. Beyond the fear she could see glimmers of stubborn hope and the quiet determination that came from a lifetime of hard work.

"It's time to build a new business here in Independence," Grandma said.

Myka felt a new energy in the room. "If we're going to do this, all of us have to get involved. Those who don't have a craft can pitch in by sharing their business experience. We'll also need everyone—from the *colcha* embroidery people to folks like Mr. Gomez, who do absolutely amazing straw inlay work on wood," she said. "It's time to think big. Halfway measures won't be good enough anymore."

"Mr. Gomez hasn't been working much lately. The churches and art museums aren't buying because their budgets are down," Lydia Baker said. Like Myka, she processed and dyed wool, but only for her own personal use—at least till now. "I'll talk to him and see what he could make for individual purchases.

I'm sure he'll join us—if there's a market for his pieces. He loves Independence as much as the rest of us."

"There are other men and women, too, who are incredibly gifted woodworkers, like Adam was," Grandma said, looking over at Joshua, who nodded. "Maybe they could sell wood carvings, simple toys or those things people put on their lawns, like miniature windmills. Who knows? We should approach them and see if they're interested."

"I like that," Myka answered. "But we all need to be aware of one thing. Doing this will mean throwing our hearts into it and working like crazy to make it pay off. Even so, we may not be able to reverse the slide. What we will do is give ourselves a fighting chance. On the internet, the world is our market."

"You're the only one of us who has an on-line shop with a following, Myka," Grandma said. "You don't necessarily need us, but we need you. Can a cooperative work?"

"Our crafts take different amounts of time, so I think it's only fair to come up with a partnership formula based on our individual contributions and sales. We could each pay a percentage of our personal earnings back to the company to cover expenses, and any company profits would trickle back down based on an individual's contribution. Those who manage the business will have to be paid by the hour, of course," Myka said. "Once we work out the details, the entire group can vote to approve our plan."

"Myka, you were a bookkeeper for IVA. You know how to do all that," Robyn Jenner insisted.

"Yes, but I wasn't the chief accountant. He set up the system and I followed it," Myka said. "Mind you, it's not that I can't do it, I've just never done it before."

"I can help you," Joshua said. "A limited liability company—an LLC—is taxed like a sole proprietorship, but profits and losses appear on each member's tax returns. The annual fees are low, at least here in New Mexico," he said. "If the LLC takes off, you can still incorporate."

"We need someone who can set up the bookkeeping," Grandma Medeiros said, "and you're it, Myka."

Myka considered this. "If we can get enough people interested, we'll have the volume and the varied inventory we need to expand the store. But we'll also have to let the world know we're here. That means advertising. Since our funds will be tight, we'll have to become more active online and join the various social media sites to tell people about our store."

Robyn smiled. "Hey, I worked publicity for years. I'll tackle that side of it if you handle the bookkeeping."

"See that?" Grandma said. "All the pieces are falling into place."

"Let's not get ahead of ourselves. Some people won't join up, so be prepared for that. In our last meeting, someone said we'd be turning our hobbies into full-time jobs," Myka said.

"That was Bertie," Robyn said, "but things are even worse now."

"Let's go to the town council meeting tonight and present a united front," Grandma said. "Between now and then, we can spread the word that Myka's found a way to save the town. Sure, it's an exaggeration, but we need a good turnout, and I'm betting people will come out of curiosity if nothing else."

"I agree," Robyn said.

"Will you help us out—officially?" Myka asked Joshua. "Like a consultant."

"I'll do my best to get you started, but I'm not sure how long I'll be in town," he warned.

"Fair enough," Myka said. "While you're here, will you take part, including coming to the town meeting tonight? We'll need to get everyone fired up."

Joshua hesitated. "I'm not sure how good I'll be with that."

"I'll sell the idea, but I need you there to answer business questions," Myka said.

"All right, I'm in."

"Okay then. Everyone pass the word," Grandma said. "By tonight we want that town hall packed."

After they all left, Myka dropped down on the couch. "Oh, help," she whispered, not expecting an answer.

Joshua smiled. "You'll do fine tonight, Myka, and I'll be there to back you up—if you need it." He grew serious. "But there's one thing you haven't considered, and it could create a problem."

"What?"

"I'm not exactly the town's favorite son. When I left, I'm sure lots of people cheered. Most everyone still remembers me as the punk who was always in trouble. They're not going to trust anything I say."

"Right now this town's fighting for survival, and everything else has to take second place. You ran a multipartner business for several years, one large enough to deal with subcontractors and all the problems that entails. We need you... I need you." She swallowed hard. "I know I talk brave, but there's so much at stake. I may be in over my head."

"Most people expanding a business feel like that at one time or another. Your first battle is against the little voice inside that says you can't do it. If you get past that, it'll be downhill from there," he said.

After he left, Myka stayed by the window and watched him walk to his truck. Everything about Joshua drew her in, from his confidence to the quiet strength he brought to bear on the very things that terrified her.

She turned away from the window and sighed wistfully, thinking some dreams were better left unrealized.

CHAPTER SIX

As JOSHUA WALKED back to his truck, he felt her gaze on him. He didn't look back, not wanting to send the wrong signals. Myka was a blend of opposites—gentle and tough, gutsy and sweet, beautiful and…off-limits.

He climbed into the truck, put it in gear and drove off. Figuring the fresh air would help him think, he rolled the window down all the way.

Today, as he'd looked into the faces of the women gathered at Myka's, he'd remembered the optimism that had filled him and his partners when they opened their architectural firm. Back then, fresh out of college, it seemed as if destiny had handed them the golden ticket. Everything they'd ever dreamed of was suddenly within reach.

Then life had cut them off at the knees. In the dark days after the economy started going downhill, they'd fought hard, combing the entire Bay Area looking for clients. Yet, in the end, nothing had helped. They'd been lucky to shut down debt free.

He wondered about Myka's future in Independence. As much as he wanted things to turn around for the community, the odds were stacked against them. The cost of failure could be steep, too. Grief and loss had taught Myka to keep her heart safely out of reach, but she cared about Independence and the people here. That made her vulnerable.

He pushed the thought aside as he reached the stop sign where Constitution Road met up with Main Street. Main eventually became State Road 718, which led to a small ski resort and lodge up in the mountains thirty miles north. Josh had never been able to afford skiing, but he had good memories of going tubing with his high school friends. He and his dad had fished for trout at the lake countless times before that, too.

He considered going for a drive in the mountains—that had always cheered him up—but then he remembered his financial situation. No sense in wasting a half tank of gas on nostalgia.

Joshua turned left instead, heading toward downtown. His architect's perspective drew him toward the old buildings along the street.

Except for the Brooks Mansion, he'd been indifferent to the buildings while growing up. Now they each held his interest.

Josh's cell phone rang. He came to a stop beside the curb of Hilltop Avenue and brought the phone out of his jacket pocket. The caller was Independence Insurance—his father's insurance company.

"This is Joshua Nez," he answered.

"Joshua, it's Mayor Phil Allen. I'm calling on behalf of the town. I'd like to hire you to do some architectural consulting, if you're available."

Joshua had to smile. The one thing he needed right now was work—and this was his second job offer of the day. Two years ago, he would have had to check his schedule, but at the moment, his only plans were buying groceries.

"Yes, I'm available, Mayor Allen, and I'm licensed to practice in New Mexico now. Tell me about the project you have in mind."

"Providing the town can afford your services, we'd like you to survey several of the abandoned or unoccupied buildings and give us some feedback regarding their potential."

"By potential, do you mean whether it's

cost-effective to renovate or restore them?" Joshua asked.

"Exactly, and for the buildings where neither option is efficient, we'd like you to determine whether any building materials can be salvaged and reused or sold," Allen said.

"I see where you're going with this, Mayor. If I recall, there's a lot of quality wood and hardware in some of the older structures. Can you email me your proposal with a list of the properties, so I'll know exactly what I'm getting into?"

"Of course," Mayor Allen replied. "You're the only available architect in the area, so I hope we can agree on a price. If you accept the terms, just fax the contract to my insurance office number. Town hall doesn't keep regular hours."

"I'm not going to let money stand in the way," Joshua said, giving the mayor his email address. "I'm away from home right now," he added, "but I'll check the email on my cell phone then fax back my signature later. Thinking ahead, where can I get the keys to these buildings?"

"Glad to see you're already on the ball, Josh. You're just like your father—sharp and dependable," he said. "The keys are kept at town hall. When you want to pick them up, give me a call at this number and I'll meet you there, okay?"

"Sounds good, Mayor. Thanks for your confidence. I'm really looking forward to this. By any chance is the Brooks Mansion on the list?"

"Sure is. It's a showpiece, and the town's determined to preserve it."

"What's your deadline for the estimates?"

"That'll be spelled out in your contract. If you need to adjust any of the dates, call me and we'll work it out," Mayor Allen said.

"Thanks again," Joshua said, then ended the call.

JOSHUA PULLED UP at Daniel's store ten minutes later. He'd begun this drive knowing he was almost out of groceries, but he'd been determined to buy only what he absolutely needed. Now, with some money coming in, he was in a far better mood and he was ready to remedy the food supply situation.

As he stepped inside, he saw Daniel setting up a display of toys and gifts at the front window. The garland circling the window frame made it clear the grocer wanted people to start thinking of Christmas, though it was still October.

"Hey, buddy," Joshua said, coming up to him. "Didn't know your place carried toys now."

"I'm keeping a low inventory, but I thought I'd give it a try this year since there's not much competition in town," Daniel said, looking up from the display showcasing high-end dolls. The "cowgirl" looked downright Southwestern with braids, Western hat, boots, jeans and a concha belt. Another doll wore a dark blue velvet dress in colonial New Mexican style with a shawl over her shoulders and a silver barrette in her long hair.

"Most of the families around here are on tight budgets right now, but I think they'll move heaven and earth to make sure the kids have a proper Christmas. I'm starting to offer layaway, as well."

Joshua looked at the price tag on one of the dolls and whistled low.

"Yeah, I know, but these are very popular, and I'm offering them at the same price as the Painted Canyon stores. I'm only carrying two of each, so we'll see what, if anything, happens."

"Testing the market is a good idea," he said, his thoughts drifting for a moment.

"So how come we haven't seen you in here lately?" Daniel asked, bringing him back to the present. "I figured you'd either given up eating or were driving to the superstore in Painted Canyon."

He laughed. "I had a short talk with your grandmother while picking up stuff for breakfast a few days ago. I'm not much of a cook, though, so I've been eating burgers at Shorty's."

Daniel nodded. "He still gets enough business to stay in the black."

"The food is just as good as when I was a kid. The chicken-fried steaks melt in your mouth, and he's got the best hamburgers I've ever tasted," Joshua said. "None of that franchise assembly line food."

When Daniel's gaze shifted, Joshua turned his head to see what had captured his friend's interest. Betty was at the front of the store holding Evie's hand and talking to Daniel's grandmother.

"Are you ever going to ask Betty out?" Joshua whispered.

"What? Nah, it's not like that between us."

A second later, Evie came over. Although

she didn't touch anything, her eyes were glued to the doll in the colonial dress.

"She's beautiful," Evie said in an awed whisper.

A second later Betty came over. "Sorry! She wandered off."

"Mom, look," she said and pointed.

"I know. It's the doll you saw in that catalog," Betty said. "Maybe someday I can get you a doll like that. For now, help me find your breakfast cereal. We also need milk and bread."

"And popcorn," Evie said.

Betty laughed. "Okay, get a box of our kind, then go find the cereal."

As Evie hurried off, Daniel touched Betty's arm and spoke in a low voice. "We're all watching our money right now, but since you buy all your groceries here, how about if I let the doll go at cost? You can put it on layaway and pay a little each week through the end of the year."

"That's really nice of you, Daniel, but I can't," she said. "I don't want to take advantage just because we're friends."

"Look at it as payback then. Your brother helped me out when I had a shoplifting problem last summer."

"That's his job," Betty answered. "I really appreciate your offer, Daniel, but I just can't. Not even on layaway. I've been living strictly off my savings and what the town pays me for delivering meals to our seniors. You know I'm also trying to get the inn back open for business, so any money left over goes to that. Evie and I have enough to get by, but not for extras."

"I'll tell you what. This doll's my display model. I'll set it aside for her at the end of the season and write it off my taxes."

Betty started to decline but then looked at her daughter, who'd returned and was arranging the cereal and popcorn in the shopping cart.

"Evie needs a little magic this time of year," he said quietly. "Let's see what we can do to bring it to her."

Betty hesitated, shook her head, then gave Daniel an impromptu hug. "Thanks for the offer."

As Betty walked away with Evie, Daniel looked at Joshua and shrugged. "I'm not her type, Josh. She always went for the ultramacho guys—the knuckle dragging 'me want woman' type."

"Seems to me like she might be ready to change that."

Daniel shook his head. "Don't try to set things up. Look around you. My only full-time employee is Grandma Medeiros, and this store's on life support. Take on the re-sponsibility of a woman and a child, even if she'd have me? No way."

Even as he spoke, Daniel picked up the box with the doll and took it off the display.

"You'll find a way to get it to her," Joshua said as Daniel put the box behind the counter.

"Yeah, yeah." Before he could say anything more, Betty came back.

"I forgot to ask, Daniel. Are you coming to the town meeting tonight?"

"Yeah. I hear there's big news in the air. I wouldn't miss it."

"He better show up," Grandma called out. "Or he's never going to hear the end of it."

Betty laughed. "I'll save a seat for you, Daniel."

"Sounds good. You want me...us..." he said, glancing at Grandma Medeiros, "to pick you up?"

"No, that's okay. I'll meet you there."

"Sure," Daniel said. As Evie and Betty left,

he glanced back at Joshua and growled, "One word and I'm going to deck you."

"You mean you'll try," Joshua said, laughing. Then he looked around the store. "Do you have any rawhide bones?"

Daniel pointed. "There, at the end of the aisle. Did you find Bear?"

"No, but I was thinking of putting out a special treat. So far he hasn't touched the kibble Myka leaves out, so I thought I'd tempt him with something else. Myka really wants to take care of this dog, so I figured I'd try to help."

"Better get the large ones on the bottom shelf. That's the kind your dad used to buy for him," Daniel said. "One more thing, Josh. Bear's slow to warm up, but once he's your friend, you'll never have to worry about him again."

Joshua heard the warning woven into Daniel's words. "*Slow to warm up? Does he bite?*"

"Don't think so, but I once had him sit on me for a half hour until Adam came home. The dog could have torn my face off—his head's beyond huge—but he just sat there, looking down at me and drooling. Just don't make him nervous or suspicious, and let him decide whether to approach you."

Grandma Medeiros came over. "I've been listening in and, Josh, I wanted to tell you not to worry about Bear. You are your father's son and he'll know. Pheromones and all that."

Ten minutes later, groceries in hand, Joshua left the store. As he looked at the bone in one of the bags, he thought about the big mutt. All things considered, that was one meeting he wasn't looking forward to.

MYKA AND JOSHUA set out in his truck a little before seven that evening. "I spent the past hour on the phone getting the word out," Myka said. "So did the rest of the women. I really hope this works, but I'm also worried about giving people false hope. There are no guarantees."

"Everyone knows that by now. What's needed is a goal, a mission. There's nothing worse than sitting around feeling helpless."

He paused, then said, "Let me tell you about the last few months of our firm." His eyes never left the road. "We all knew that, logically, we should walk away but, instead, we put our own money together and gave it one more try. In the end, it wasn't enough, but you know what? None of us regretted that final push. We were all broke by then, but we went down swinging."

He glanced over at her and shrugged. "If you don't fight for what you want, you've already lost something that's far more important—a piece of yourself. Stay confident and look to the future."

"I'm not looking toward the future, Joshua. We have to deal with the here and now first. But, yes, I'm ready to come out fighting."

They pulled into the parking lot, and in the glow of the light posts, she could see that nearly every slot held a vehicle. Cars and pickups also lined both sides of the street.

"I think your phone tree worked," Joshua said, finding one of the few remaining spots at the dark end of the lot.

"Wow. I didn't even know there were this many people left in town. Any hints on how to persuade them to get involved?"

"When you address the group, try to make eye contact with as many people as possible," Joshua said. "Speak from the heart and make it personal."

"Got it." As she exited the truck, Myka felt her hands shaking. She never had any problem speaking in small groups, but tonight's large crowd was another matter entirely.

Together, they walked inside the meeting hall, which was filled almost to capacity. People were seated side by side on rows of gray metal folding chairs. There was an aisle in the center, but even that was crowded with recent arrivals searching for a place to sit. A big folding table had been placed at the front of the room, where Mayor Allen and three councilors were seated.

At one time there had been eight people in the town council, but the three men in the group had resigned and moved away with their families, taking jobs in other communities.

After the Pledge of Allegiance, customary reading of the minutes, and some announcements, Mayor Allen told everyone about the possible school closing. Though the news had already spread, there was an angry rumble around the room.

Someone in the back shouted. "I don't want my seven-year-old daughter to spend an hour each day on a bus when we have a perfectly good school just down the street."

"We have to face facts," Mayor Allen said. "There's no fast or simple solution to what we're facing. Some of our craftspeople want to start a new business selling online, and that's all good, but this town needs major surgery, not a Band-Aid."

Grandma stood, threw her shoulders back and faced the crowd with an air of authority. "We keep hearing about what we can't do. Let's hear from someone who actually has a plan. Myka Solis has an idea, and we need to hear her out. It's not a cure-all—the mayor's right about that—but it's a step in the right direction."

Exasperated, Mayor Allen ran a hand through his thinning hair. "Elise, starting a new business now will take funding, and the one thing we all need to hang on to most of all is our money."

Knowing she had to speak now, Myka stood. Her hands were shaking so badly, she hid them inside her pants pockets. "We're all in trouble, and we can't continue on the way we have been. We've got only one choice now—to go forward."

Myka began to explain how they could bring the town's most talented artisans together. "Made in the U.S.A. means something to Americans and we're second to none here in Independence. We've got something special to offer."

"Myka, girl, you're dreaming." Chuck Martinez's voice echoed from across the room. "You think a bunch of artsy-crafty women are going to jump in and save our economic butts? It won't happen unless you have some golden fleece I don't know about." Several people laughed.

Anger rose inside her, but she forced herself to clamp a lid on her temper. Chuck was a chauvinistic jerk and she wouldn't let him derail her. "I'm not talking about saving the town, Chuck, I'm talking about reversing the slide, and giving some families a chance to turn things around. I've been selling skeins of my own hand-spun yarn for the past seven months and making a good, steady profit. I even have a waiting list for some of my dyed lots. Working together, we could double our output, and by purchasing the raw materials we need locally or regionally, we'd also be infusing cash into the economy here. That would eventually create jobs, too. Shipping clerks and website people, for example."

"And those of us who can't knit will herd sheep down Main Street. You're kidding, right?" Chuck shot back.

He was the only person who laughed this time.

"That's enough, Chuck," Mayor Allen ordered. "I think we all need more information on this proposal. If it'll help keep just five or ten families in their homes, I'll learn to crochet. And who knows? The wealthiest company in the country began with two college-age kids in a California garage."

Myka continued her presentation, wrapping up by mentioning the possibility of local woodworkers creating crafts and toys to add to the inventory. She finished by saying, "This is our chance to help ourselves."

"Let's open the meeting to questions," Mayor Allen said.

The hall became so quiet Myka was sure that if she tried, she'd be able to hear the heartbeats around her.

Will Solis, who'd been sitting in the back wearing civilian clothes, stood. "You all know me. I'm a no-nonsense kind of man. I listened to what Myka proposed, but I stayed grounded on the facts, and here's what I see. An operation like the one Myka described will require licenses, tax accountants and maybe even a start-up loan. Or let's say that we pony up the cash ourselves. How many of you can afford to gamble on something like this?" He looked around the room.

Myka jumped to her feet. "Are you saying

it's better not to try at all? Nothing worth-
while ever gets done without taking a risk.
Let's not give up yet."

"Great words, Myka, but that's all they
are," Will said gently. "You need to face facts.
You just don't have the necessary know-how
to start up anything bigger than your online
store."

"You have *no* idea what I'm capable of,
brother-in-law. Don't ever sell me short!" Her
words came out more forcefully than she'd intended. "Besides, I have backup—someone
who does have those skills," she said calmly,
looking over at Joshua.

Mayor Allen followed her gaze. "Josh? I'm
not sure I understand. You had your own architectural firm in San Francisco, and you're
doing some consulting work for the town, but
what's that got to do with the type of company Myka's proposing?"

Josh stood and looked at the people gathered there. "For those who don't know me,
I'm Joshua Nez. I grew up in Independence.
Most of you probably remember my dad,
Adam. Like the mayor pointed out, I'm no
expert in selling handmade crafts, but I did
start my own company, and most of the initial
steps are the same. I can help you all navigate

the sea of forms and licenses that the chief mentioned."

"Folks, take a hard look at who's talking," Will cut in. "Are you really ready to trust someone with a history as a troublemaker? Here he is back out of the blue, telling you how to spend your hard-earned money. Does listening to him sound like a good idea?"

There were several murmured comments among the crowd.

"I seem to recall you standing in front of the high school principal more than once, Will, yet you're the town's police chief now. I'll match my integrity to anyone else's in this room, including yours," Joshua said, then he turned away, clearly dismissing Will. "What I'm offering you are the skills I've acquired since leaving this community. I can help with the paperwork, but I won't join the partnership Myka's proposing. The company will belong to you all."

"Why are you doing it, then?" Henry Vaughn called out from the back of the room.

Myka knew Henry well. He was one of the best furniture makers in the area and he'd been a friend of Adam Nez. Since his pieces couldn't be easily shipped, and the train no longer serviced Independence, Henry's orders had dwindled and he'd had to close the doors of his shop. He'd be a good candidate for the partnership—if he could be sold on the idea.

"If I can help my friends while I'm here, I see no reason not to," Josh said. "But your futures are in your own hands. I have plans of my own. My firm took a hit and had to close down, but I'm still an architect. I haven't given up on my dream and I'm looking to start a new company—elsewhere."

"It's hard to follow someone who doesn't plan on sticking around," a man off to the right said.

"There is no 'follow,'" Joshua quickly responded. "Whatever happens tonight depends on all of you, not me. I've offered my skills and knowledge free of charge—for as long as I'm here. If you don't want my help, that's fine." Joshua looked around, then turned and walked out.

The room suddenly became quiet.

Myka looked at the faces around her, angry at Will and his vindictive attitude, yet pleased with Joshua's response. "The way to get through tough times is to toughen up, take every helping hand that's offered, and fight your way out," Myka said. "We either join forces now or end up like Soledad, with empty streets and abandoned homes and schools. The choice is ours."

"I'm with you, Myka," a woman's voice piped in from the right.

More heads nodded, and soon people began asking questions about creating the new business, including Henry Vaughn.

"Joshua Nez is outside, and we need him to fill in the details," Myka said. "He can guide us as we take those first few steps."

"So go get him back," someone called out.

"What if he refuses now, all things considered?" said one of the men in the front row.

"He cares about this town, which is why he came tonight, but if he says no, I can send the police to haul him in for questioning," Myka said.

Will laughed despite himself, and soft chuckles went around the room as she walked out.

Myka found Joshua sitting on the steps, arms crossed, looking up at the stars.

"Sorry, Myka, but I can't help you with this. They see me as the punk I was—not the man I've become. They'll second guess everything I say or do."

"They're ready to listen now, Joshua. Forget about Will—he's a jerk. Give the others a chance."

He stared into the distance for several long moments. "You stuck your neck out by speaking on my behalf tonight. That might come back to haunt you."

"If it does, I'll deal with it."

"If I say yes, what's going to happen once I leave town? My future lies elsewhere."

A chill spread all through her. Loss. She'd dealt with that before and had avoided it in any way, shape or form since. Refusing to let him see her insecurity, she smiled and spoke in a steady voice. "By then, hopefully we'll have things set up and running like a well-oiled machine, but if we don't, we'll cope."

"There's something I need to know first," he said. "When things don't go as planned, even if it's only a temporary setback, people begin to assign blame. It's human nature. Are you really ready to face that kind of pressure without letting it eat you up inside?"

"The responsibility for the company will be a shared one, but you're right, some will automatically look to me. If that happens, I'll face it squarely, and do what has to be done. Like you, I stand up for myself."

He nodded.

"I know all about dreams that go south, Joshua. I had a loving husband, a good job and a wonderful home." She swallowed hard. "When all that ended, I was lost for a long time, but these days I take pride in knowing I can do whatever I have to. Asking for help isn't easy for me, but this isn't about me. It's about a place we all love. If I end up losing it, too, I want to know I had the guts to fight for it."

"Then I'll help you. Let's go back inside and get started."

CHAPTER SEVEN

FORTY-FIVE MINUTES later the meeting ended, and people began streaming back to their cars. What a crazy thing life was! The same people he'd considered his enemies at one time were now looking to him for answers and advice.

The last to leave, Myka eventually met him on the steps. "We've got lots of people ready to jump in. Henry's getting some of his friends together to decide what wood crafts and toys they could sell. Also, several women will send me photos of their work. Then I'll decide what can be marketed."

"The pressure begins. Do you think some will want to sell the equivalent of Evie's refrigerator art?"

She smiled sheepishly. "Yeah. I'll just have to find a way to play the bad guy."

"*You* playing the bad guy?" He laughed, but Myka poked him in the ribs.

They were walking toward Joshua's truck

when Will and Betty stepped away from a group of a dozen or so people and approached.

Will glanced at Myka, then cut in front of Joshua and fixed him with an ice-cold glare. "This town may be ready to trust you, but I'll be watching every step of the way."

Will turned to Myka, and in a gentler voice, added, "Josh will make a move on you—it's just a matter of time."

Myka tensed, not knowing how to respond.

"Okay, that's it, big brother," Betty said, grabbing Will's arm and tugging at it. "Let's go."

Will kept his focus on Myka. "Be careful. He's got time on his hands now, and you're living right next door."

Myka watched Will walk away with Betty and Daniel. "I don't understand why he behaved so badly tonight," she said. "You seem to bring out the worst in him."

"In his shoes, I might not act any differently."

"What do you mean?"

"Will misses his brother, Myka, and seeing you going on with your life is just another reminder that Tanner's gone for good."

She took a breath, nodded and climbed into his truck. "You might be right, though I felt like smacking him a couple of times tonight. Accepting that someone's never coming back is incredibly hard. When Tanner passed away, the reality that he was gone forever almost crushed me. Then one day I realized it had been hours since I'd thought about him. That was the first step of many, but life is like that. No matter how much it hurts, the sun still rises and days go by."

"I'm sorry you had to go through all that," he said, driving slowly down the street. He'd listened to her carefully, wondering if Myka was still in love with Tanner, but what he'd heard in her voice hadn't been grief. The wound had healed, but the scar remained.

"Dad has some old snapshots, and your folks are in a lot of them. You and Tanner, too. Why don't you come over and take the box? I've already separated the ones I want. If there are any you'd like to keep, you're welcome to them."

"Okay, thanks."

The drive home didn't take long, and soon Josh parked in his driveway. As they were approaching his front door, they heard a creaking sound coming from the back of the house.

He stopped in midstride and held her back. "Do you have many break-ins around here?"

"Not at all. Even if you left a door open, which is my guess, no one's likely to just walk in."

"I haven't settled into a routine, so it's possible I may have left the back door unlocked," he said slowly. "I've done some heavy duty cleaning lately, and I remember propping it open to let the fumes out. Stay here while I go take a look."

"Wait," she said, reaching for his arm. "Let me call Will or one of his officers. That's their job."

"No, I'll handle this myself," he said, and jogged around to the back of the house. Will was the last person he wanted to ask for help. Joshua slipped silently through the open door. As he entered the kitchen, he immediately spotted the intruder and froze. A big mutt was standing on its hind legs reaching for the bag of dog treats on top of the fridge.

As Joshua drew in a breath, he nearly gagged. The massive dog had clearly been sprayed by a skunk.

The mutt grasped the bag in its jaws and calmly turned around to look at Joshua.

This had to be Bear. He was black with an enormous head, floppy ears, and a short wide muzzle. His body was heavy boned and muscular. Myka had mentioned that the dog was big, but this animal was a tank with legs.

"Good boy," Joshua said calmly, not wanting to alarm such a powerful creature in close quarters. Moving slowly, he reached over and flipped on the overhead light switch.

The dog didn't move, but it growled, a low, menacing sound that made Joshua's skin crawl. He remained perfectly still, trying to figure out his next move. Right now, he was between the animal and the door—its only way out. A cornered tank...

Joshua took a slow step to one side, granting it passage, but instead of bolting for the exit, the dog just barked, a sound that was deep and menacing.

A second later Myka appeared. "Bear, you big dummy! You scared me half to death! Where have you been all this time?" Suddenly she gagged and put her hand over her mouth and nose. "Aw, gross! You tried to make friends with the skunk again, didn't you?"

She crossed the kitchen and grabbed the dog by the collar. "Come on, Bear, we need to get that stink out before you choke us to death."

The animal's growling became softer but,

if anything, the sound was more menacing than ever. What was worse, he never took his eyes off Joshua.

"We've got to get him into the bathtub," Myka said, but Joshua didn't move a muscle. "Joshua, move. He needs a bath, and we can't do it outside. It's already too cold."

"He doesn't want me to move," Joshua whispered. "Look at him." No way Myka would be able to hold that beast back if he lunged. He had to come up with a plan.

"Relax. He's just trying to figure out who you are. Now get moving and find some towels," Myka said, trying not to choke.

As Joshua stepped aside, Bear growled, but Myka jerked on his collar. "No!"

The dog stopped immediately.

"Meet me in the master bathroom," Myka told Joshua. "Your dad and I had to do this before. He kept a special skunk descenter in the pantry so get that and some baking soda, too." She coughed. "Hurry."

Moments later, he met her in the bathroom. The dog was sitting at one end of the tub as she soaked him all over with the handheld shower wand.

Myka pulled her shirt up to cover her mouth as she lathered Bear with the emzyme shampoo, but the smell seemed to increase the wetter the dog got. Pretty soon, both Myka and Joshua were gagging hard. "Get something to cover our faces. Bandanas, anything," she managed.

Joshua returned moments later with two dishcloths. He'd tied one around his face, and he started to do the same for her when the dog growled.

"Quiet, you big dummy!" Myka said, and the dog stopped. "Get me some vinegar. The descenter needs a little boost."

"Don't have any. I've got beer and I've got water."

"Run over to my place—the key's beneath the planter. Go to the cupboard on the right, beside the kitchen sink, and grab the vinegar. It's in a big plastic bottle. Then get towels from my hall closet, *lots* of towels. He's got a short coat, but there's a lot of dog here."

"Hadn't noticed" he said.

ALMOST THIRTY MINUTES LATER they were both soaked to the skin, but the dog had stopped smelling like an exploded septic tank.

They sat in the kitchen, cups of warm coffee in hand, while Bear lay at Myka's feet, happily snoring away.

"That animal doesn't trust me," Joshua said.

"You helped me towel dry him, and he didn't grumble, so he's okay with you. Now that he's had something to smell besides skunk, he understands that you're a friend."

"He knows I'm *your* friend, but I don't think he's ready to consider me his bud."

"Now that he's cleaned up, would you like him to spend the night? Both of you could get to know each other," she said, and added, "oh—and before I forget, he sleeps on the bed. Adam let him have the left side."

Seeing Joshua's eyes widen, she laughed. "I'm kidding, I'm kidding." She placed her hand on the dog's back. "Unless you really want Bear, I'd like to take him home."

"Fine by me."

"Great. Now help me carry his bed, dishes, and toys over to my place." She curled her hand around Bear's collar. "Come on, guy. You're mine now."

The dog looked up at her and wagged his tail.

"You've got a real way with animals," Joshua said, walking over to pick up the enormous doggie bed.

"No, I just know this particular dog and I like him a lot."

Once Bear's stuff was placed in his new home, Myka immediately reached on top of the cupboard and brought down a stuffed toy squirrel. She tossed it to the dog, who caught the toy in midair, shook it, then brought it back to her.

She played tug of war with Bear, ignoring his growls.

"Are you sure you're going to be okay with him?" Joshua asked.

"Oh, yeah! He's just playing. Look." She stopped tugging, looked at the dog and said, "Bear, sit!"

The dog obeyed instantly.

"Your dad trained him." She hugged Bear, then glanced at Joshua. "Can I borrow some of your aftershave? I'd like to add a nice boy scent to his coat, not just skunk deodorizer."

"Yeah, but for him, you're going to need a gallon, not just a splash."

She laughed. "A few drops will do. I just want something nice smelling in my bedroom."

That was the last thing Josh should be thinking about, Myka was alluring without even being aware of it.

Bringing those thoughts to a crashing stop, he added, "Tell me something, Myka. Why does this dog mean so much to you? You were really hoping I didn't want to keep him. Am I wrong?"

"Yes and no," she said, leaving Bear with his toy and joining Joshua at the kitchen table. "Bear needs someone. The person who was his entire world passed away. I know what that feels like. And, like him, I wanted to run away, too," she said. "Bear and I are two of a kind. The difference is that he'll always need someone to look after him, and I learned to take care of myself."

He glanced down at the dog, who seemed perfectly at peace now. "I'll go get some aftershave."

By the time he returned, Myka had offered the dog a bowl of kibble, and the animal had made himself at home. Josh watched as Myka put a few drops of aftershave on her hands, then rubbed Bear's coat along the flanks.

"Thanks!" she said, returning the bottle to him. "Nice aftershave. I've noticed it before—on you. Very masculine." She reached out and touched his arm, inching closer. "I really appreciate all your help tonight."

"We make a good team. Remember that car wash back in eighth grade? Raising money for the field trip?" He smiled, recalling the details.

"What I remember was the water fight we had with those garden hoses. We were both sopping wet, and Mr. Kelly drove us home in the back of his pickup. Under that blanket together…"

"We were both too shy to cuddle and stay warm."

"That was then, this is now." Myka let go of his arm, then sat on his lap, wrapping both wet sleeves around his neck.

Bear barked and came over, resting his big muzzle on her leg.

"Another chaperone. I can't get a break," Joshua moaned, careful not to make any sudden moves.

"Yeah, I'd better get off before he gets possessive," Myka replied, standing. "Next time, our pal here gets sent outside."

Joshua gazed through the open doorway into the living room and saw Tanner's photo on a shelf. Had she placed it there to keep his memory alive, or had it been there for so long she'd stopped seeing it?

"As much as I'd like to stay, I'd better go home," he said. "I need to do some more research on LLCs and New Mexico regulations before calling it a night."

"Well, here's to a great evening." She stood on her tiptoes and gave him a quick kiss.

After saying goodbye, Joshua walked home slowly. Maybe Will was right and he should stay away from Myka. Tonight, he'd caught a glimpse of just how vulnerable she really was. In their own ways, they'd each been to hell and back. Yet, at the end, she'd shown they could still have fun together.

Once inside, Joshua checked the back door, wondering how the dog had gotten in. A moment later he had his answer. The mechanism was sticking, probably from accumulated dust, and the bolt had stayed open. Bear could have opened the door with a push from his muzzle or paw.

Josh tracked down some spray silicon below the sink, fed a little into the works, and moved the knob and bolt until it worked smoothly again. Then he locked up.

Crossing the main room, he went to his laptop. His dad's computer was still sitting on the large wooden desk. He took a deep breath. He might as well start using it. It had a larger display and files that might be important now.

Joshua began going through his dad's many

emails. Most of the ones between Mayor
Allen and his dad dealt with restoring rail
service to the town. The trains came in via a
spur located on land that had once belonged to
Silas Brooks. Without proof of ownership—
supposedly in Brooks's missing will—the
town hadn't been able to cut a new right-of-
way deal with the railroad. Going through the
courts so the county could assume ownership
could take forever, so the best solution was
for them to find the will.

The mayor and his dad had searched everywhere, including Brooks's safety deposit
boxes, but the document had yet to surface.

Joshua sat back, lost in thought. The company Myka was working to get off the ground
would benefit from having rail service. That
would really cut shipping costs, particularly
on the larger items. It made sense for him to
continue his dad's work and see where it led.

After a moment, Joshua checked his own
email account. Most of the messages were
spam, but two were from architectural firms
he'd applied to. The first was a generic "thank
you for your interest" rejection letter from an
Albuquerque firm. The second, from a consulting company in Seattle, informed him that

the owners had decided to retire and were in the process of closing down for good.

He gazed out the window and, seeing the lights were still on at Myka's, his thoughts drifted. He'd dreaded coming back, yet now that he had, he realized everything had changed, including his own perceptions of Independence and its residents. The only place where things had remained the same was in the landscape of his mind.

As he watched, the lights over at Myka's went out one by one. He'd hoped they could be friends, but the attraction between them was too strong. The longer they were around each other, the more dangerous the situation would become.

He was falling in love with her all over again, and she might feel the same way. His plans were set—he was going to resume his career, which meant he'd have to leave Independence. Yet this was where Myka's roots were firmly planted. If he stayed because of her—and that would be the only reason—he'd end up a failure, at least to himself. There was no guarantee that their love would endure anyway. And for Myka's sake, he couldn't ask her to give up all she valued and go with him. They just didn't have a future together, un-

less he or Myka surrendered what each valued most. The sacrifice would come back to
haunt them sooner or later.

He muttered a curse and turned back to
the computer. The sooner he got out of this
town, the better. With that in mind, he got
down to business, creating a plan that Myka
could follow to set up her company. Once that
was done, there would be no reason for him
to stick around.

CHAPTER EIGHT

MYKA GLANCED OUT the window and saw Will's squad car go by. Since the town hall meeting a week ago, he'd been driving past at night more often. She'd seen him cruising down the street at midnight last night, and now here he was at eight-thirty in the morning.

Myka padded to the kitchen in her bunny slippers, poured herself another cup of coffee, then walked out onto the back porch with Bear. "Okay, guy, playtime."

As the dog wandered off, she sat down on the stoop and sipped her coffee. She was dressed comfortably in a pair of jeans and her favorite old, baggy wool sweater. Over the past few years, she'd repaired the worn spots by embroidering over them. The dark blue wool was now decorated with multicolored daisies, their size depending on the hole that needed to be covered.

Myka kept an eye on the dog as he meandered around, sniffing the various places that caught his attention. He stayed away from the sheep, who were feeding, and when he was finally done, he came back to her.

Myka put her coffee down and hugged him. "I'm glad you're here, Bear, and that you're mine."

"Are you going to change his name?" Joshua's voice came from the far side of the house.

Myka jumped, and Bear placed himself between her and Joshua.

"You almost gave me a heart attack," Myka said. "How do you move so quietly?"

Joshua stayed where he was. "That dog's on edge. Maybe you should put him inside."

Myka placed her hand on the dog's head and instantly his tail started to wag. "He's okay. You startled both of us, that's all. Believe me, if Bear had really considered you a threat, you'd be flat on the ground with him on top of you."

"I heard about his run-in with Daniel," Joshua said.

"So what brings you here this morning?" she asked, warming her hands on the coffee mug.

"I made a list of items you need to take

into account when you write up your business plan."

"I'm still trying to sort out the partnership details," she said. "Everyone will get a share of the profits, but there should be some kind of incentive for the most productive members of the company, too."

"I'm sure there are business software packages that can be adapted to whatever formula you come up with." He watched her for a moment longer. "But something else is bothering you, isn't it?"

She gave him a tired smile. "This morning I tried to expand my website to include the various kinds of merchandise we'll be carrying, and everything crashed. I'll have to revamp the entire site. On top of that, I still have to write copy and post an image for each new item and package current orders so they ship on time," she said, her voice rising, though she was trying to stay calm.

"You'll need to start delegating some of those duties. If you apply for a start-up loan, you can hire someone. Let's go to your computer, and I'll show you where to begin."

She pointed down the hall. "My office is the first room on the right." Myka followed Josh inside with Bear at her heels.

"I've got a basic outline for your executive summary. Of course you'll have to fill in the blanks, but I'll help you as much as I can. You'll also need a license and insurance. The sooner the better," he said, taking a flash drive from his pocket. "If we start the paperwork right now, we can get the bulk of it done by the end of the morning."

"Slow down, will you? I haven't even finished my coffee," she said, and took a shaky breath.

"Setting up an LLC can be complicated. Ask Robyn to come over and do some of the computer work while we take care of the rest," he said. "I'll upload the file and start filling out some of the forms while you contact her." He inserted the flash drive into a USB port. "I've got this."

"Will you give me a minute to think?"

"Go call Robyn. I'll handle this part."

"Stop it. You're issuing orders."

He glared at her. "I'm trying to help you."

"You're not. You're taking over," she snapped.

He rose to his feet, his hands trembling slightly. "Handle it on your own, then. I've got other things to do. See you around." He strode out the door without looking back.

Alone in her office, Myka listened to the silence, then bent down to hug the dog. "He doesn't get it, Bear. Taking over and helping are two very different things."

The dog sighed softly and wagged his tail.

STILL ANGRY AT the way things had gone with Myka, Joshua grabbed a printout listing the properties Mayor Allen had included in his contract. He had work to do, so why was he still thinking about her? Even if he had come on too strong, he'd only been trying to help.

He pushed Myka from his mind. Today, he'd go and take some photos—starting with the Brooks Mansion.

Grabbing his pocket camera—he'd sold his expensive Nikon during the attempt to save his business—Joshua went outside. As he walked to his pickup, he glanced at Myka's house. No one was about.

Josh slipped behind the wheel. Next stop, town hall to pick up the keys.

SEVERAL MINUTES LATER, Joshua parked his pickup on Main Street in front of the Brooks Mansion and climbed out. The estate was comprised of two sections. This structure, a blend of Moorish and Spanish Mission architectural styles, had been the business offices of Brooks Enterprises. The rear structure, the residence, was traditional Territorial, and they were linked by a tunnel in the form of an arched corridor.

Joshua stood on the sidewalk and looked up at the imposing doorway, which featured an ogee arch. The double doors were thick oak, five paneled, and chip carved by hand. The lock, however, was modern and secure. He took a step up and inserted the key.

Once inside, he looked around and smiled. The front room was spacious and meant for entertaining. Large chairs and benches were scattered about, but he paid little attention to the furnishings. Instead, he concentrated on the mosaic tile bordering the large fireplace and the Southwest landscape fresco on the largest wall. He brought out his cell phone and began taking pictures.

As he walked from room to room, he noted the places where ceramic flooring tiles were missing or loose and checked for thin lines on the walls showing where masonry was cracked. These were all minor cosmetic problems, however; not structural issues.

Next, he headed for the underground corridor. The passageway between the two structures was built in a New World Spanish Mission style with a plain white arched hallway, brick floor and very few decorations. The light fixtures were leafy, wrought-iron wall sconces with electric candles.

A large oak door gave access to the residence, up one flight of stairs. Inside, the older adobe house was solid but simple. There were *nichos,* boxlike hollows built into the walls, used to display religious icons.

Several of the rooms had kiva fireplaces, and all but the smallest featured vigas—large, peeled round logs used as ceiling beams.

There were a lot more drawers, cabinets and storage spaces here. He opened a few out of curiosity, wondering if the missing will and other papers might be hidden in one of these. Then again, his father had undoubtedly searched through them already.

Finally, he stepped out to the courtyard, floored with brick and tile, and decorated with stone tables and metal chairs. There were five small, bare trees surrounded by a thick blanket of leaves. Organic debris had blown everywhere, and nearly filled the empty compound circling the decorative fountain. Josh could tell it wouldn't take much to restore what had been a quiet retreat.

He put away his cell phone, having taken dozens of photos already. Then he looked at his watch, knowing he still needed to check out the other properties. After that was done, he'd come back and spend some more time exploring. The Brooks Mansion had exceeded even his childhood imaginings. Someday, perhaps, a son or daughter of his would be sitting beside a fountain like the one out there, dangling their toes in the cool spray and laughing with the innocence only a child could have.

MYKA WAS SITTING at her desk looking through Joshua's file when she heard a knock on the front door. Answering it and finding Sophie, Myka invited her inside.

"I saw Josh leave about an hour ago," Sophie said with a tiny smile. "Did he spend the night?"

Myka drew in a sharp breath. "Are you nuts? No! We're just friends—at least we were. Right now I'm not so sure."

"You two have a fight?" Seeing Myka nod, she added, "Did you get into it as friends, or were you arguing with the company's consultant?"

"Both—I think," she said, walking back

to the kitchen with Sophie and offering her a cup of coffee.

A moment later they sat at the table, mugs of fresh brew in front of them. "Okay, fess up. What happened this morning?" Sophie asked.

Myka explained, then added, "I hate being rushed into making decisions. It reminds me of what happened after Tanner passed on, when the insurance people and lawyers came out of nowhere, all wanting me to give them instant answers."

"To do things the right way, you're going to need his input, Myka. Don't shut him out."

Myka took a deep breath, then let it out slowly. "I know. You're right, but having Joshua tell me what to do was hard."

"Because he's so hot?"

"That's *not* what I was going to say," Myka answered, biting back a smile. "It was difficult because I wanted to prove to myself that I could handle it, not just follow directions."

After finishing her coffee, Sophie left, and Myka went in search of her boots. She had to check the water for her sheep, then lay out some more hay. The pasture was getting a bit bare, and with winter coming on, she needed to compensate.

Once she finished with that, she'd go talk

to Joshua. Sophie was right. This was no time for sore egos.

She thought of all the work he'd put into the business plan and the research that had involved. She needed to thank him and apologize.

She was the real problem, not him. Joshua's energy and his relentless pursuit of whatever goal he fixed on made him exciting to be around. He was strong, masculine and sure of himself, and she'd have to fight not to get swept up in all that.

She stopped by the hall mirror and took a hard look at herself. The truth was as clear as the image staring back at her. Although she needed to keep it strictly business between them, a part of her longed for more than was wise.

Two WEEKS PASSED in a whirl of activity and she still hadn't caught up to Joshua. He was seldom home, and when he was, she was invariably busy. People had been dropping by practically nonstop, bringing all kinds of handcrafted items and hoping to take part in the online shop.

Hearing a knock and realizing it was ten in the morning—time for the package express guy to come by—she stepped away from the keyboard, where she was writing advertising copy, and went to greet the delivery man.

She opened the door, but instead of the driver, she found Robyn.

"Hi, Robyn. I guess my deliveryman's late this morning. Come in. Did you bring me more of your mom's pieces?"

Robyn shook her head. "I need to talk. You have a minute?"

Myka gave her a wan smile. "No, but I'll make time anyway. Tea or coffee?"

"Coffee would be great."

They sat down in the kitchen and Myka brought the coffee pot and cups to the table. "So what's on your mind?"

"I spoke to Joshua earlier at the post office. He said you got upset when he tried to help, that you were finding it difficult to delegate responsibility."

"There's some truth to that," she admitted.

Robyn glanced around the front room, filled with boxes, and shook her head. "Myka, this place looks like a warehouse. If you try to do everything on your own, work will bury you. You have to get a staff."

"*Staff?* Are you kidding me? Where would

they work? I barely have room to walk down the hall."

"You need to accept Josh's help setting things up. If he's a little heavy handed, it's probably because he has a lot at stake, too. Josh lost his business, and by helping us run ours, he's getting a chance to make a place for himself here in town."

"I don't think you've got Josh figured out. He's helping because he wants to stay busy until he decides what's next. The future of Independence directly affects him, too, because he'll eventually sell his father's house and he wants a fair price for it."

"Maybe so, but the bottom line's still the same. We need his help, and you need to delegate some of the work. I'll handle the marketing, write copy and take care of the updates on the website. Ask Sophie and the others to pitch in, too. They can package orders and everyone will need to get busy promoting our site online."

Myka shook her head. "We can't take on any more business, not yet anyway. There's a problem I hadn't foreseen—raw materials. I've been supplying people in town with the yarn they need to make our products but I'm almost out of wool. I'll have to call around and see if anyone who raises sheep has some wool on hand we can process."

"That may take contacting people outside Independence. No one here has a large herd. Let me look into it."

"Winter's coming up, and shearing time is still months away," Myka reminded her.

"So it's bound to be a challenge," Robyn said. "Don't worry. I'm up to it. If there's raw wool out there somewhere, I'll find it."

Myka was walking Robyn to the door when a loud knock sounded. Robyn reached it first and opened it.

Joshua stood there with a box of Grandma Medeiros's handmade doughnuts.

Robyn sniffed the air and smiled. "I know what's in the box, and I'm not leaving unless you share."

Laughing, he lifted the lid and offered her a doughnut.

As she took one, the scent reached Bear. He pushed past Myka and nudged Joshua.

"Forget it, guy," Josh said.

"If this is your idea of a peace offering, remind me to pick a fight with you as often as possible," Robyn said. "I'll get back to you, Myka, and don't worry. I'll hurry." Robyn headed toward her car.

"What's up? Is something wrong?" he asked Myka.

She nodded, glad to see him, and waved him inside. "This morning I realized that we're running low on wool. I've been selling my yarn at reduced prices to Liza and Millie and some of the other women. They make the sweaters, afghans, bedspreads and crafts we're selling online. I was also selling some of my hand dyed skeins under a special label, but with increased demand, my wool's almost gone."

"So you've got a crisis?"

She nodded. "I didn't realize how fast I was going through my reserves. Before, it wouldn't have mattered as much. We would have waited until next shearing season and, in the interim, used commercial yarn. Now it's different. We sell high-end merchandise for top prices, and we promise customers completely handcrafted products. We'll need to buy first-rate wool and process it ourselves."

"So, how many people in town raise sheep?"

"Only two, but their flocks aren't much bigger than mine. I have a feeling that what they could offer us won't be nearly enough."

"I have relatives on the Rez who raise sheep. Let me put out the word," he said.

"Could you call them?" she asked. "It might speed things up a little."

"Most of them live in rural areas where phone service is spotty at best, but I can leave word at the trading posts and eventually the message will reach them."

As they talked, Bear brought Myka an old tennis ball and dropped it by her feet.

"This guy's been so good this morning. Would you mind going out back with me so I can throw the ball for him?"

"Let's do it," he said. He followed her outside and they walked to a place away from the sheep.

Although she tried pitching, she wasn't very good at it, and the ball never went far. Bear caught up to it easily and immediately brought it back. "He needs more exercise. Can you throw it for him?" She handed Joshua the ball.

He pitched it across the yard in a high arc and it traveled at least three times the distance it had for her. Bear lumbered after it, clomping along like a horse then scooping it up.

"Nice throw! Can you do that a few more times? He'll love it."

Bear trotted back proudly, the ball clenched in his mouth.

"No problem," he said and after Bear dropped the ball in front of him, he threw it again. "Myka, I hope you don't mind my saying this, but you look exhausted. I've seen your lights on long after midnight. Have you been getting enough sleep?"

She shrugged. "I wake up at two or three in the morning, then start thinking about what needs to be done. It's hard to roll over and go back to sleep after that."

"I put in eighteen-hour days or longer when we first opened our firm. After a while exhaustion took its toll and I started making mistakes. One might have proven to be a disaster if it hadn't been caught."

"You think I'll do that, too?" she asked, now worried.

"You're overworked and you're human. I don't want to scare you, Myka, but you need to stay sharp and that requires sleep."

This time, instead of bringing the ball to Josh, Bear raced past both of them and went directly to the back door.

"Okay, he's had enough," Myka said, going inside.

A moment later, Bear sprawled on the cool

tiles in the kitchen and began to gnaw on his bone.

"I'm glad he likes my present," Joshua said.

"Are you kidding? He loves it. He carries that bone everywhere." She paused for a moment, collecting her thoughts, then continued. "Before we go on, I need to apologize to you, Joshua. Last time you were here we had a problem. Too much was coming at me at once. I'm not just running Myka's Wooly Dreams anymore, and sometimes I forget that."

"It might help to come up with a new company name," he said. "Also, try looking at what you do in a different light. It isn't just a business. You're producing things that bring a touch of beauty into people's lives."

"Broaden my outlook," she said with a nod. "Is that what you did?"

"Yeah. I never saw my work as just designing buildings to suit a client. To me, it was about creating spaces people could call home, or buildings that became the heart of a growing business. Each design had to speak to the owners in a special way. Once you shift your focus, things fall more naturally into place."

She sighed. "See that? That's exactly what

makes it so darned hard to work with you," she muttered.

"What do you mean?" he asked, surprised.

"It's way too easy to come to you for answers," she said softly. "The problem is your own future will take you away from here all too soon. I can't get used to having you around."

"Then let me set your mind at ease. You have my word that I won't go anywhere until after Christmas."

"You can't promise that, Joshua. Christmas is almost two months away. What if the perfect job comes along next month—or next week?"

He shook his head. "There's no such thing, Myka. 'Perfect' was owning my own company. What I'm doing now is searching for a job that'll allow me to recoup financially. I need to start saving so that eventually I can reach my goal again. The problem is that the industry has slowed almost to a standstill. I've sent out dozens of applications and made a lot of calls, but very few firms are hiring right now."

Remembering Robyn's frustrating job search, she nodded. Myka took a doughnut from the box he'd brought and offered him another. "Is living here as hard for you as it used to be?"

He stood by the window, looking back at his father's house. "There was a time when this place seemed like a giant black hole, one that sucked up dreams and squashed them out of existence. Dad moved through each day just getting by. I wanted…more."

Joshua lapsed into a long silence, and she came up from behind and silently placed her hand on his arm.

He turned to face her. "I reached my dream once, and I can do it again, but this pause is useful. It gives me time to reassess what I want and where I'm headed. What's even better is that right now I'm needed here, and I'm spending my time doing something that matters."

"Our company does need you, Joshua," she said, then smiled slowly. "Of course it would also help a lot if I could learn to accept advice gracefully."

He laughed. "Yeah, there's that, but don't worry. I may come on strong sometimes, but I'll still have your back. You can trust me."

He brushed a gentle kiss on her forehead, but as the warmth of his body touched hers, other feelings stirred to life inside her.

"We'll look out for each other, Joshua," she said, and walked him to the door.

Myka stayed by the window and watched Joshua head home. Determination defined his long-legged strides. After he disappeared from view, she walked down the hall to her office.

Halfway there, she tripped over some boxes. Myka yelped, but managed to catch herself before hitting the floor.

An office…a real one somewhere away from home…was that even possible? She needed to look at the spreadsheet and see where they stood financially. That start-up loan Joshua had mentioned was looking more attractive by the minute. Office space would mean she could restore order to her parents' home. If her mom could see the place now, she'd swear Myka had lost her mind.

She had to stop letting fear hold her back. It was time to move forward.

CHAPTER NINE

WORK SEEMED NEVER ending, and the weeks passed, ushering in November. Taking a break and sitting back in her chair, Myka suddenly realized that, with the exception of throwing the ball for Bear and having an occasional cup of coffee with Robyn or Sophie, she hadn't done anything fun in ages.

She stared at the pile of paperwork on her desk. More crafters had joined their LLC since Joshua had helped her file the articles of organization and operating agreement with the state. They were forty-two members strong now. In the spirit of renewal, she and Robyn had come up with a list of possible company names, and after a majority vote, they'd officially become Handmade in Independence, or HMI, for short.

With additional production and sales, business continued to grow. Robyn had completely taken over the webpage, too, and traffic was increasing, keeping up with their listings.

Sophie came over every morning to help Myka package the orders, except for the crafts belonging to the woodworkers, who handled their own shipping. Hearing a knock and seeing it was eight-thirty, Myka went to let Sophie in.

"How's the search for office space going?" Sophie asked, looking at the crowded living room, then bending down to pet Bear.

"Joshua has been searching for just the right place. We need to make room for our crafters as well as the woodworkers group headed by Henry Vaughn. People from both divisions have said they could do more if the company would provide them with work areas. At home, they tend to be in cramped spaces and they get interrupted. The woodworkers have also mentioned that their neighbors are complaining about the constant din of saws and lathes day and night."

"Working from home isn't all it's cracked up to be," Sophie said. "It's not that Mom interrupts, but there are too many temptations to get away from my desk, you know? It lacks…structure."

Myka looked at her spinning wheel, now

sitting in the corner and hemmed in by packing boxes. "HMI will need wool processing rooms, too. We should be far away from residences and other businesses so the noise doesn't become a problem. That means we're looking for a lot more than office space. We need a whole new working environment—maybe two sites."

For the next half hour they worked in silence, then Myka reached for the last skein of russet-colored yarn. "Uh-oh."

"That's the last one?" Sophie said, her voice rising in panic.

"Yeah, I'm afraid so. We have other colors, but they're going fast. Robyn and Joshua have been trying to find more local suppliers, but it's been tough. Ideally, we'd like to buy a year's worth of wool, wholesale, from a seller who'll let us set up a payment plan."

"Any luck so far?"

"No," Myka said. "I never realized that finding a new supplier would be this hard."

Hearing a knock on the screen door, she glanced up and saw Joshua standing there. "Hi, ladies. Is there a problem? I just overheard Myka say something about finding a supplier."

"Come on in, Joshua," Myka said, waving

her hand. "You already know that we're running out of wool, and it's the most important raw material to keep us in business."

Joshua nodded. "And you're going to need a constant, dependable supply. I meant to try to find a tribal source that might work out, but I haven't made any calls yet."

"Get started, then, Josh, if you don't mind. We really need quality wool, and we need it soon," Myka said.

Sophie finally spoke. "Josh, your mentioning the tribe just reminded me of something—someone—who might be able to help."

"Really? That's great." Myka stopped what she was doing and gave Sophie her undivided attention. "Who do you have in mind?"

"Before I came back home for good, I lived with a roommate in Albuquerque. From time to time she'd talk about her aunt, an Iraqi vet who lives on the Navajo Rez. She's got a huge herd of *Churro* sheep."

"Whoa, I think I know who you mean," Joshua said. "The woman you were talking about…any chance her name is Maxine Redhorse?" Joshua asked.

"Yes! Do you know her?"

"Only by reputation. Since Dad died, I've

been in touch with people he knew on the Rez, uncles and old friends, and her name came up. She's a decorated war veteran who apparently returned to the Rez after her hitch was up. That was seven years ago. The *Diné,* The People, leave her alone for the most part, because she'll wave a shotgun at you if you approach her place without permission. She has a reputation as being kind of a hermit. And now that you mention it, I recall some-one saying she raised sheep."

"Then let's call her," Myka said quickly.

"That's part of the problem. She has no phone."

"This doesn't sound promising," Myka said slowly.

Joshua shrugged. "We do have an edge. The reason I heard about her is because she gets her groceries at the trading post owned by my aunt and her husband."

"I don't think I've ever met them. Were they at your father's service?"

He shook his head. "They're Traditional-ists. They don't attend funerals or memorial services."

"You told me why that was one time, but I can't remember. Something about the per-son's ghost?"

"Not quite. The chindi isn't a ghost, it's the evil side of a man, and since that can't merge with universal harmony, it stays earthbound. Traditionalists believe it can create big problems for the living, so they do their best to avoid contact with it," he said. "My aunt and uncle take things like that very seriously. My uncle's a *hataalii,* a Navajo medicine man. He and Dad had trouble getting along, but I think he'll help me."

"Can you call and find out?"

He shook his head. "No. They'll see a phone call as a sign of disrespect, that I didn't care enough to come ask them in person."

"All right. Then we'll both go," Myka said.

"I can take care of this," he said. "It may be dangerous for you. I understand Maxine doesn't trust Anglos—whites—particularly those she doesn't know."

"I have to be there, Joshua. I'll need to establish a connection with her if we end up doing business. After you leave, she'll have to deal with me."

"*Leave?* Josh, are you taking off on us now?" Sophie asked.

"The soonest I'd go is after Christmas, and that's only if I find a position as an architect," he said.

"Even so, I'm going to the Rez with you, Joshua," Myka repeated.

"Then can you be ready to leave early tomorrow? It's nearly a three-hour drive, and I'd like to be there about the time they open the trading post," Joshua said.

"When's that?" Myka asked.

"Eight o'clock," he answered.

"Sure," she said. "Sophie, can you box tomorrow's orders?"

"No problem. My cousin's daughter Paula can help me get everything ready. We can also feed and water your sheep."

"Thanks so much! One more favor?" she asked, glancing over at Bear, who was playing with his squeaky toy. "Can you guys take care of him, too? I'll pay you myself for that part."

"No problem. Paula loves dogs. I'll give her the job of babysitting him until you get home. She'll keep him company, so no more running away."

"Perfect. That way I won't have to worry," Myka said, then looked back at Joshua. "Okay, we're all set. I'll be ready."

As he walked out, they both watched him, and after a moment, Sophie glanced at Myka and grinned. "He's still got the best butt in the county."

"I wasn't checking out his..." Seeing Sophie give her an openly incredulous look, she laughed. "Okay, busted."

JOSHUA STOPPED BY Daniel's market next and found that his friend was assisting a customer at the meat counter. That wasn't a problem, because he'd come looking for Grandma Medeiros anyway. He walked over to the back room and glanced through the open doorway. The spry, elderly woman was making coffee.

"Excuse me, ma'am, do you have a moment?" he asked.

"Certainly, Joshua, come on in and sit down. What's on your mind?"

"Thanks," he said, finding a seat on one of the three-legged stools beside a counter. "I'm hoping you have some information about my father—work he was doing before he died."

"We spoke a lot about the community—and family—you father and I," she replied, reaching for a coffee mug with a hand-painted daisy on the side. "What, exactly, do you want to know?"

"Before Dad passed on, he was trying to help Mayor Allen find Brooks's revised will.

The town needs it to restore the railroad right-of-way. I've decided to see if I can finish what he started but I have some questions."

Grandma Medeiros looked through the door and saw Daniel checking out a customer at the front register. Taking her mug, she sat down in an old stuffed chair with an embroidered cushion. "Silas Brooks was one wily, crazy old codger. He cheated people left and right all throughout his life, and toward the end, he was convinced that his enemies were out to get him. He didn't trust his own lawyers, so Silas hid all his legal papers as soon as they were drawn up. Mind you, he may have been right about his attorney, Jonah Patterson."

"What makes you say that?" Joshua asked.

"The town's former attorney, Bill Yarrow, caught Jonah presenting a forged codicil to Brooks's old will. Bill checked into some of the details and proved it was a fake. The document would have given Jonah most of Silas's assets. After he was charged, Jonah committed suicide rather than go to jail."

"And Patterson never made copies of Brooks's papers, like the new will?" Joshua asked.

"Silas's old will was in Patterson's safe deposit box. That's why the town now owns the Brooks Mansion. No one's ever found the amended will. That one left the railroad right of way to Independence, too. Silas showed it to our mayor at one time, but Silas wouldn't allow Patterson or anyone else to keep a copy."

Joshua nodded. This confirmed what he'd read in his father's emails to Mayor Allen.

Grandma Medeiros glanced at her grandson again and shook her head. "Daniel's having a tough time of it these days," she said quietly, changing the subject. "He blames himself for the fact that the store's not doing so well. I keep telling him that when you're self-employed, business has ups and downs. If he's patient, it'll turn around."

"I'm sure it will," Joshua said. "HMI will generate a rebirth in Independence. I feel it in my gut."

"Me, too," Grandma said and smiled. "I'm glad you're back, Josh. You're good for Daniel. He doesn't have as many friends these days. Most of the boys he hung around with are gone. The ones who remain…well, too many have chosen to take it personally when he tells them he can't afford to extend them any credit."

Joshua sighed. "He does what he has to do. He wants the store to remain open."

"This store's his legacy. The Medeiros family has owned it for generations, but my time as a shopkeeper will come to an end sooner rather than later, and the only reason I'm staying on is because I'm receiving a share of the family profits instead of a salary. I'd like to hire someone to take my place, but we just can't afford it right now. Don't tell Daniel I told you, please."

Joshua shook his head. "Of course not."

She poured herself some coffee. "I know you've stayed busy, fixing up your dad's house and doing that survey work on town-owned properties, but do you miss it? Architecture, that is. Building things."

"Yeah, I do, but eventually I'll find the right position and be back in business. I'm not worried. There's one thing architecture teaches—patience," he said.

"I heard you're working with Betty and Will on the B and B," Grandma said. "That'll take a lot of patience."

He laughed. "Betty's fine. In fact, I've got some new drawings I need to show her. Will…isn't sure of me. Myka thinks he's trying to look after the women in his family."

Grandma shook her head. "There's more to it than that." She stared into her coffee mug for a moment, lost in thought, then looked up at him. "I don't know if you've heard about this, but after Tanner died, Myka didn't get out of bed for nearly a month. Her mom finally forced her to snap out of it by refusing to cater to her. She stopped bringing Myka food, and wouldn't go shopping for her any more."

Grandma paused, gathering her thoughts and sorting her memories. "Tanner was the other half of Myka. People saw them as a unit, not two separate people, and they saw each other in much the same way. After he was gone, she had to redefine herself and find her own footing.

"Myka's a different woman now," Grandma added. "She's stronger and more independent, and can stand on her own—but Will hasn't realized that yet. He continues to worry about her."

"And he sees me as a potential problem," Joshua replied. "I'm no threat to Myka. I'm only here for a while, then I'll be gone again. My career lies elsewhere."

"I know, but a lot can happen between now

and then," Grandma said. "That's what worries him."

"You're right."

A long silence stretched out between them. "You're working on the Brooks Mansion, I hear," Grandma said at last. "Will you be restoring one or both of the buildings as a public attraction, or will they be offered to potential tenants? Either way, the town could certainly use the money."

"I'm not sure what the mayor plans to do with them yet," Joshua said, explaining what he'd been hired to do. "Both structures are still in very good shape. I had the electrical and plumbing systems checked out after my first visit and it turns out there are no major issues. The building facing Main still has potential as a business. The adjoining adobe is already zoned as a residence, so maybe the town can find someone who likes living close to their work, as Silas Brooks did."

After she'd finished her coffee, Grandma excused herself and returned to work. Joshua picked up some canned goods and brought them out to his truck. Placing the bags in a portable cooler, he grabbed the sketches he'd made for Betty and decided to walk down

Main Street. He'd stop by the inn, then maybe take another pass through the Brooks estate.

As he walked down the narrow sidewalk, Joshua recalled how Myka had gone on the defensive the first time he'd come to her with detailed business plans. She'd been so enthused after the town meeting, he'd expected her to want to act quickly, and her reaction had thrown him. Now he finally understood. No wonder she'd been so reluctant to follow his lead. She'd worked hard to blaze her own trail and having him prodding her must have seemed like a step back in time.

A few minutes later he entered the lobby of the Blue Spruce Inn.

As the door jingled, Betty looked up from behind the counter.

"Hey, it's good to see you!" she said with a bright smile.

He showed her the plans he'd drawn up.

"I love this! When everything's done, the archways are going to look great!"

"Once the framing and the wiring are complete, the masons will be able to lay in the brick for you. After that, the finish work should go pretty fast," he said.

"I can't wait!" Her eyes sparkled with excitement. "Features like that will help the inn retain an Old West feel, and they'll lighten the place up. But I'm also thinking about replacing the flooring, if I can afford it."

"What did you have in mind? I don't think you want to use brick or ceramic tile, but you could consider oak or pine. Resawn lumber would be attractive—it's less expensive and practical."

She thought about it a moment, then smiled. "I have an idea, Joshua, and it should be well within my budget. I've heard you've been given the keys to a lot of the abandoned houses and businesses, and you'll be deciding what gets salvaged. I'm guessing that the old Mabel Soto house is going to be torn down. What if I put in a bid for the wood plank floors? Those beams might take a lot of finish work, but I'd love to use them here. They'd give the inn a more rustic look."

"You're right. I looked that place over yesterday. Work up an offer in writing. I'm sure you'll be able to get them at a great price," Joshua said.

"Can I go in and take a look around?" Betty asked. "Maybe there's something else in there that'll catch my eye."

"It's not safe for you to go alone. I'd have to come with you or you could go with Will.

Since he's the town's fire marshal, he's got legal access to all the abandoned buildings in the community."

Joshua showed Betty some additional plans he'd drawn for remodeling the other rooms at the inn. "We can alter anything at this stage, so if there's something you don't like, just say so."

She studied the detailed images. "Josh, these are perfect—exactly what I had in mind! Can I hold on to these for a while? I'd like to show them to Will."

He nodded. "Take as long as you want. Just be aware that your brother might hate anything I come up with on principle."

"Yeah, I know." She shrugged. "He's just… hurting."

"He and Tanner were close," Joshua said.

"Yeah, they were…"

After saying goodbye, Joshua headed toward the Brooks Mansion. He still hadn't walked completely around the compound, which spanned the entire block. It was time for a closer look.

Once he arrived, he studied the condition of the building's exterior. Everything looked good, with only normal signs of weathering. As he went to the north side, he saw that the wrought-iron gate leading to the courtyard was open about a foot.

Joshua hurried over and saw that the locked chain had been slipped off over a broken weld. Someone had pried it loose.

He stepped inside the courtyard and glanced around, wondering if he should call the police. Nobody was in sight, however, and no doors or windows were open.

He was halfway across the courtyard when he heard someone running through the pile of fallen leaves behind him.

He turned just in time to see the back of a person in a denim jacket and tan pants slinking out of the gate. Joshua raced out into the alley just as the fleeing man disappeared, ducking around the corner.

Joshua followed, hoping to get a better look at the intruder, but before he reached the far end, he heard a car door slam and a vehicle race away, tires squealing.

Wanting to see if the person had actually broken into the buildings, Joshua jogged back. As he reached the gate he saw a police cruiser entering the alley from Main Street. Will stopped and climbed out of his car.

"You're too late," Joshua said.

"For what? Get away from that gate," Will ordered. "Breaking and entering is a crime."

"I didn't break in. The gate had been forced open so I went inside the courtyard to check things out. Whoever it was sneaked out behind my back, ran down the alley and raced off in what sounded like a pickup. I never got a good look at the intruder or the vehicle."

"I heard the squeal of tires one street over. That must have been the guy. Anyone else still inside?" Will asked.

"Don't know."

Will gestured with his chin for Joshua to move aside. Hand on the butt of his weapon, he called out a warning to any potential intruder, then stepped into the courtyard.

"Stay here," Will snapped, then he disappeared.

CHAPTER TEN

WILL CAME BACK a few minutes later, his shoulders tense. "No sign of a break-in, but we've had a problem with vagrants squatting in empty houses all over town. Most of the time they're harmless, just seeking shelter, but you never know." He rubbed the back of his neck with one hand. "Generally, if I catch someone I recognize from town, I cut them some slack. With the weather turning cold, the homeless are desperate to find shelter, and this town cut public assistance programs over a year ago."

"Lots of people are down on their luck these days," Joshua said with a nod.

Will's eyes narrowed as he gazed at Joshua. "What the heck are *you* doing wandering around the Brooks estate? Treasure hunting like your old man?"

Joshua felt his muscles tensing up, but as he looked at Will he sensed he wasn't being baited. "This house is one of a dozen the mayor hired me to evaluate."

He reached into his jacket pocket and brought out a big key ring. "I've been given access to all of them, but you're right. I'm also conducting a search. My dad was working to find some papers for Mayor Allen, and I've taken on that job, too. Like Dad, I love solving puzzles."

"Your dad was a real history buff. He knew more about these old buildings than anyone else in town. He, Benjamin Bruce and Elise Medeiros formed their own historical society. To my way of thinking, if they couldn't find the missing Brooks will, it's gone for good."

"Wait—Mr. B. is still around? He was older than Dad by a good fifteen years," Joshua said.

"He had a stroke about a month ago, and he's in a home in Painted Canyon. His mind... is gone."

"I'm sorry to hear that," Joshua said.

Will looked around slowly, his gaze thorough. "If you see anyone wandering around who doesn't belong, let me know. I'll handle it."

"I'm not sure I'd know who belongs and

who doesn't anymore. A lot has changed since I left Independence."

"You'll know," Will said. "Look for someone duded up, not a regular Joe with jeans."

"Sounds like you've got someone in mind," Joshua said slowly.

"Just keep your eyes open. And if you have the key to the padlock—" he pointed to the gate "—could you lock up?"

"No problem. I'll also be checking out other empty buildings. I'll let you know if I find signs of intruders."

"Watch your back," he said, then added, "I'm on the clock, so I better shove off. I can be anywhere in town within four minutes, so keep that in mind if you spot trouble."

"No problem, but I won't be working for the mayor tomorrow or this weekend."

"Job interview?"

Joshua noted that he'd sounded almost hopeful. "No." He didn't have to give Will any details, but he decided it was better to get it out in the open. "Business trip for HMI. The ladies are running out of wool and the company needs to find new sources. I'll be introducing Myka to some shepherds on the Rez. Hopefully, they'll have wool to sell and that'll open new doors for the company."

"You two are going alone, the entire weekend?" he asked, an edge to his voice.

"Ease up. If we do stay overnight—which is highly unlikely—we'll have our own rooms. This is a *business* trip, nothing more. More likely we'll drive straight back and get home late."

Will's gaze was glacial. "Step out of line with Myka and I'm going to make your life hell. Got that?"

"Your intentions are good," Joshua said, refusing to flinch or step back when Will got in his face. "But I don't have to explain who I spend time with to anyone—including you."

"That's where we disagree," Will said, then strode off.

After Will drove away, Joshua stepped back inside the compound. He walked across the porch that ran the length of the territorial home, inspecting the exterior carefully, then opened the door.

As he entered the foyer and looked around, he smiled. He loved this place. The old vigas, the brick floors, the old world feel of the place appealed to him on every imaginable level.

As he walked around, he tried to imagine how it would feel to own a place like this. His gaze took in the beauty already there—

and what could be. In his mind's eye, he saw the updates he'd make, like opening the second-floor landing to create a double-height space and a balcony that went over and into the space below. He'd also enlarge the windows and add more corbels. A little manpower could make the Brooks Mansion the place of elegance it had once been.

After locking up, he walked back into the alley, then reattached the chain and padlock to a solid portion of the gate. A few minutes later, he was walking back up the sidewalk along Main, headed for his pickup.

Daydreams could be beautiful, but they weren't much if they remained dreams. His real future was far away from Independence. Joshua glanced back one last time, then kept his eyes on the path ahead.

MYKA AND SOPHIE worked side by side, sealing the cardboard boxes scattered around Myka's living room and affixing mailing labels on each one. As the minutes ticked by, Myka noticed that Sophie was uncharacteristically silent.

"Okay, spill it. What's wrong?" Myka asked.

"There's something I want you to hear from me first," her friend said softly.

"What's up?"

"You've probably seen Will's squad car driving up and down our street a lot lately," she said.

Myka smiled. "Yeah, but don't worry. He feels the need to keep an eye on me. We're not having a surge in crime."

"It's not just you he's keeping an eye on," Sophie answered.

"You think he's harassing Joshua?"

Sophie shook her head. "Will and I are seeing each other."

"What?" Myka asked, surprised.

Sophie nodded. "Sometimes he can't get away until late, and he'll drive by slowly to see if Mom's light is on. If it isn't, he doesn't stop. I've told him that it's okay as long as he doesn't ring the doorbell, but he won't risk waking her," Sophie said. "He's like that, real sweet in a rough-around-the-edges kind of way."

"You and Will... Wow! I never saw it coming. For the record, I think it's wonderful news!"

Sophie smiled. "He's caring and strong, and he makes me feel special."

"Is it serious?" Myka asked.

"It's too early to know, but I really like him."

"I'm happy for you, Sophie," she said, giving her a hug. "Will's a good man. He's old fashioned, and the kind you can always count on."

"That's what I like most about him. He's…" Her words trailed off.

"Steadfast?"

"Yeah, that's it exactly." She grinned.

Myka and Sophie finished packing the boxes, then Sophie left, and Myka set up the new bookkeeping software.

She was tired by the time she finished it all, and as she leaned back, Myka saw it was nearly ten.

Bear had laid beside her the whole time, so she bent down to pet him. "What a great buddy you are! I'm so glad you're here with me."

Bear licked her face, and Myka laughed.

THE NEXT MORNING, it was still dark outside when Myka heard a light knock at her door. Bear stood, but he didn't bark or growl. Though she was certain who it was, she played it safe, turning on the porch light and checking through the peep hole before opening the door. Seeing Joshua, she invited him inside.

"Your light's been on for almost an hour, so I figured you'd probably be ready to go," he said. "I've got directions to the trading post. It should be an easy two-and-a-half-hour drive. Since we're leaving early, and the roads will be clear, I expect we'll make good time."

"Assuming we get the wool, we'll need lots of room to process it quickly. Have you made any progress finding a home for HMI?"

"I've got the search narrowed down to two buildings. The mayor's checking out the legal status of both places for us." As headlights illuminated the street, Joshua went to the window and glanced out. "Will's cruiser," he said. "And I thought we were up early today."

"He's seeing Sophie, did you know that?"

Joshua's head snapped around, and he stared at Myka for a second. "Sophie...from across the street? Are you serious? Those two don't seem right for each other. Sophie's always upbeat and all smiles," he said. "I can't remember seeing Will smile—ever."

"He does—just not around you." Myka, laughed. "Will's really the perfect guy for Sophie. He's strong, honest and dependable.

He'll treat her right and that goes a long way. When Will commits he gives his all and that's just what most women—including Sophie—are looking for…a forever love."

"Does that include you?" he asked after a beat.

She shrugged but didn't answer directly. "There's no such thing as forever. That belongs only in fairy tales."

He didn't reply right away, but when he did, his voice was low and gentle. "You're wrong, Myka. When we get to the Rez, look at the sacred mountains. You can see forever etched in every cliff, snow covered peak and sandstone ridge. Forever is written in traditions as old as these mountains and it's at the heart of our clans," he said. "Forever exists, though maybe not where you've been looking."

"Handmade in Independence… Maybe it'll become a forever thing, something that'll be there from one generation to the next, like the mountains," she said in a wistful voice.

"Only time will tell."

FIVE MINUTES LATER they were on their way, armed with snacks and strong coffee in an insulated metal bottle. The GPS on the truck had been programmed, and just in case, Joshua had brought maps of the area.

"How about a muffin?" she asked, reaching into the small woven picnic basket she'd brought along.

"Sure, but don't fill up. Once we get to the trading post Aunt Emma and Uncle Rudy run, you'll want to taste their *naniscaadas*. You've never tried handmade tortillas like these. Pour honey on them, fold them over, and you'll think you've tasted heaven. We'll have coffee there, too, and take our time visiting. That'll give me a chance to learn about Maxine Redhorse."

"Sounds good," she said, handing him an oatmeal applesauce muffin.

"I think you're going to like my aunt and uncle," he said, eyeing the muffin. "Dad didn't get along with them, mostly because he was a Modernist and they're Traditionalists. Those are two very different paths." He took a bite of the muffin, nodding his head to show his approval.

"And you walk a path different from all of them," she said.

"True, but I don't challenge Uncle Rudy like Dad did," he said. "One word of caution—don't mention Dad by name. Traditionalists believe that's one way to call the chindi."

"I'll be careful. Any other advice?"

"Yeah. Listening is more important than talking when you're trying to establish trust—and never interrupt a long pause in the conversation. There's no such thing as awkward silence among the *Diné*."

"All right. I'll remember," she said.

As the miles stretched out, she leaned back in her seat. Though she wasn't looking at Josh, she was aware of everything about him, from the aura of roughness his black leather jacket gave him, to the way he squared his strong shoulders when he drove. For a moment she wondered what it would be like to rest her head against him and have him drape his arm over her protectively.

Realizing those thoughts would get her nowhere, she pushed them out of her mind and forced herself to focus on something else. "Do you ever think of how far we've come? Independence is starting to show signs of life and new businesses have started cropping up."

"You're gaining ground, and that's something, but it's too soon to celebrate. You may still have a fight ahead of you."

"True, but I want to celebrate the little wins along the way," she said.

Myka knew he was worried, but for the first time in months, she wasn't. Thinking about the future no longer filled her with fear. What she felt now was hope and the excitement that came from high expectations. The best was yet to come.

JOSHUA GREETED HIS UNCLE, who was standing on the wooden porch of the trading post, with a friendly smile and a nod of greeting. According to custom, they didn't shake hands.

"Is this a bad time, Uncle?" Joshua asked, noting that his uncle was wearing the white sash of a *hataalii*.

"Not at all. Come in."

As they stepped inside the store, Joshua glanced around. The building dated back to the 1950s, when it was constructed to replace one of the earliest trading posts on the Navajo Nation. As he went farther into the room, he detected the aroma of freshly ground coffee, fry bread and spicy burritos.

At the Turquoise Bear Trading Post, the old ways and the new coexisted naturally. The store carried farm and ranch supplies, Spam, powdered milk and bags of flour along with microwave pizza, CFL light bulbs and rental movies on DVD. In the corner, up on a shelf, was a TV set broadcasting a network news program, thanks to a relay tower on the nearby mountain. Reception was pretty good through the rabbit ears, Joshua noticed absently, looking up at the screen.

The tall man led them around the old oak-and-glass counter filled with Navajo jewelry to a spot beside a very modern ceramic heater. "I had to do a Sing earlier, but my healing work is done for today." He waved Joshua and Myka to chairs beside a small table. "Sit and make yourselves comfortable."

Moments later, Joshua's aunt joined them, bringing a tray that held freshly brewed coffee, *naniscaadas* and honey.

They ate slowly, enjoying the food and coffee, and after they were finished, Joshua's aunt spoke.

"Nephew, tell us what brings you here today."

Joshua told them about HMI and their need for high-quality wool, then he waited.

Myka followed his lead and remained silent.

"The woman you're searching for is…difficult," Rudy said at last. "When she came

back home I did an Enemy Way Sing for her."
For Myka's benefit, he added, "That's a ceremony to rid a person of the evil they come into contact with during war."

He took a deep breath, then continued. "It helped her, but she still struggles. That's why she's chosen to live a solitary life. Of course that's not unusual for a Navajo. Great distances often separate us."

"What we have to offer would be a blessing to her and us," Myka said.

"It's good that you think of it that way," Rudy said with an approving nod. "That's the essence of harmony, when both sides are in balance."

"Do you think it's safe for us to pay her a visit?" Joshua asked.

"That depends. If you drive up and wait in the truck until she asks you to approach, you'll be fine. If you go up there like the *bilagáanas,* the white people," he said, "and knock on her door, you'll probably not get the welcome you want."

Myka bit back a smile at what she would classify as the understatement of the year. She'd heard about Maxine's shotgun-style greeting.

"We'll stay in the truck," Myka said. "We don't want to offend anyone."

Rudy smiled at her. "Respect will get you far here."

"She's been in a better mood ever since she adopted that horse, a mustang from the Bureau of Land Management. She's training it, and working with the animal makes her happy," Emma said. "The horse, too, has found its purpose."

"Can you give me directions to her place? This is what I've got," Joshua said. He showed his uncle the hand-drawn map he'd made based on information from a friend of his father's.

"The rain last summer washed out part of the road, so you'll need to turn here and go through this canyon," Rudy said, and gave him more precise directions. "It's actually a few miles shorter this way, too."

Soon Joshua had what he needed. "Thank you, uncle."

"Walk in beauty, nephew," the man said.

"Ask about her native blue dye, too," Emma told Myka. "Blue has always been difficult, but she's found a way to create a particularly beautiful shade."

"Thank you. I'll do that," Myka said.

As they set out, Myka felt a touch of excitement. "We use mostly commercial dyes, so that sounds really interesting."

"Remember that out here knowledge isn't shared easily. It's considered a living thing, something to be protected. Lead the conversation, but don't force it. You'll get farther that way."

"What an incredible place the Rez is. It's like entering a different country—with its own rules and customs."

"A lot of our young people can't wait to get away from here. It's hard to make a living off the land, and not everyone has the motivation to farm or raise livestock. Those who are able to move away generally leave."

"Like your dad?"

"He left the Rez at eighteen, but I was never really sure why."

"Maybe he had dreams, too, and those led him away," she said, and in a thoughtful voice, added, "it takes a special kind of courage to leave everything that's familiar to you and reach out to the unknown."

"A quiet strength, the hardest of all for a teenage son to see or appreciate," he said, his words all but drowned out by the rumble of the engine.

CHAPTER ELEVEN

As THEY TURNED off the main highway, the path ahead became nothing more than two ruts lined with bone-jarring holes that forced Myka to hold on to the armrest.

"How much longer do we have to drive on this washer board track?" she asked, then clenched her teeth as another pothole bounced her hard from side to side.

"The house should be up ahead, two miles."

They continued traveling at a slow, steady rate, then at long last, she saw a huge, fenced-in pasture extending up and over a low rise, then down into a low area along a shallow creek. Sheep were everywhere. "That's the largest herd of *Churros* I've ever seen! And look at that wire fence. It must be eight feet high."

"Helps keep most of the predators out," he said, turning toward the house and driving down the fence line. A moment later he parked the truck in full view of the main house, a cinder block home with a gray scratch coat of mortar instead of paint. Beyond, adjacent to the fence, was a large red barn.

He leaned back, prepared to wait. "She's got it better than most. Out here you see lots of single wide mobile homes or three-room houses with sheep pens nearby, but usually no overhead cover."

"Even with such a tall fence, it must be hard to keep out the coyotes."

"Yeah, it is. They might not be able to jump that high, but some can climb or dig under. She probably has some dogs to help discourage attacks." He shifted in his seat, making himself comfortable. "There they are." He pointed toward three large mutts who'd come over to the fence to check them out. Just as he spoke, the animals began to bark.

"So how long does it take before a person invites you in?" she asked.

"Depends. Things run on Indian time out here."

After about ten minutes, Myka began to get restless. The dogs had stopped barking, having disappeared somewhere across the large enclosure. "Do you think this is her way of telling us to leave? Her truck's parked over by the barn, so she's probably home and keeping an eye on us, right?"

"Not necessarily, and it hasn't really been that long, not by Indian standards. Also, keep in mind that if she's working in the barn she may not have heard us pull up. She probably ignores the barking dogs except at night."

Josh had parked in the sun, and after a while, the truck's cab began to heat up. He rolled down the window.

A second later, Myka sat up. "Did you hear that?"

"What?" he asked, glancing around.

"That frantic whinnying. When I took riding lessons in high school I learned about horses, and that sound means trouble. Something's not right."

He stepped out of the truck and listened. "Yeah, you're right. That's probably what got the dogs' attention, too."

"Your uncle told us not to leave the car, but if she's in trouble…"

"Hang on for a bit," he said. The whinnying stopped, then started again, followed by the sound of barking dogs.

"Come on, we'll both go," Myka said. "If she gets angry, you can blame it on me."

Myka took a small baggie from inside her

purse, then ran along the wire fence toward the barn.

About five feet from the entrance, she heard someone yell, "Quiet!" The dogs instantly stopped barking.

As Myka ran up, she saw the dogs sitting inside the fence, staring at something in the turnout area just beyond the stall. She tried to get a closer look, but a large black horse was running back and forth inside a welded pipe corral, snorting, pacing and pawing the ground. He had a halter on and was dragging a lead rope behind him.

Myka walked up slowly. "Easy, boy." As she approached, Myka saw a tall, slender Navajo woman in jeans and a flannel shirt on the ground in the center of the small enclosure. Her black hair hung in a single braid down her back.

"Hang on!" Myka called to her in a soft voice. Out of the corner of her eye, she saw Joshua moving slowly toward the woman, staying outside the enclosure, and trying not to spook the horse more than it already was.

"Don't come in while he's upset. If he runs at you or spins around and kicks, I'll get trampled," the woman said.

"All right. Are you hurt?" Myka asked.

"I twisted my ankle when I fell, but I'll be fine." She reached down, gingerly feeling the side of her scuffed Western-style boot.

"I'll call 911," Joshua said in a quiet voice, his eyes on the horse.

"Don't bother. They'll take an hour to get here and I'm not lying on the cold ground that long. Give me a few more minutes," she said firmly. "I'll be fine."

Myka slipped between the fence rails into the adjoining turnout area. Standing at one end, she took some apple slices from the baggie she'd brought and placed them on the palm of her hand. "Come on, big guy. You like apples, don't you?"

The horse sniffed the air, nostrils flaring, but didn't approach.

"If I get the horse to come over to me, Joshua can help you out of there," Myka said.

"He won't come to you," the woman replied. "He's ornery."

"What's his name?" Myka asked.

"Frank—short for Frankenstein. He's… moody. One second he's great—the next, nuts."

"Wild mustang?" Joshua asked, slipping through the rails and drawing closer while Myka kept the horse's attention.

"Not so wild anymore, just unpredictable."

Myka placed a second piece of apple on her palm, then reached into the baggie, and began eating one herself. "These are good, Frank," she said, holding out her hand a little farther.

Frank came over slowly and took the apple slices. As soon as he did, Joshua went to the woman, lifted her into his arms, and carried her out of the enclosure.

Myka watched him, realizing how strong he was and wishing she could be in his arms like that. With a tiny sigh, she focused and went to meet them.

Although Joshua would have carried her all the way back to the house, the woman refused. "Just let me lean on your shoulder. I'll hobble back."

"You'll need to see a doctor to make sure you haven't broken anything," Myka said.

She shook her head. "I handle things differently. There's a *hataalii* at the trading post near here. He knows the Plant People—the plants that grow on the Rez," she added for Myka's benefit. "He makes a herbal salve for sprains and swollen joints that works wonders. I'll call him as soon as I'm inside."

"He's my uncle," Joshua said.

She looked up at Joshua. "I'm Maxine Redhorse. Did your uncle send you?"

"No, we came on another matter. I'm Joshua Nez and this is Myka Solis."

"I'm really glad we came by when we did," Myka said, helping Maxine along by giving her another arm to hold on to.

"So am I," Maxine said. "I would have crawled back to the house, but it's a ways."

Myka heard the pride in her voice and understood. When all else failed, sometimes that was the only thing that kept you going.

Once they were inside the house, Myka helped Maxine into a weary-looking sofa placed beneath the window.

Maxine shifted, sitting sideways with both her legs up. "Would you be willing to get me some of that salve from your uncle?" she asked Josh. "I'll pay you for your time. There's money in that desk drawer."

"I'll go, and there's no need to pay me," Joshua said. "Will he know what you need?"

"Ask him for the yellow salve. It's made of rabbitbrush, asters and some other ingredients." She gestured with her chin toward the drawer. "Take thirty for the *hataalii,* and some to cover your gas."

"While he's gone, why don't I help you slip your boot off and get some ice?" Myka said.

"I'll take the boot off myself, but you can get me some ice from the freezer and wrap it up in the dishcloth by the sink."

Myka returned moments later with the makeshift ice pack. By then, Joshua was gone.

As Maxine held it against her ankle, Myka walked to the display case hung on the wall. "Wow, so many medals and commendations!"

"Most are campaign ribbons for Iraq, then Afghanistan. I'd stuck all of those in a drawer, but the seniors at the local VFW made me that case and I didn't want to disappoint them." Maxine remained quiet for a moment, then added. "They display their medals because they've had time to move on. My memories are still too fresh."

Myka said slowly, "The pain from a wound that has yet to heal can be nearly overpowering."

"Yeah, it can. Did you serve overseas?"

"I'm not a vet," Myka said. "I'm a widow."

"Did your husband serve?"

"No. He was in an industrial accident," she said.

Maxine nodded, but respecting her privacy, didn't ask any further questions. "So tell me, Myka, what brought you and Joshua here today?"

Rather than give the sales pitch she'd rehearsed, Myka told her about Independence and HMI. "Things are finally turning around for us, but we need more quality wool if we're going to meet the demand. You were recommended to us," she said.

"Once a year my aunt and I shear the sheep and wash the wool. We don't process it any farther than that—it's not carded or anything."

"What were you planning to do with it?"

"Sell it, eventually, but I don't have much to do with people these days, and I'd need the right contacts. Since it's all properly stored, I'm in no rush. Reach into that first drawer," she said, pointing. "There's an envelope with a sample of my wool. Take a look."

Myka did, studying the color, fiber diameter and staple length. "It's very good quality. Can I see the rest?"

"There's a storeroom inside the barn, first door on your left. If you want to open one of the bags, go ahead, but when you're done, make sure you reseal it properly."

Myka went outside, and following Maxine's directions, found the storage room. The wool had been placed in vacuum-sealed bags stacked ceiling high atop a layer of wooden pallets. There was enough wool there to keep HMI going until next shearing season.

Ten minutes later, Myka returned to the house. "I'm interested. Let's talk terms."

BY THE TIME Joshua returned, Myka had closed the deal. They loaded as much wool as Joshua's truck could carry, covered it with a canvas tarp and tied it down. Then they made arrangements to have the rest delivered.

"You got a very good price for all that wool," Joshua said as they pulled out of the ranch.

"I thought so, too. That's why I bought all of it. I also offered her a percentage of the profits for any wool we process using her special dye. She mixes sumac and blue clay to make an amazing shade of violet."

"Good deal all the way around," he said, "but it was still a lot of money. I didn't realize HMI had that much cash on hand."

"Our company's still running on a tight budget. That's why I took the money from my personal account."

He felt his blood run cold. "Myka, you

never use your own funds. I learned that the hard way."

"You were willing to take the risk. Besides, the company can pay me back later."

"Myka, listen to me. If a company's going to survive, it has to be able to stand on its own. When you start funneling your own funds into it you lose the dividing line that protects you, personally and professionally. More importantly, you can end up putting an unbelievable strain on your own finances, particularly if you're pulling out money intended for your food, home and gas."

"It won't be a problem," she said in a whisper-soft voice. "It's from an account I've done my best to ignore. It didn't feel right to spend that money on just anything."

"I don't understand."

"It's the settlement IVA offered me after Tanner died. I got the initial payment, but after the company filed for bankruptcy, I never got the rest."

"So they admitted Tanner's accident was their fault?"

She nodded. "After corporate knew they were going to shut down, safety inspections outside the production lines were given a low priority. They fixed obvious problems, but the emphasis was on cost cutting, not preventative maintenance," she said. "Tanner was inside the freight elevator when the wiring in the shaft caught fire. He died of smoke inhalation before anyone could get to him."

There had been very little emotion in her voice, but he saw her quickly wipe a tear from her eye.

"I'm sorry, Myka. I didn't mean to bring up painful memories," he said, reaching for her hand and giving it a gentle squeeze.

She didn't pull away. "I try not to dwell on things I can't change." She took an unsteady breath. "I've been waiting and holding on to that money because I wanted to use it on something Tanner would have liked."

"And you think he would have approved of Handmade in Independence?"

"Oh, yeah. He would have supported anything that helped Independence get back on its feet. You know how much he loved this place."

"Is the success of HMI important to you because of him?"

She looked at Joshua in surprise. "No, Tanner's gone. I'm only dealing with what's in front of me right now. Independence needs

HMI, and we all need our town. It's a marriage that can't fail, right?"

"I don't know about that, but it *is* a good partnership," he said. After a brief pause, he added, "Tell me something, Myka. Do you ever think about getting married again?"

"Not really, but if that time comes, I know one thing. It won't be like the marriage I had with Tanner. I'm not a kid anymore. I can't define myself as just the other half of my husband. I have my own identity."

"Do you think you'll be able to put Tanner's memory behind you and love as deeply as you did then?"

"Of course. Tanner will always be part of me but love isn't something you use up. You just add to what's already in your heart."

Joshua nodded. She wasn't the same Myka, but he liked the woman she'd become even more than the girl she'd been.

FIVE DAYS AFTER their trip to the reservation, it became clear that HMI desperately needed a facility where its newly acquired wool could be processed. Working individually wouldn't give them the uniform quality the company needed to maintain. In Myka's mind, the search for a suitable building had become top priority.

Myka stepped over Bear, who was snoozing in the hall, lost her balance, and crashed into the boxes stacked waist high against the wall. As everything tumbled down, Bear jumped out of the way, bumped into Myka and pushed her over. She careened onto the carpet, smashing more boxes as she fell.

At that precise moment the doorbell rang. Myka cursed, picked herself up and went to answer it.

"Are you okay?" Robyn asked, looking her up and down. "We heard the crash!"

Standing next to Robyn was Joshua. As Myka looked into his eyes, she suddenly realized how much she'd missed him. "I'm fine, just clumsy," she said with a weary smile.

Robyn and Joshua looked past her and saw the dented and squashed boxes. "Okay, that's it," Robyn said, looking at Joshua. "We settle on a new location today."

"I met with Mayor Allen earlier this morning. We can have one of the buildings IVA used to lease from the town—rent free," Joshua said. "Mayor Allen will meet us over there right now with the keys if you can get away, Myka."

"Which IVA building?" Myka asked.

"He suggested the main assembly plant. He'll be parked next to it," he said.

"You said rent free, right?" Myka asked, making sure she'd heard right.

"Yes, HMI will pay for utilities and taxes, which will directly benefit the town. The building is move-in ready, too. Trust me, this is the time to go for it," Joshua said.

"Let me grab my tote and we'll go take a look."

"You two will have to handle that without me," Robyn said. "I'm on my way to pick up some computer supplies. I just dropped by to let you know that we've been getting a record number of hits on our webpage. Orders keep flying in."

"I know. Look at my house," Myka said, laughing.

After Robyn left, Myka locked up and followed Joshua to his truck. "Where have you been? I haven't seen you since the trip."

"I went out of town for two days. I had an interview in Albuquerque."

"And?" Myka pressed, looking at him.

"Turns out the job wasn't right for me, and the interviewer and I both knew it," he said.

"Either way, I told you I wouldn't leave before Christmas, and I meant it."

"You know I'd never hold you to that, right?"

He nodded. "Here's the thing, though. I'm not ready to leave yet, so I've put the job search on the back burner. There was a time I hated Independence, but things have changed—or maybe I have," he said.

Myka remained silent, unwilling to let him see how happy she was to hear the news. Joshua's future was his own, and she had no right to interfere. Even if he stayed in Independence, it didn't guarantee they'd have a relationship. Yet it was hard to hide her elation. As she turned to look out the window, she couldn't help but smile.

On their way to town, he was surprised to hear her humming. "I don't recognize the song, Myka, but you realize you're humming, right?"

"Too bad I can't carry a tune." She laughed. "I'm just happy HMI is going to have a home. When I first suggested we start our own company, I had no idea how complicated things would get. These days I barely have time for myself, but as crazy as it sounds, I've never been happier."

He smiled. "I think you're getting a taste of what I loved most about running my own firm. Knowing you're creating a product or providing a service that will be valued is an incredible rush."

"Do you get that same feeling working with us?" she asked.

"Yeah, but it's not only because of HMI, or my surveying for the town. I've also been poring over Dad's historical papers and trying to figure out where Brooks may have hidden his will. I'd really like to complete what Dad began," he said.

"That would be wonderful. Everyone in town would benefit from having rail service restored, particularly HMI."

"I've discovered that Brooks may have been a loon, but he was also crafty. Getting into his head has been one major challenge."

She smiled. "Right now you sound just like your dad. Adam's face would light up just like yours when he talked about that will. Neither of you can stand unanswered questions. They drive you nuts."

He laughed. "Busted!"

They arrived at the old compound, but

Mayor Allen was waiting by the redbrick building that housed IVA's business office and custom order shipping department, not the assembly plant next door. Her stomach clenched as she climbed out of the pickup. This place still held too many bad memories for her.

The mayor came to greet them, then led the way to the main entrance. He looked up at the piece of plywood that had been nailed over a busted window and turned back to Myka.

"At first I thought you'd need the bigger building, but then I realized this overgrown office would serve HMI better. For starters, it'll cost a lot less to heat and cool than the assembly plant. That one's basically a big room configured for massive machines and wired mostly with two-twenty outlets. This one, on the other hand, has an emergency sprinkler system and already meets workplace safety standards," he said. "What do you think?"

She swallowed the enormous lump at her throat. "This is the building where Tanner died. I worked here, too, before and after. Let's just say it wouldn't have been my first choice."

"I understand, but think about it. This really is the best place for HMI," Phil said. "It's got storerooms, an attached loading dock, and defined work spaces." He paused a moment before continuing. "This building was also the heart of a company that once defined Independence. It would be wonderful to rewrite its history and see it become a symbol of renewal and our return from extinction." He smiled. "That's part of our new town logo. Did you know that?"

The abrupt change in his tone and subject threw her momentarily. "What is?"

"Back from extinction. We've erected a new sign above the entrance to town hall—a dinosaur inside a circle with a red line drawn through it. It's a daily reminder that we're coming back to life!"

"HMI's still growing. With the woodcraft workers, we have nearly a hundred people involved, but we'll never rival the auto plant," she said.

"You're right, but HMI's success has given our town a badly needed shot in the arm. Every day people are coming up with new business ideas. The biggest stumbling block we've faced so far has been access to funding." He looked directly at Joshua. "That's where your ideas really helped out."

"How so?" Josh asked.

"You'd mentioned special grants. I found out that the state's rural development council supports efforts to promote Rio Grande traditions. So far two locals have received financial help. We'll have a New Mexican *panaderia*-style bakery opening next to the Blue Spruce Inn, and Mr. Mora, our saddlemaker, will open a shop across the street from the feed store."

"I had no idea!" Myka said. It all sounded great, but it was way too early to know how HMI would do in the long run. If they went crashing down, then what? She'd started this journey to help her town, but now it was possible she'd end up financially devastating the very people she'd tried to help.

Determined to hide her fears, she braced herself and tried to focus on the reason they were there.

Mayor Allen took them inside the building, then handed her the keys. "Take your time. Of course you'll need business insurance and liability to protect everyone concerned. I'm ready to offer you the best rate, so talk to me when you're ready."

"We will, but first, I want to look around. After that, I'll need a day or two to think it over," Myka said. "I have to make sure this place will suit HMI."

"Of course." The mayor looked at his watch. "I've got to get back to my office, but feel free to poke around. Just be sure to lock up when you leave. You can return the keys later."

Once he left, Joshua and Myka walked through the empty building. Myka avoided the area near the small loading dock and focused on the administrative and employee space.

Aware of Myka's tense silence, Joshua took her hand and brought her around to face him. "Okay, talk to me. I know Phil changed which building we'd be touring at the last minute. His motives were good, but we don't have to stay if you're uncomfortable."

"It's okay. I'm fine," she said. "I worked here after the accident—but I won't go near that freight elevator."

"All right."

Knowing in her heart that Tanner would have approved of her using this building, she took a breath. Ready to move forward, she nodded. "Come on. Let's go verify that this place can be adapted to HMI's needs."

She reached into her tote and brought out

a folder with pages of notes. "I've discussed things with Sophie and Robyn, and this is a list of what we'll need. First, a large processing area where we can prepare the wool for spinning, which means access to hot water and space that can hold the drying racks. I'm thinking that the kitchen and cafeteria upstairs might be best for that. We'll use hand carders as much as possible to work the wool into rovings, then set up adjoining rooms for spinning wheels."

Myka went down the long hall, glancing into each of the former business offices. "Some of these will become our administrative offices. The meeting rooms can be used for storage, packing and shipping."

"This way. Let's take the stairs," he said, and pointed directly ahead.

As they reached the second floor, Myka glanced around. The tiled floors made their steps echo with a hollow emptiness as they walked. It was as if the building itself were calling out to them, demanding to be filled with the sounds of life.

She walked into one of the large executive offices and looked around. The empty walls still held the outlines of paintings, diplomas and photos long gone. The carpet also showed the ghostly indentations of file cabinets and desks.

"They didn't take all the furniture," Josh observed, pointing to a few metal desks and file cabinets. "HMI could make good use of those, I'll bet."

"Absolutely."

They walked down the hall and went inside the kitchen facility. Joshua pointed to the large stoves still in place, though the electricity and gas had been turned off long ago. "Water needed for scouring could be heated here and with some remodeling, that bread storage bin would make a perfect drying rack," he said. "Wool could be hung from racks attached to the ceiling, too"

"It makes sense," she said, then looking around, she took a shuddering breath.

"Myka, are you sure you're okay?"

She nodded. "It's not the past I'm worried about, Josh. It's the present. A lot of our people have gambled everything on HMI's success. I'm really afraid I'll become the proverbial lemming that led the others off a cliff."

"People make their own choices, and you're a good bet," he said, taking her hand and brushing a gentle kiss on her palm.

The unexpected, tender gesture made her ache for more. "I'm glad you're here."

"As I told you from the start, I've got your back. Life never comes with guarantees, but you can count on that."

She smiled, but before she could even say thanks, he continued.

"For what it's worth, I don't think it's fear of failure that's really troubling you. Success can be just as scary—but take it from me, it's a lot more pleasant."

Myka laughed. "Yeah, you're right. Maybe I just need to relax. The company's growing, and people have extra money in their pockets. Not a bad deal at all." She glanced around and after a long beat, added, "When you first came to town, I remember saying these abandoned buildings would make a great business opportunity for someone. I never figured I'd be taking advantage of it."

He laughed. "You've surprised yourself, but not me."

"Aw, come on."

"No, really. You're one of the strongest women I've ever known."

For a moment they stood face-to-face, his steady gaze holding her spellbound. At that moment all she wanted was to feel his strong arms around her and rest her cheek against his hard chest.

"Myka," he whispered, and cupped her face in his hands.

A delicious warmth spread all through her as his mouth closed in over hers. He coaxed her lips open and kissed her deeply.

When he drew back and eased his hold, she sighed softly, disappointed it had ended so soon.

"Kiss me like that again." It was a new time in an old place…life in a building of shadows.

The taste of his mouth and the tenderness of his kiss left her weak at the knees.

After a moment, Myka moved away from him. Was she crazy? Sooner or later, Joshua would find the job he wanted and leave Independence—and her—far behind. She needed to remain on her guard. Loss cut deeply, and a heart that had been repaired, like hers, was never quite as strong as one that hadn't been wounded at all.

CHAPTER TWELVE

As much as he wanted to take her in his arms again, Joshua remained where he was. Myka was right to step away. He was a bad bet for anyone, particularly her. She needed security, and he had no idea where his life was headed. He couldn't offer her anything except more risk and uncertainty, and she already had enough of that in her life.

"Myka, this building is all but perfect for HMI. You and Robyn could both have proper offices and the crafters can all work here if they choose, including the woodworkers. The basement has enough room for their tools and working underground will take care of the noise issue. The best part is that you'll finally be drawing a line between home and work."

"You're right. HMI would become my job—separate from my private life. Maybe I'll even find 'me' time now. It's hard to get away from work when it's right there in your living room, kitchen and bedroom."

"Exactly," Josh replied. "Getting a company off the ground is really a challenge. Working impossibly long hours is part of the process, but we all need downtime."

"I give work one-hundred-percent, but I've missed being able to leave it at the office when I go home," she said. "There's still a problem, though. I don't want our people to be reminded on a daily basis that their former employer sold them out. I want everyone focused on what we're trying to accomplish now."

"Then let's do something to change the look and feel of the building. We can paint some of the walls with cheerful colors, arrange for background music and maybe even use the mayor's logo—that 'no dinosaurs' thing. We'll remind people that the past is gone and we're moving toward the future."

"I like that." She smiled broadly. "Let's place that logo on the entrance doors so it's the first thing people see when they come in."

He nodded. "I'll make sure the inspections are done and that the utilities are up and running ASAP. In the meantime, you can decide what layout you'd like in the wool processing rooms and other specialized areas. Have Henry Vaughn check out the basement for his people, too. Then get your combined wish list to me. I'll draw plans based on the feedback you give me."

"Let's take one last walk through," she said.

"Good. As we go along, tell me what you're envisioning for each of the rooms."

As they explored the building, including the basement, they brainstormed different possibilities. Finally back on the ground floor, Joshua pointed to a closed door beside the stairs.

"What's in there?" he asked. "More electrical panels?"

"I don't remember."

Joshua tried the knob, but it was locked. Finding the right key, he unlocked the door and looked inside. The small closet was filled with brooms, mops, buckets and other janitorial supplies.

Joshua's gaze was drawn to the faded jacket hanging on a hook behind the door. The name tag over the breast pocket read Nez.

"Dad's," he said, his voice quiet. "I guess he didn't want to bring home any reminders."

"I'm sorry, Joshua." She looped her arm around his and held on to him. "It's hard, I know. You miss him."

"I wish we could have had one more talk. Something haunted him throughout his life and I think that's what ultimately held him back, but I never figured out what it was. I remember trying to convince him to work smarter, not harder, and go up the next step in the ladder. I wanted him to start his own janitorial firm, but nothing I said ever got through. He'd given up wanting anything other than what he already had."

"Joshua, you're forgetting something important. Your dad worked very hard, that's true, but he was living the life he chose and was happy. Isn't that what we all want?"

"That's just it, Myka. I don't think he was happy. To me, he seemed like a man who'd given up and accepted his fate. I know he loved woodworking, but he'd come home too tired to do anything except sit in his easy chair."

"Your dad was an incredibly skilled woodworker. He could carve a piece of wood and give it life. I remember seeing some of his animal figures."

He sighed. "I'd fish them out of the trash and try to get him to sell them, but he wouldn't allow it. He said it was just whittling. Most of those I saved are still on the windowsill in his library."

"Your father seemed like a man at peace with himself, Joshua. That's worth something, even if you don't agree with his choices."

He looked at her, her words slowly sinking in. "You may be right. I hadn't thought of it that way. I've always focused on finding what's at the end of the rainbow, but maybe his rainbow was different from mine."

Joshua closed and locked the door. "We need to get this building move-in ready, so let me start right away. Which office do you want?"

"I'd like the upstairs office that's down the hall from what will be the wool processing area. Robyn will have to choose the one she wants. We'll also need internet connections, battery backups for the computers and an emergency generator. Without functioning dryers the wool could be ruined by a power outage."

"Okay then, we've got a plan," he said. "Let's get going."

LATER THAT AFTERNOON Myka was back home, balancing HMI's books. After finishing her work and backing it up, Myka lingered over a cup of her favorite vanilla cinnamon tea. These little pleasures were rare for her these days.

She'd just finished the last sip when the doorbell rang.

Bear looked up at her and sighed.

She laughed. "Bear, that's positively anti-social of you. Let's go say hello to our company."

Myka opened the door and waved Robyn inside.

Reaching into her purse, Robyn brought out a huge rawhide bone and gave it to Bear. "Here you go, pal."

"You've made a friend for life," Myka said as Bear took the bone to his bed and started chewing it.

"We need to talk, Myka."

"This sounds serious. How about we sit down and I'll make some tea?"

"Perfect."

Robyn took a seat at the kitchen table, staying silent while Myka boiled the water.

"You're starting to worry me, Robyn. What's wrong?" Myka asked, bringing the teapot and two mugs to the table.

"It's not *bad* news. I've just got a concern." She waited as Myka poured the tea. "I've been doing a lot of free online publicity, but I've taken that as far as it can go. Traffic on the webpage is good, but analytics tells me we're getting more repeat business than new. To generate more traffic, I need an advertising budget, even if it's small. We've got to tell the world that HMI is here. That means special targeted promos, and those cost money."

"We can squeeze some money out of the budget, but you'll have to think small scale."

"I'll make every dollar stretch, I promise."

"So what are your plans?"

"For starters, I'd like to run a few online ads. I'll design them and write the copy myself, but I'm going to need new software…and a real office. I've been contacting specialty stores who might be willing to carry our merchandise, particularly our large tapestries. We haven't sold many through the site because shipping is expensive," she said. "The problem is that at Mom's, no matter which room I choose, the customer I'm talking with through Skype sees a family photo collection on the wall behind me."

"Working from home has been tough on a lot of us," Myka said, "but I've got good news. We've found a home for HMI!" Myka told her about their plans for the former IVA office building.

"Great! One more thing. I hate to push, but how about a new computer? Can we afford it? Something with more RAM, storage and a faster processor for multitasking would make my work a lot easier."

"Come up with several computer choices that'll meet your needs and I'll see what I can do. Joshua is going to make sure we get good internet."

Robyn sat back, now more relaxed. "We're all working hard, but it's exciting, isn't it? Each day is filled with challenges, and there's a surprise around every corner."

"All that can also be exhausting," Myka said with a thin smile.

"True, but I've never been happier. I love networking," she said. "Speaking of that, did you know J. R. Vega came back into town?"

"Who?" Myka asked.

"We knew him as Jerry Vega."

"I remember Jerry," Myka said. "He was super smart but lived in the shadow of his big brother."

"J.R. started out as an IT tech at Insomuch Software in Albuquerque, then he hit it big."

"How'd that happen?"

"He invested heavily in the company, which became a major player in the business software market. By the time Jerry sold his shares, he'd already made a small fortune. Now he can do whatever he wants."

"Wow, and he's back home?"

Robyn nodded. "You know what a great artist Jerry's father is, right?"

"Yeah, he painted a lot of murals in public buildings until the funding dried up."

"Exactly. Jerry set up a website for his dad, and since then, Mr. Vega has been selling his paintings all over the world."

"That's great! What a wonderful idea."

"I've got a lunch date with J.R. today. I'm hoping he'll give me some ideas on how to market our brand."

"Good thinking!" With a mischievous smile, she added, "Back in high school, you told me you had a thing for Mr. Vega's son. At first, I thought you meant Luke, the hunk. I never dreamed you liked Jerry."

Robyn laughed. "Luke's muscle and charm, but I was always in awe of Jerry. I remember him going into these long discussions about algorithms and abstractions for manipulating data structures. Half of what he said was over my head, but I'd pretend I understood because I loved listening to him."

"You've always picked brains over brawn."

"I still do."

Myka blinked. "Wait—do you have a crush on him?"

"Maybe," she said. "We're not kids any-more, but that just makes things spicier. You know what I mean. Look at you and Joshua."

"There is no me and Joshua."

"Sell that to someone who doesn't know you, Myka."

"No, I'm telling the truth. There's nothing between us. He's here for now, but once he lands a job, he'll disappear again," she said. "I don't need that kind of heartache. I've had it with goodbyes."

Robyn gave her an impromptu hug. "You've been through hell and back, honey, and I'm so sorry!"

"I'm fine—now."

"But you're lonely," Robyn said.

"Not really. I've got Bear, and once I start working in an office again I'll be around peo-ple all day long."

Bear looked up at her and stopped chewing.

"Don't worry, big guy. You're coming to

work with me. You can even have your own official title. How's 'Security' strike you?"

Bear gave her a huge panting grin and they both laughed.

"I better get going, Myka. I'll let you know how things work out with J.R."

After Robyn left, Myka decided to fix herself a sandwich. She opened the cupboard, then the fridge, and realized she was out of everything except tea, coffee and one pint of emergency ice cream. The milk was sour and the few slices of bread that were left were trimmed in gray fuzz.

"You have plenty of food, Bear, but I'm out. Wanna go for a car ride?"

The dog got up, a two-step process due to his size, the rawhide bone sticking out of his mouth like a cigar.

"Okay, you can take it with you, but just so you know, that makes you look far less ferocious."

The dog wagged his tail in response.

As Myka walked outside she saw Josh loading up his truck. Deciding to offer her help, she walked over.

He set a box down on the tailgate and smiled at her. "I'm glad you came over."

"Need a break?" Myka glanced down and

saw that he'd packed up many of his father's books, maps and papers. "Are you giving those away?"

"Yeah, I'm taking them over to the library in Painted Canyon. They can use reference materials." He rubbed the back of his neck with one hand. "I've cleared out most of Dad's things, but this part takes longer."

"Are you sure you won't need them in the search for Brooks's will?"

"I've already read them over, and they're no help. It should have been a snap to pack them up and give them away, but they're part of Dad's collection…"

"I hear you." He sat down on the porch's front step, and she took a seat beside him. "Some things are just harder to part with than others. That's how it was for me, too. Tanner's favorite book, his class ring, his special tie…"

"I can see that with a spouse," he said, "but a parent… It's different. It's the natural order, you know? Why does giving these things away bother me so much?"

"Maybe you're just not ready," she said, putting a hand on his arm.

He covered her hand with his own and didn't say anything for several long moments.

"Maybe it's the act of saying goodbye…I think the reality of it is just hitting me."

"Grieving is tough, Josh. Those emotions don't come when you think they should."

"Maybe that's it. I never got a chance to make my peace with it."

"You need time," she said. "There aren't any shortcuts to something like this."

He took a deep breath then let it out slowly. "There's one thing I have to do." He showed her a small leather pouch. "This belonged to my dad. It was his *jish,* his medicine bag. These can hold a variety of things, but Dad's held only corn pollen, which brings peace and signifies the continuity of all life. It was a gift from Uncle Rudy, given to him after Mom died. I've held on to it, not sure what to do, but as I was packing up Dad's maps and books I got an idea."

She looked at him, waiting.

"I'm going to scatter the pollen at Dad's special place." He met her gaze and held it. "I think he would have wanted you to be part of that." He looked at an indeterminate spot across the yard, then back at her. "It's not just that. I want you there, too. Will you come with me?"

"I'd like that." This was the first time he'd

ever asked her for anything. More importantly, he'd trusted her to see a side of him he never showed the world.

"You don't even know where it is, yet," he said with a ghost of a smile.

"It doesn't matter. I'll be there."

He took her hand. "Then let's go. It's not too far to walk."

"Let me put Bear away," she said, standing up.

"No. He was Dad's friend. Let him come."

Bear followed as they headed out through the back gate into the piñon juniper woodlands that lay a quarter of a mile from the house. They'd hiked up and down these hills in their youth, but it was clear that one place in particular had been important to Adam Nez, a place he'd shown only to his son.

After about ten minutes, they encountered the pebble-strewn base of an intermittent stream. The water flowed only after heavy summer rains, a rarity these past few years.

"Sometimes we'd wade around and watch the little shrimp that flourished in the pools before they dried up again," Myka recalled. "I remember you saying that they hid inside their shells during the dry seasons but would come back again next year, or the year after."

"And they did, right? I learned about them from my father. They're some kind of brine shrimp that love bracken water," Joshua replied.

"Are we going to the top, where the water sometimes flows over the ledge?"

He nodded and continued climbing up the dry wash. As they progressed along the gentle slope, the path narrowed, and before long they were in a gully with sloping sandstone walls. Ahead was a low rock cliff, layered in shades of tan, gray, yellow and reddish orange. Sagebrush, thin grasses and a few hearty junipers grew along spots in the ledge where eroded sand and soil had found refuge.

Joshua stopped, then pointed toward a shiny, almost varnished layer of sandstone along the lowest section of the water channel. "We'll have to circle around a little to get to the top. It's just too steep here."

Several minutes later they were standing on the bowl-shaped bed of sandstone above a cliff that descended about ten feet in a nearly vertical drop.

Against the rock face was a cairn of stones with one small turquoise bead near the top. "This was Dad's special place. Cairns like this can be found all around the Navajo Nation. Most of the time they mark someone's passage or journey, but to Dad, this one signified peace…and memories. He'd come here and make an offering to Earth Woman whenever he was troubled."

Joshua took the pouch from his pocket. "I'm going to sing a *Hozonji* he taught me. It's a good luck song that brings protection and can aid a person facing a challenge. This song has been passed down through my family, and it's seldom shared with an outsider."

"Whatever happens here stays here," she said, meeting his gaze.

"By scattering the pollen in this particular spot, where rainwater collects, I'm asking Earth Woman for the blessing of rain. Pollen, like rain, is life."

As his voice rose in song, a range of emotions flowed through his chant. She didn't speak Navajo, but understanding the meaning of each word seemed less important than listening with her heart. What she heard was the cry of a warrior mourning his father and moving on to face new battles. It was beautiful and powerful, each note filled with the strength that came from centuries of tradition.

As he emptied the pouch, she saw the

breeze catch the motes of pollen, swirl them in its grasp, then let go, allowing them to drift gently back to the earth.

Some of the golden grains fell over the cairn, a few adorning the turquoise bead and glistening with the light of the afternoon sun.

When the song ended, there was only stillness around them. Bear was lying down, his muzzle on his front paws and his eyes closed, asleep. Even the birds were silent. Joshua placed the empty leather pouch by the cairn.

She wasn't aware that she'd been holding her breath until he turned around. His eyes shone bright and there was new strength in him.

She understood his pain, remembering her own. Yet another stronger emotion pushed aside the remnants of sorrow. In the wake of one ending, life whispered to them about uncharted beginnings, urging them to follow the new path unfolding before them.

He took her hand and pulled her to him. He didn't kiss her, he simply held her. She rested her head against him, enjoying the hardness of his chest and knowing that he needed her softness, too.

For that moment in time, nothing else mattered. They were two people who'd known pain and needed the comfort of an embrace, two souls who yearned for more in their solitary lives.

He brushed a kiss on her forehead. "Thank you for being here with me."

"You said before that you'd always have my back. I'll always be there for you, too. That's what friends are for."

He met her gaze and held it. Awareness, sweet yet dangerous, flickered to life between them. She wanted to stay in his arms, but found the will to step away.

"Let's go back," he said as if reading her thoughts.

THIRTY MINUTES LATER, she and Bear were on their way to Medeiros Market, Bear in the backseat and her insulated cooler behind him in the rear storage area.

The parking lot was almost full when she arrived. It had been a long time since she'd seen so many people there.

As she walked inside, Myka heard her name being called. Grandma waved at her from the back of the store. As Myka came over she noticed Grandma was setting up the life-size cutout of a Thanksgiving turkey in a special display.

"Business is brisk for a weekday," Myka said.

"The town's renovation efforts have added several dozen construction jobs, and we've got a lot of new faces." She looked around at the crowded store with a smile. "I've made something special for you, Myka. It's a thank-you. Come to the back."

"What for?" Myka asked.

"Look around you, girl. Business is way up. We've sold more steak in the past month than in the previous three. Folks have some extra money in their pockets again and they're looking ahead to a brighter future." Grandma reached behind a counter and brought out a small box. "Homemade cake doughnuts—the ones you like."

"Thank you, Grandma! But you didn't have to do this. Share one with me."

Grandma smiled. "If you insist."

Myka held out the box, and they each took one. "These are incredible, Grandma."

"I'll make some for Joshua, too. You two are a terrific team."

"He's really helped me get HMI off the ground."

"My advice is hold on to him," she said.

"The company sure does need him," Myka agreed.

"And so do you," Grandma said quietly. "Life and love are calling to you again."

Myka shook her head. "What I feel when I'm with Joshua isn't love, Grandma," she said. "I know love. I lived it every day with Tanner. With Joshua, it's more about excitement and attraction, but love—the real kind—doesn't need fireworks. It's gentler and much quieter."

"There are as many ways to define love as there are people," Grandma said.

"Maybe, but the fact is that Joshua and I are a bad mix. His dreams for the future are way different from mine."

Grandma stood, ready to go back to work. "That's logic talking, but you know what? The heart almost never listens to common sense."

As Grandma walked back out into the market, Myka stuck another doughnut in her mouth. They were light as a feather and practically melted on her tongue. With a contented sigh, she finished her shopping, then went back to the car.

With the windows halfway down, she was able to reach in and pat Bear on the head. He was still happily chewing on his bone. She smiled and the dog wagged his tail, which thumped loudly against the back of the seat. "You're great company, you big moose," she said as she placed her groceries in the cooler. Not that it was needed. The weather was in the low fifties, and she hadn't bought anything frozen, but it would keep the milk and glass containers from tipping over or rolling around.

As she drove down Main Street, Myka noticed that the bakery next to the Blue Spruce was sporting its new sign. Wanting to know more about the M&S Bakery and Coffee Shop, she decided to pay Betty a visit. If anyone knew the details, it would be her.

This time Bear came with her. Evie would be happy to see her pal.

As they walked through the front doors, Myka noticed that the arched doorway Betty had wanted was now a reality. Bricks lined the interior of the arch, making it look like a passageway in some old fortress, and the black, wrought-iron chandeliers with their candle-shaped lights made it all come together.

Evie came out from behind the counter. Seeing Bear, she smiled and ran over to give him a hug. "Can I take him outside to play? I have a ball I can throw."

"Sure, if your mom says it's okay, but not out front," Myka said, looking over at Betty. "Bear's dying for some exercise. How about it?"

"Okay, Evie, you can play with Bear, but stay inside. You can roll the ball instead of throwing it. That way you won't break any lights."

As they ran down to the main hall, Myka said, "The weather's beautiful, and the lawn's perfect for play. What's going on?"

Betty hesitated, then said in a low voice, "For the past few days, I've had a feeling that someone's watching me. Most of the time, when I look outside, I see absolutely nothing, but I'm getting a little creeped out."

"Wait—*most* of the time?" Myka asked, trying to stay calm.

"Sometimes I'll catch a glimpse of a shape or shadow that disappears as soon as I try to focus on it. If it's anything other than my imagination, I'm guessing it's a drifter looking for a place to sleep."

"You should trust your instincts, Betty. Have you told Will?" Myka asked quickly.

"No, I'm not sure it isn't all in my head. I've been putting in some superlong hours and I'm really tired."

"Yeah, I know how you feel," she said, but before she could continue, they both heard a familiar voice. Myka turned and saw Sophie rush in, white paint all over her pink sweater.

"Have you told her yet?" Sophie asked Betty.

Betty laughed. "I haven't had a chance! Why don't you?"

Sophie smiled widely. "I've got super news. One morning I got to thinking how hard it is for us to get together like we used to. Talking over coffee and cupcakes kept us sane, even when things were really bad," she said. "Now we're not doing that because we're all so busy working. It just didn't seem right."

"So you've decided to…what…sell cupcakes door to door?" Myka asked.

"No, silly! I'm opening my own bakery and joining forces with Mabel's place. She still has the best coffee around, but the bakery that supplied her closed down months ago. At first she bought homemade goodies from Betty, but Betty's been too busy with the inn to do much baking. That's where I stepped in. Mabel and I are opening the M&S Bakery and Coffee Shop. We'll serve Mabel's coffee and all the extras, including New Mexican specialties like *biscochitos* and fry bread."

"Are you sure you'll have enough traffic?" Myka asked.

"Oh, yeah. Mabel's business tapered off when customers couldn't buy a pastry to go with their coffee, so together we're going to bring her customers back." She paused to take a breath. "But the main reason I wanted to open a bakery is because people need a place where they can sit and talk."

"I love it," Myka said.

Evie suddenly raced past them, laughing, Bear trotting beside her. Myka watched them for a moment and smiled. "You're so lucky to have her, Betty."

"Yeah, I am," Betty said softly. "My marriage to Tony was a train wreck, but when I look at Evie I know it was worth it."

After promising them the bakery's first batch of cupcakes, Sophie left to resume painting.

Myka lowered her voice so Evie wouldn't hear. "Have you heard from Tony?"

"Yeah. He finally agreed to a divorce, but Will thinks Tony's going to pull a fast one and try to get custody of Evie. That's why he helped me dig up the arrest reports and restraining order. If I need them, I'll have everything ready to present to a judge," she said.

"Good. It never hurts to be prepared. What's Tony doing these days?"

"Selling used cars in Albuquerque."

Bear's loud barking interrupted them. It wasn't his normal playful bark, so Myka hurried to the sunroom to find Bear standing on his hind legs and looking out the window into the garden.

Myka stood beside Bear, following his line of sight, and saw movement by the juniper hedge inside the wall. She moved to the right for a better angle, but whatever had been there was gone.

"It was probably a squirrel going over the wall," Myka said and smiled at Evie.

"Can Bear and I play some more?" Evie asked, looking at Myka then her mom.

"Sure, honey. Just stay inside," Betty said.

As they both ran off, Myka glanced at Betty. "Someone was out there. Tell Will, okay? It won't hurt to have him patrolling this area more often. With construction activity on the rise, there are more unfamiliar faces in Independence these days."

"All right," Betty said.

Myka glanced out the window again, but this time her gaze went to the train tracks on the raised roadbed that curved toward the plant.

"What's on your mind?" Betty asked, coming up next to her. "The train?"

"Exactly. If we want to grow the town's economy, we need to give tourists a reason to visit. Offering families that Old West experience could make Independence a real destination."

"You're right. We used to get quite a few visitors when the train was still running."

"I'll ask Joshua how he's doing with the search for Brooks's will. That'll hopefully clear the title to the crucial piece of land," she said, then added, "I might even offer to help."

Myka returned home with Bear a short time later. As she walked inside the house, the silence was deafening.

"Come on, Bear. Let's see what we can rustle up for dinner," she said, trying to fill the quiet emptiness.

The dog padded along with her as she headed back to the car, emptied the cooler and brought the groceries inside. Passing by the small framed photo of Tanner and her at the harvest festival, she stopped—setting down the last bag—and studied it for a moment.

Tanner was gone, but so was the Myka who

had stood beside him. After a beat, she placed the photo inside a drawer.

Independence's rebirth had also been her own. The future—good and bad—was waiting to unfold.

CHAPTER THIRTEEN

ANOTHER FIVE DAYS PASSED, and IVA's former office building was ready to be occupied. Myka had spent most of the morning moving equipment and supplies into the various rooms and getting her own office set up. Now, after giving Bear a much needed outside break, Myka headed back upstairs. As she passed the wool processing area, she saw half a dozen women inside the former kitchen, setting up dyeing stations and drying racks.

Seeing Myka, Fran Brown, one of their spinners and a member of the town council, came over to meet her. "Myka, I'm glad I caught you! Have you spoken to Robyn yet? She said we've received several special orders."

"What kind?" she asked, instantly wary.

"Two ladies want us to process and spin their poodles' hair into yarn."

"I have no idea what kind of yarn we'd get from that," Myka said.

"Neither do I. Maybe we could experiment by shearing Bear's coat and making him a sweater," she teased.

Almost as if he'd understood, the dog looked at her and snorted.

"I think that's a no," Myka said, laughing. "On those special orders... Let's suggest that the customers ask us again after New Year's. By then we'll be running at full capacity."

"Fair enough. Oh, and before I forget, Joshua's been looking for you, too."

"Where is he now—do you know?"

"Last time I saw him, he was downstairs helping Robyn in her office."

"Okay, thanks."

Myka found Joshua on the floor beneath Robyn's desk, tying off computer cables while Robyn organized software CDs in a storage box.

"Hey, guys," she said.

Joshua came out from under the desk and sat up. As their eyes met, Myka felt a rush of warmth envelop her. "Hi, Josh. I haven't seen you in a couple of days. Where have you been hiding?"

"I finished my reports on the town properties, so now I'm working part-time renovating some of those buildings along Main Street," he said, standing up. "I'm also lending a hand with facade restoration. From a design point of view, that's really important because it sets the tone for the entire building."

Joshua's face seemed to light up as he filled her in on the details, and she realized this was the happiest she'd seen him since he'd returned. It was as plain as the sunlight streaming through the glass window that he'd missed working as an architect more than he'd admitted.

"Thanks for helping me get set up, Josh," Robyn said, sitting down at her desk.

"Anytime." Joshua looked at Myka and cocked his head toward the doorway. "I'd like to take the office at the end of this hall. It's got perfect lighting and lots of room for my drafting table. Almost all my blueprints and sketches are done using computer assisted design software, but I can use the table surface to study Dad's old maps and papers."

"No problem," Myka said, following him to the room in question. "I can help you move your stuff in, too, if you'd like."

"Nah, I've got it."

"Do you have a minute? Something's been bothering me, and I'd like to talk to you about it," she said. Seeing him nod, she closed the door. "The prospect of renewed rail service is becoming more and more important. Where are you on the search for Brooks's papers?"

"I haven't made any progress. Dad's notes are all I've got to go by, and those are sketchy. He, Grandma and Ben Bruce were trying to get inside Brooks's head and figure it out, but that didn't go anywhere."

"Ben can't help us, but I think I know someone who might," she said. "Edgar Vega's always been reclusive, but he was one of your dad's oldest friends, and they shared a love of town history. You should talk to him."

"That's a good lead, Myka, but I'm not sure how welcome I'd be. I never got along with Mr. Vega's oldest son, Luke. I clocked him one time for shooting off his mouth. After that, Luke left me alone, but I'm guessing I'm still not one of his favorite people."

"So we'll go over there together. The Vegas don't live too far from here. Can you use a break?"

"Okay. Let's go."

After leaving Bear in her office with his favorite toy, they walked to Joshua's truck, which was parked in the loading zone alongside the train tracks.

Myka gave Joshua directions as he drove across town and soon they entered one of the neighborhoods west of Main Street. The houses here were evenly spaced, checkerboardlike, on half-acre lots.

"It's the last house on the right—the blue-and-sand-colored stucco one," Myka said. As Joshua drove slowly down Cottonwood Road, she told him about J.R. and how he'd helped Mr. Vega.

"I always liked Jerry," he said. "It took guts for him to stick with his own interests and not run with the pack."

As Joshua pulled up against the curb across from the Vega residence they saw Robyn coming down the front walk toward her car.

"Interesting," Joshua observed. "I didn't expect to see her here."

"She's got a thing for J.R.," Myka said, "but she'll kill me if you tell her I said so."

"Don't worry, your secret's safe."

As they crossed the empty street, Robyn waited on the sidewalk to greet them.

"Let me guess, Robyn. You're just following up on that lunch meeting," Myka whispered, grinning.

"Exactly," Robyn replied, her face flushing slightly.

"Okay, seriously now. How did your lunch with J.R. go?" Myka added.

Robyn smiled. "It was perfect. He gave me some great marketing ideas. I'm going to start a blog giving people special insights into HMI. I'll focus on the artisans and the different crafts they practice."

"That sounds great!" Myka said. "Will it be part of our webpage?"

"Yes, and I'll also start a newsletter. We'll ask visitors to the site to sign up," she said. Robyn looked from Myka to Joshua. "But what are you two doing here, if I may ask?"

"We're going to ask Mr. Vega if he and my father ever learned anything more about Mr. Brooks and all his secrets," Joshua replied.

"Trying to find out where those documents went?" Robyn asked.

"That's right. My dad and Mr. Vega were and are this community's best amateur historians," Joshua answered. "Hopefully, we'll learn something new."

"Well, I've got to get going, so good luck with that. I'll catch you guys later."

As Robyn walked off, Myka and Joshua went up to the Vegas' front porch.

Before they could ring the bell, J.R. opened the door and greeted Myka with a smile. "I thought I heard a familiar voice," he said. "Robyn and I were just talking about you, Myka."

The awkward-looking kid Myka remembered was taller now, about six foot one, and although he'd put on some weight, he was still slender. He wore brown framed glasses that made his hazel eyes seem owlish.

"You've done a great job kick-starting Independence," he said. "It's good to see people taking charge of their destinies."

As his glance shifted to Joshua, Myka introduced them.

"You remember Joshua Nez, don't you?"

"Long time, dude," he said with a nod, then waved them inside.

"I hear you're retired now," Myka said.

"Too young for that. More like between careers. Right now I'm keeping busy helping Dad with his business."

"Myka, is that you?" Edgar Vega called out from farther inside the house.

"Yes, Mr. Vega," Myka answered. "Where are you?"

"He's in the den," J.R. said. "Dad spends a lot of time in there, but it's awfully cold in winter. I want to put in a fireplace, some skylights and full-length windows as soon as possible. His eyesight isn't what it used to be and he needs more light." J.R. looked at Joshua. "At your convenience, I'd like to talk remodeling with you."

"Anytime," Joshua said. "You have my number?"

"Got it from Robyn," he replied. "I'll be in touch."

As they entered the den, Edgar Vega, a slender man in his early seventies with thinning gray hair, was wiping his hands on a rag. The painting before him was still in the early stages, sketched out with thin strokes, but it was clearly a Southwestern landscape. He gestured to the closest chairs, then placed the rag on a small worktable covered with paints and brushes.

"Hi, Myka, Joshua. Make yourselves comfortable," he said, pushing the rolled-up sleeves of his plaid flannel shirt farther up his arms.

"It's good to see you, Mr. Vega," Myka said, noting the faint scent of turpentine. "I hope we're not interrupting."

"Sir," Joshua greeted.

"I was ready to take a break, so your timing's perfect," Edgar said, taking a seat on a tall, three-legged stool beside his art supply table. "So tell me. What brings you here today?"

Myka glanced at Joshua and gave him a nod, knowing this would be better coming from him. As she sat back, he explained about his dad, the maps and the historical documents.

After he finished, Joshua added, "I was hoping that maybe you and Dad had discussed his research, or that you've looked into Brooks's legacy at one time or another."

"I've done both. The questions surrounding Silas Brooks have always piqued my curiosity, but your father's research was more comprehensive than anything I've done. He'd spend hours studying those old newspapers and reading whatever he could find about the man. It was personal for him. Your dad identified strongly with Brooks."

"Really?" Joshua asked. "How so?"

"You have to look past the surface to see it. Although one was wealthy and the other not, there was a lot more to their stories than money."

"Like what?" Joshua pressed, curious.

"Let's start with Brooks. Although his family diversified their holdings, their biggest moneymaker was a firearms manufacturing plant in the Midwest. Silas despised weapons, but he did what his father expected and took over when the time came. Yet as the company prospered, he became guilt ridden. After Silas's wife and baby died during childbirth, he was convinced that he'd been cursed by the ghosts of those killed with his family's weapons."

"I'd always heard he was a troubled man, but I didn't know the whole story," Myka said. "Did you ever meet him?"

"He commissioned me to do a painting of a prominent New Mexican historical site. He left the choice to me and I took months to decide."

"And he was okay with that?" Myka asked.

"Yes. He wanted something special and knew I'd come through," he said. "That painting turned out to be one of my best. It focused on the Cross of the Martyrs in the Sangre de Cristo Mountains near Santa Fe. It's a monument dedicated to the Franciscan friars in 1920. Since Brooks rarely left his house, I took the finished painting over to him. He loved it and asked me into his home for some cognac. He didn't have many guests, so I was incredibly flattered."

"That house was really something in its heyday, I would imagine," Joshua said.

"It was. I've never seen anything like it—before or since." He lapsed into a long silence. Eventually, he continued. "When it came time for me to get paid, he asked me to wait for him, then closed the door and stepped out of the *sala*. I heard what sounded like furniture being moved and the clack of wood. I thought something was wrong, so I went into the entryway and called out, asking if he was okay. He met me a second later, annoyed because I'd left the room. He handed me my money, all cash, and told me to leave."

"Did you ever figure out what was going on?" Joshua asked. He was beginning to understand his father's fascination with Brooks. Every detail he uncovered led to another, even more interesting one.

"Since he paid me in cash, I figured he must have had a secret panel stuffed with money in the house somewhere, but I don't know for sure," Edgar said. "Your father checked for loose floorboards or a trap door just last year, but he didn't find anything."

"Does Mayor Allen know this story?" Joshua asked.

"I doubt your father would have said anything unless he'd actually found those missing documents."

Joshua nodded. "Yeah, Dad was like that."

"If Brooks really did leave a will behind, my guess is that it's still somewhere in his house."

"Thanks, Mr. Vega," Joshua said.

"I know you and your father had differences, but he was very proud of you, son. You always came first...no matter what the cost."

In a thoughtful voice, he added, "Like Silas Brooks, your dad paid the price for family."

The change in Mr. Vega's tone caught Joshua's attention. "You mentioned before that my dad and Brooks were alike. How do you figure that?"

Edgar started to speak then shook his head. "It's not for me to say."

"He's gone, Mr. Vega. If it's something that might help me understand Dad better, I'd sure like to hear it."

After a long moment, Edgar finally nodded. "When a son looks at his father, all too often he sees only part of what's there. There's judgment, history, sometimes pride, and all that colors the reality," he said. "You saw a hardworking janitor that some misguided people in the community looked down on, but he, like you, had bigger dreams once."

"He never mentioned anything like that to me."

"Probably because there was nothing more to be said," Edgar answered. Looking directly at Joshua, he continued, "Your father was a first-class woodcarver, and although you may not know this, he had his own shop at one time. He loved his work, but business came in spurts, and when your mom got pregnant, he realized he needed a steady paycheck. His job at the plant gave him a salary and health insurance, so he closed his shop and never looked back."

"If he loved woodworking so much, why didn't he open a shop once I was in college and on my own?"

Edgar shook his head. "As we age, our dreams change, Josh. He no longer had the energy nor the inclination to deal with the ups and downs of an unreliable career."

"I wish he'd told me." Joshua felt as if he'd been kicked in the gut. He'd misjudged his father for years and there was nothing he could do to make it right.

"Adam was a proud man. He never felt the need to explain himself to you or anyone else."

"Proud, he was," Joshua agreed.

They left the Vegas' home soon afterward, and Joshua didn't speak until they were back in his truck. "My dad and I weren't so different after all."

Myka reached over and took his hand. "You two loved each other, and that's all that really matters, Joshua."

"I know now how hard it must have been for him to walk away from his dream." He took a deep breath, still reeling from what he'd learned. "When our firm closed its doors, I knew in my gut I'd rebound, but Dad faced overwhelming odds—and he did it with grace."

"Hemingway defined courage as grace under pressure," she said.

"That was Dad…"

He lapsed into a heavy silence, lost in thought. At long last he spoke. "I can't change the past, but there's still one thing I can do for him. Dad loved this town. To him it was home. I'll continue to play my part in bringing it back, not just through HMI, but by restoring the buildings on Main."

"Independence is your home, too, Joshua."

He shook his head. "No, Myka, this is *your* home…and Dad's. Sooner or later, I'll have to leave. There's just not enough work around here for an architect, and that's part of who I am. I have to make a living and plan my future."

"You've been working part-time for HMI as an unpaid consultant, but the company can afford to pay you now. It won't be a lot, but let me see what we can offer. Maybe your future is here and you just don't know it yet."

He wanted to say no, but the truth was he needed the funds. He'd agreed to a minimal fee for his consulting work for the town, but the first stage of that was already over, and he'd used most of the money for living expenses and supplies to paint and fix up his father's house. At the moment he was getting by, but not by much.

"All right, thanks," he said.

As he looked at her, he realized that their parting was as inevitable as the next sunset. Myka belonged in Independence as much as HMI did, but he'd worked hard to become an architect. He had something of value to offer the world and he wouldn't let Independence bury his dreams. Myka lived in the here and now, and it would hurt leaving her behind, but his own brass ring was on the horizon, and he had to chase after it.

CHAPTER FOURTEEN

THREE MORE DAYS flew by. Though she still avoided it, the freight elevator had been repaired. The new wool processing areas were in use and work areas were available to their special crafters—like Mr. Gomez, who did straw inlay work. The basement housed the woodworkers and their noisy tools.

Myka walked down the hall, smiling, Robyn at her side. No matter how busy it got, she could always hear the sound of laughter. As they passed the dyeing room, Liza came out holding a sample of dyed roving. "Look at this blue. We used the mixture your contact gave us. Have you ever seen anything more beautiful?"

Myka drew in a breath. It was an exquisite blend of violet and indigo. "It's gorgeous! Let me know when it's spun. I have a feeling this will fly off our shelves."

"That's good news," Robyn said. "I put a

small description online, and we've got orders coming in already."

"You priced it correctly? We need to charge extra," Myka said.

"Oh, yeah, and the price hasn't kept people away."

"That's fabulous!" Myka glanced at her watch. "I better go, I've got to meet the mayor. He asked me to stop by his office as soon as I could."

"Is there a problem?" Robyn asked.

"I don't think so. It's probably just paperwork."

As Myka headed toward the stairwell, Robyn reached for her arm. "Come on. Let's take the elevator. I'll ride down with you."

Myka shook her head. "No, I can't go in there." She hated the way the two women looked at each other but pushed it out of her mind. "It's only one flight anyway, so it's no big deal."

Myka hurried downstairs. People didn't understand how stubbornly memories could cling to certain places. She couldn't go into the freight elevator without being overwhelmed by the past. It was far easier to avoid it altogether.

Myka drove down Main Street alone, glad

that Bear was with Sophie's cousin today. Paula had offered to take the big guy on a long hike, so Myka had readily agreed.

Minutes later she parked in the rear lot of the insurance office where Phil worked half days. As she was getting out of her SUV, Mayor Allen stepped outside to meet her. "Good! You're here," he said. "Come in."

He escorted Myka into his small office and offered her a cup of coffee. "I've got to tell you, when you first came up with the idea for Handmade in Independence, I thought the business end of it would eat you alive. I gave you a month before you ran away screaming."

She laughed. "There've been plenty of times I wanted to do just that."

"You've proved that your greatest strength is the ability to work around obstacles. That's why I wanted to speak with you," he said, leaning over and resting his elbows on the desk. "Municipal revenues are still hurting, and when our fire chief asked me for sixty-five thousand to repair and purchase essential equipment I had to turn him down. Unfortunately, that means our fire station will close. We'll have to depend on County and a much longer response time, so our insurance rates, both business and residential, are going to skyrocket."

She sat back, dismayed by the news and desperately trying to come up with a way around this new hurdle. "So you called me here to give me a heads-up?"

"Yes, but also because you always manage to pull the proverbial rabbit out of the hat, and that's what we need right now."

She ran a despairing hand through her hair. "I don't know what to tell you except we've got to find a way to save our fire department."

"I've been looking for alternate funding sources, but I keep coming up empty."

"There's an answer to this, Phil, I'm sure of it."

"That's exactly why I came to you. You believe there *is* an answer and, somehow, I know you'll find it."

"You have more faith in me than I do. I'm not a miracle worker."

"Actually, Myka, I think you are."

AN HOUR LATER, Myka was walking down the long hallway to her office when she noticed the doors to the freight elevator had been screened off with a band of pink fabric. She knew yellow was the color of crime scene tape, but what was pink?

Passing Sara Chase, one of their most experienced spinners, Myka pointed to the closed doors. "What's going on?"

Sara hesitated. "The electrician is double-checking the new controls. Molly needed to block off the elevator while testing the system," she said. "We put a pink ribbon across it because Liza had several spools in her purse—she's using it for baby afghans."

Sara hurried off, but figuring that the woman was as pressed for time as she was, Myka quickly put it out of mind.

She entered her office, and after leaving voice mails asking Joshua and Robyn for a morning meeting, Myka stood by the window staring at her reflection in the glass. Now that she was running HMI, everyone seemed to look to her for answers. Yet she was still just Myka. Did they see more?

"What's up? I got your message," Joshua said, stepping into her office.

"Sit down. I was hoping we could do some brainstorming. Robyn's coming, too."

"I'm here," Robyn said, hurrying inside. "Sorry, the website crashed when I rebooted the system. Too much traffic."

"So we're off the air?"

"We were, for about twenty minutes. Now we're up and running and better than ever. I got J.R. to redesign our site and it looks amazing! You can click on any item, then hover over it with your mouse to see the details. He's also standing by to set up a widget that'll lead customers to instant live help during business hours instead of the email question-response system we're using now."

"Live help from whom?" she asked.

"I wanted to talk to you about hiring someone full-time to take those calls. During business hours, of course."

"We can't afford it," Myka said.

"Part-time then, and not live, but responding no later than next day?" Robyn pressed.

Myka considered it, then nodded. "Okay, let's try next day and see how it works out." She reached up and adjusted the collar on her blouse. "Right now we've got a more immediate problem." She told them what the mayor had said about the fire department.

"Myka, that's really bad news, not only for us, but for everyone in town, especially all the new businesses still in start-up mode. Most are operating on a shoestring and a prayer. Look at Sophie. She and her mom used all their savings to open that bakery. They figured if we could do it, so could they, and they've been counting on lunchtime business from our workers," Robyn said.

"No one realizes just how close to the margin we've played things," Myka added.

"HMI is taking the place of Independence Vehicle Accessories in people's minds, but this time, it's a success they've helped create, and some of them want their own chance to dream big," Joshua said.

She drew in a sharp breath. "IVA was a *huge* corporation with manufacturing facilities all around the country. We're a tiny dot on the map, with barely a hundred workers."

"You started a company in a town that was all but dead, and now it's showing a profit. When the people around us look at HMI, they see...possibilities...for themselves and Independence," Joshua answered. "They see their future."

"I'm more worried about the present. We have to keep the momentum going, and right now, that means finding a way to save our fire department," Myka said.

Robyn paced around the room as a heavy silence descended.

"This won't work, Myka," Joshua said at

last. "When you try to force an idea, you get nowhere. We need to go about our jobs and see what comes to mind as the day goes on."

"All right," Myka said. "We'll meet back here sometime tomorrow."

"Just don't forget this weekend," Robyn said. "It'll be good PR." She glanced from Joshua to Myka. "Are you two going together?"

"Huh?" Myka said. "You've lost me."

"I hadn't gotten around to asking her yet," Josh said.

"Then get busy!" Robyn shook her head as she strode out.

"What's she talking about? What did I miss?"

"Nothing yet. Mayor Allen wanted to hold a town social this year as a sign that bad times are over. He's found a band that'll play for free, too. The Heartsongs. Have you heard of them?"

Myka laughed. "Yeah, but I wouldn't exactly call them a band. It's more like one senior gentleman with a fiddle, his retired son who plays guitar and Mabel at the piano."

"Good enough for me," he said. "We should go together."

Myka hesitated. "As colleagues, or are you asking me on a date?"

"Whichever one will get you to say yes," he answered with a grin.

"Okay, but let's keep it informal. I'll meet you there."

"What are you worried about, Myka?"

"Headaches," she said. "Will, for one."

"Let me handle him."

She shook her head. "He's *my* problem and I have to deal with him. You're just caught in the middle."

"Maybe, but I can take whatever he throws at me."

"There's something else you should keep in mind, Joshua. What you do, or don't do, matters more than ever. You're working as an architect for the town and helping HMI. You've got to ignore Will's negativity. People see you as part of the solution. You've earned their trust."

He grew serious. "I know, Myka. These days, when I look at the faces around me, I see respect. That means more to me than you know."

"It's what you've always wanted…"

She started to say more, but just then she heard a loud commotion outside her office.

"What on earth—" Myka hurried into the hallway. A large wheeled cart filled with supplies slated for the dyeing room was blocking the doors of the freight elevator.

"What's going on?" she asked, seeing Sophie and Liza.

"Myka, good! I was about to find you! Can you and Josh take that upstairs?" Liza asked, pointing to the cart. "Sophie and I are running late. We're supposed to pick up some supplies at Painted Canyon and we have to get there before the vendor closes."

"Go," Myka said without hesitation.

As the women hurried off, she suddenly realized what she'd agreed to do.

"Come on," Joshua said. "I'll pull the cart into the elevator, you maneuver it."

"I…" She swallowed hard. "I'll help you roll it in, then meet you upstairs."

"It's not the same elevator anymore, Myka," he said gently. "It belongs to HMI now and it doesn't even look the same."

"What do you mean?"

"Come see for yourself."

Curiosity got the better of her, and she followed him. Joshua pushed the button, the elevator dinged and within a few seconds the doors opened.

Myka stared at the interior, blinked, then continued to stare. She wasn't sure what she'd expected, but this...

Pink was her favorite color, and the interior of the freight elevator had been painted a light rose. Beautiful, small butterflies had been hand drawn over its metal walls, and each had a name inscribed below it.

"All the people who work here have a butterfly, including you, but you'll have to sign your own. It's the pink-and-lavender one at the center, below the quote."

As she read what was written there, tears welled up in her eyes.

"'The future belongs to those who believe in the beauty of their dreams'—Eleanor Roosevelt," she said. "When did they..." Her voice wavered.

"Everyone knows how hard it was for you to use this elevator and they wanted to help. They asked me to come up with a design that would welcome you." He took her hand and pulled her farther inside. "So what do you think?"

"I love it. It's beautiful, and thoughtful and... I'm speechless!"

He placed his arm around her shoulders and pulled her closer to his side. "In almost all cultures, butterflies represent renewal and transformation. It seemed fitting for HMI."

"It's lovely," she said, signing her name below the central butterfly with the special pen he handed her. "I don't know how to thank you."

"I do." He pulled her into his arms, then took her mouth tenderly. The warmth of his body and the power of his kiss wove a spell all their own, pushing the past away and welcoming the present.

After a brief eternity, she stepped back, but left her hand in his. "What an incredible gift this is, Joshua."

"It's from everyone. I just gave it form."

She smiled. That's what drew her to him most—his belief that imagination was the doorway to new realities. "It's just perfect."

CHAPTER FIFTEEN

THE NIGHT OF the social was blustery and cool with autumn leaves flying freely, but it didn't dampen anyone's spirits. Fortunately, organizers had decided to host the dance inside the community center rather than in the courtyard.

The auditorium had been transformed into a giant dance floor and it was filled to bursting. Familiar faces pressed in all around her, most dressed in their finest Western wear. Myka had chosen a denim dress with her silver concha belt and her favorite handcrafted turquoise leather boots with cream embroidery on the shaft.

Across the way, she could see Robyn wearing a long denim skirt. It was the first time in ages Myka had seen her in something other than jeans. She smiled the second she saw J.R. next to her friend.

The mayor, wearing a Western-cut suit complete with a big turquoise and silver bolo tie, stepped onto the small stage beside the band and opened the festivities with a prayer of thanks. A moment later, he stepped down and the band began to play.

Although no alcohol would be served, there were plenty of soft drinks. Myka went to the buffet table, picked up a cola and filled her paper plate with two turkey and cheese tortilla pinwheels. Unable to resist the temptation, she took a pumpkin spice cookie, as well.

Taking a seat against the wall, she ate and watched the line dancers in the center of the room.

The fast-paced music picked up her spirits. Tonight was for play, not business, and it felt good to get away and just have fun.

Myka tossed her paper plate into the trash and was about to join the dancers when a strange feeling crept over her. She paused and looked around. There'd been a change in the atmosphere of the room—the music was just as loud, but there was less laugher, and people had stopped talking.

She wondered what was going on and saw Will, wearing his uniform, standing at the entrance. With him was a man she hadn't seen in over a year—one she'd hoped never to see again.

Distracted by the unexpected visitor, she jumped when she felt a hand on her shoulder.

"Sorry, I didn't mean to startle you," Joshua said and smiled.

He was wearing a dark blue Western shirt with snaps, not buttons, beneath a leather vest. At his throat was a handcrafted Native American silver bolo tie with a bear paw inlay. He looked darned near perfect, all the way down to his jeans and black boots.

"You okay?" he asked.

"Yeah, I'm fine," she said, glancing back at Will and his companion.

"Who's that?" he asked, following her line of sight. "Everyone seems to be looking in his direction."

"He's a jerk...and I'd hoped he had left town for good."

"What did he do?" he asked, moving closer to Myka.

"He played us all for fools. His name is Carl White, and he worked here in IVA's business office. When the plant closed down he was one of four employees offered a job at one of IVA's sister companies in San Diego. What really ticked people off is that Carl knew our plant was closing long before anyone else here. Carl sold his house and summer cabin before Independence's real estate market crashed—which happened the moment everyone got their pink slips. Word was that IVA paid Carl to keep his mouth shut."

"And *he's* Will's friend?" he said, watching as the police chief walked with Carl toward the refreshment table.

"From way back," she said. "Will bought Carl's story—that he'd sold his properties because he intended to quit and move closer to his girlfriend."

Joshua was quiet for several moments. "There's more to Carl White than you're saying, isn't there?" he asked, watching her closely.

She shrugged but avoided looking at him. "It's ancient history…and it's personal."

"All right, then. Forget him. Tonight's for fun. Let's dance," he said and took her arm.

Just then, Carl came up.

"Myka, you're a sight for sore eyes."

"Hello, Carl," she said with a tight-lipped smile.

"I'm glad to see you're enjoying life again, darling. We were all worried about you for a while there."

Myka drew in a breath. She wanted to kick him as hard as she could with her pointed toe boot. "Thanks, I appreciate that. If you'll excuse me…"

She started to go around him, but he reached for her arm. "Can we talk for a moment?"

"Not now," she replied coldly.

Joshua stepped forward, coming shoulder to shoulder with the man. "Myka wants to dance," he said, turning his steely gaze to Carl.

"My bad," Carl said. "You know I work for American Vehicle Accessories in San Diego, right?" Seeing her shrug, he continued. "We're always donating to one project or another, and since you dealt with most of the execs, I figured you'd want to talk to me about the fire department's funding problem."

"The person you should be speaking to is Mayor Allen," she said, forcing her voice to stay calm.

"Phil doesn't have your insight. I'd have to pitch it to my boss in just the right way. Since you know Mike Petersen, our CFO, I thought you could give me some ideas on the best way to approach him."

Myka drew in a breath. That was true. As bookkeeper, she'd dealt with many out-of-town corporate VIPs, including Peterson.

"All right," she said after a moment. "Let's talk."

"Step out to the lobby with me. Give me a few ideas on how to approach Peterson with this, and I'll take it from there."

"Can this wait?" Joshua said.

"No, actually. I'm heading out tomorrow at first light. I'm only in town to see my aunt, and she insisted on coming to the social tonight."

"It's okay, Joshua. I'll join you in a few minutes," she said, and left the auditorium with Carl.

With the sound of the band behind them, she could now speak at a normal level.

"With Mike, you have to give him the soft sell along with all the details up front," she said, getting right down to business. "Give him the dollar and cents amount the fire department needs, then explain that if it's handled right, the donation could be part of a public ceremony that'll include the press. Publicity like that can be rebroadcast and used in other promotions, so it'll give AVA a lot of bang for their buck. Let me know if you need anything else." She started to walk away, but he moved in front of her.

"Myka, relax," Carl said softly, closing the

distance between them and putting his hand on her shoulder. "It doesn't have to be all business between us, not tonight. You know I had a thing for you even when you were married, but there's no need to hold back now. We're both unattached. Be nice to me, and I'll be nice to you."

She brushed away his arm and stepped back. "If you touch me again, you creep, I'm going to scream loud enough to wake the dead."

"Myka, I heard all about the insurance fiasco. *Your* business depends on the fire department, as do a lot of other companies here. Many are bound to sink if the insurance rates triple. You need what I have to offer. Admit it."

She took another step back, but he reached out and snaked an arm around her waist.

"Stop teasing," he growled.

Myka stomped on his toe and jerked free. "Back off!" she yelled.

Carl made another grab for her just as Joshua came into the lobby. He swung Carl around and decked him with a punch to the jaw. Carl landed on his butt, tried to stand, but only made it to his hands and knees.

People rushed into the lobby to see what

was going on, but Will was one of the first to arrive. He placed Joshua in cuffs as Carl staggered to his feet, insisting that he was fine.

Mayor Allen, pushing his way through the crowd, tried to calm everyone down.

"Stop it, Will," Myka said, grabbing her brother-in-law's arm. "Joshua was protecting me."

"Myka, back away. I'm handling this," Will snapped.

"Listen, you're making a mistake," Myka said, but Will ignored her and pushed Joshua out the front door.

Myka started to go after them, but Robyn pulled her back. "*I* get it. Carl's pulled those same moves on me, too. Come on, I'll drive you to the station, and we'll talk to Will there."

"Carl was way out of line and Joshua was defending me. I've got to make Will understand what really happened."

"He can see it for himself," Robyn said, pointing to a security camera. "Remember when those were installed last year? Kids were tagging the place and climbing onto the roof."

Myka smiled. "You're terrific, Robyn. Now

let's go turn the tables on Carl, the sleaze-
ball," she said. "I've got an idea."

"What do you have in mind?"

"First, we spring Joshua. Then, we'll talk
to Carl—together."

WHEN THEY ARRIVED at the station, Will was
at his desk and Joshua sat inside a cell across
the room.

Seeing Myka, Joshua stood up. "You okay,
Myka?" he called out.

"Yes, and I'm here to set things right," she
said firmly, turning to glare at Will. Robyn
remained by her side, her expression hard.

"I already know the facts," Will said. "I
was standing in the doorway, and out of the
corner of my eye I saw Joshua throw the
punch."

"Yes, he did, and if he hadn't I would have,"
Myka said. "You couldn't see me, could you?"

"No, just Joshua. Keep talking," he said.

Myka explained what had happened, starting from the moment Carl first came up to
her. "And if you still don't believe me, check
the security camera covering the lobby."

Will looked at Joshua, who'd been listening, then to Robyn, who nodded. Finally, he

responded. "Myka, maybe Carl misunderstood..."

"No. This all started when I was working at IVA. Back then Carl went out of his way to make my life miserable. He'd mouth off and make crude, suggestive remarks, always when no one else could hear him."

"Why didn't you tell Tanner?" Will demanded.

"Because Tanner would have confronted him, maybe even taken a swing. Carl outranked him, and might have filed assault charges, so I handled it my own way. I recorded some of Carl's comments, and planned to play them for my supervisor. Then I found out that the last woman who'd accused an exec of sexual harassment was fired. She'd even had a witness. The exec was forced to apologize and she was transferred to another department. Then, after a few months of lousy performance reviews, she was let go."

"You should have come to me. *I* didn't work there."

"At the time, Tanner and I had just bought the house, remember? I couldn't afford to lose my job, and neither could Tanner, so I made it my business to avoid Carl. He was eventually promoted and began spending most of his time traveling."

"And tonight he hit on you again?"

"And he grabbed me," Myka said. "Twice. He was going for a third time when Joshua stepped in."

Will picked up his keys and unlocked the cell. "Looks like I owe you an apology."

Joshua met his gaze and waited. "I'm not getting one, am I?" he asked, grinning.

"Hey, I said I owe you one, not that it's going to happen. Take it as a win."

Myka looked at Robyn and shrugged.

"Looks like Carl and I need to have a talk," Will said, heading to the door.

"Wait. Hear me out first. I have an idea that'll work to everyone's advantage, but we'll need backup just in case things go wrong," Myka said.

Will gave her a puzzled look. "What exactly do you want to do?"

"Whatever it is, count me in," Joshua said.

A HALF HOUR later, Myka and Robyn caught up to Carl in the parking lot outside the community center. He was heading for his car, but seeing them, he stopped and waited. "Hello, darlings. Are you here to smooth things over and maybe strike a deal? It's going to take more than a smile and a handshake to change my mind now. How far are you ladies willing to go?"

"You might want to watch what you say, Carl," Myka said, then pointed to a pickup parked just down the street. "The police chief is right over there, and I know for a fact he's watching your every move."

"My word against yours," Carl said. "Unless he's a lip reader."

"I could just play back the recording," Myka said, holding up the small digital recorder.

"I could also provide statements from the women at IVA who endured your sexual harassment, including me," Robyn said. "Want that on your next work evaluation?"

"You trying to blackmail me?" he growled.

"No, not at all. We're giving you a preview of Robyn's article for the Independence Times."

Robyn smiled. "One of my many jobs these days is writing for our local online newspaper," she said. "I'll be reporting what really happened tonight and adding the security video to my story. Everyone will have the opportunity to lip read or follow the script

I'll provide. I figure it'll go viral, but even if it doesn't, AVA will get a copy."

"Keep in mind that if anyone you're currently working with adds to these revelations, you'll quickly become a liability to the company. They'll probably toss you out." Myka paused, then added, "Jobs are scarce these days, so after the video goes online, you'll have to search for a new job in countries with no internet."

"Okay, I get the picture. Let's deal. How can I make this go away?" he snarled.

"Make sure AVA actually donates the money for our fire department." Myka said. "And deal directly with Mayor Allen."

"Even if I can swing the deal with AVA, how do I know you two will keep the incident to yourselves?"

"That's a chance you'll have to take. One thing's for sure, if you don't do the right thing people are going to see the real you," Myka said.

"Hardball, huh?"

"Payback," Robyn said.

"It's your only way out, Carl," Myka added.

He glared at both of them, then noticed Will approaching from across the parking lot.

"You'll get your safety equipment. I'll make sure of it," he whispered harshly.

Will came up a second later. "This is our town, Carl, and you're not welcome here anymore."

"Are you threatening me, cop?" Carl asked.

"No, just trying to keep you out of trouble. You've gained a couple of enemies tonight. Here, we stand up for the women in our lives." As if on cue, Joshua stepped out of the shadows.

"Next time you and I meet, it'll be just the two of us," Joshua said with a feral smile.

"Get out of here, Carl," Will said.

As the man walked away, heading for his car, Joshua stood next to Myka. "Still wish I could have had a few minutes—just him and me," Joshua said.

Will replied, "One punch was enough. You did just fine—for a city boy." Then he walked away.

Joshua chuckled softly.

"Looks like you made a friend tonight," Myka said.

"Maybe."

"Well, if you two don't need me anymore, I'm going back inside to find J.R.," Robyn said.

Myka smiled.

As Robyn strolled away, Joshua took Myka's hand. "The wind's died down and the moon's out. You want to walk for a bit?"

Myka nodded and fell into step beside him. The breeze was cold but it felt wonderful when he put his arm around her and brought her closer. Enjoying the warmth of his body and the steady strength of his arm, she smiled.

"What are you smiling about?" he asked with a look that told her he'd already guessed.

"I love this town," she said, avoiding the question and looking up at the old-fashioned streetlight with its ornate stand and curved top. "Life here has a timeless quality. I find that...comforting."

"Things are always changing, Myka, even here." He pointed to the Western facades being constructed on some of the stores lining Main Street. "Creating new elements that'll remind people of the past while focusing on the present—that's the part of architecture I love most."

"Change can be tough. Reminders of what was make the transitions easier," she said. "I think that's why I resisted changing the name from Myka's Wooly Dreams to HMI, but in a lot of ways, HMI is an even better company."

"In a lot of ways…but not in others?" he asked, voicing what she'd left unspoken.

"I miss my downtimes, those days when I could just sit on my front porch and drink a cup of coffee without having to check my watch."

"Sometimes you have to take what you need."

The street was almost deserted, and the peace that surrounded them was marred only by the sounds of laughter coming from the community center. Myka looked up at him, and following her heart, moved into his arms.

He held her tightly against him, brushing a kiss over her hair then nuzzling her neck. Lastly, he took her mouth.

Enjoying that brief pause in time, she pressed herself into his kiss, wishing the moment could last forever.

When he eased his hold at long last, they began walking back toward his truck, hand in hand. "So many dreams are starting to unfold right here in Independence," she said. "There's room for yours, too."

"Parts of it, yes," he said in a quiet, thoughtful voice.

"Are you happy right now?" she asked.

"At this very moment?" Seeing her nod, he

answered, "Yes, I am. But tell me something, Myka. When you think about the distant future, what do you wish for most?"

"I haven't thought about anything far off in ages," she said.

"Think about it now. What would you like your life to be further down the road?"

She considered it, then answered honestly. "I love my work, but someday I want to get married again and have a home big enough for several kids. I hope to raise a family here."

He nodded but didn't answer.

As silence descended over them, Myka felt him slipping away to a place she couldn't reach.

CHAPTER SIXTEEN

MAYOR ALLEN CALLED Myka at the end of the week. American Vehicle Accessories would be awarding the town of Independence the grant they needed to keep their fire station open. This meant that the government sponsored loan he'd been preparing to apply for could be canceled. A special press conference would cover the presentation.

The mayor, with a chuckle or two, also read her a small newspaper article AVA had included in their email. The article, a paragraph from a business supplement, reported that Carl White had arranged for the grant, his last official act before resigning from AVA for personal reasons.

Myka smiled, knowing that "resigning for personal reasons" was corporate jargon for being fired. Somebody must have finally reported Carl's behavior to his bosses. Justice had been done, at least in a roundabout way, and once again, they'd averted disaster.

In a great mood, she left work at five-thirty, but instead of going straight home, she decided to take a walk down Main Street with Bear.

Enjoying the red-and-orange sunset so common here in the Southwest, Myka found it easy to ignore the cool breeze that stung her cheeks. She walked slowly, taking her time. Fall was her favorite season. Each tree was ablaze with color, and the excitement of the holidays was just around the corner.

Humming under her breath, she stopped by the Blue Spruce Inn. As she walked inside and looked around, she was amazed by the results of Betty's hard work. Southwest tapestries woven in rich earth tones hung on the walls. The roaring fire in the oversized fireplace added to the inn's welcoming feel.

"Wow," Myka said as Betty came to join her. "This place looks amazing."

"I'm glad you asked me to showcase some of HMI's tapestries. Every time we change them, the Blue Spruce gets a new look. They're so eye-catching, I'm sure out-of-town guests will want to buy some of them."

Myka walked to the adjoining room and looked down at the old wood plank floor. "This is gorgeous!"

"That was Joshua's find. He's been salvaging materials like weathered lumber, flooring, tiles, bricks and fixtures from some of the old houses around town," she said. "The mayor posts a list and photos at town hall. Any resident can make a bid, and the best offer gets the materials. What's left over is sold to contractors in Albuquerque and Santa Fe. Come and see the crown molding in our dining room."

When Myka went through the arched doorway, she saw that the room had been transformed. The hand-carved molding—featuring a simple pattern of lines and grooves—added a touch of rustic elegance.

She walked around slowly, taking everything in. Most of the floor space was taken up with tables covered by plain white tablecloths. All were embroidered at the bottom in a white-on-white design that gave the room a classic touch without overpowering the down-to-earth feel of the inn.

"It's just beautiful, Betty," Myka said.

"I've got other news, too! I've cut a deal with Sophie. She'll be providing all the breakfast breads for the inn and we're using Mabel's coffee. We'll tell the guests that the M&S Bakery and Coffee Shop is just next door in case they want to do a little shopping before they leave."

"That's terrific! Everything's coming together."

Hearing the rustle of leaves, Betty walked to the window and looked outside. Bear followed her but didn't bark.

Seeing the worried frown on Betty's face, Myka went to her side and placed a hand on her shoulder. "What's wrong?"

"I finally heard from Tony. He wants half of my share in the inn before he'll agree to a divorce. If I say no, he's going to take me to court and demand visiting rights with Evie, and maybe joint custody." She turned around and faced Myka. "I can't allow that. If he's alone with Evie, I'm afraid he'll take her and I'll never see her again."

"When did he learn about the inn?" Myka asked.

"I have no idea. My guess is that he's been keeping an eye on me. I'd gladly give him a share of the inn if he'd leave us alone, but I have a feeling he'd do just the opposite."

"Please tell me that Will already knows about this," Myka said.

"Yeah, I told him, and he's furious, but legally, there's not much he can do." She paused. "I'm not afraid of Tony anymore, not for myself, but..."

"Will would never allow Tony to lay one finger on you or Evie. You know that, right?"

"Yes, and that worries me even more," she said, her voice unsteady. "Tony's a big bully, and he'd like nothing more than to take a swing at Will. If my brother got hurt because of me..."

"Would you feel safer if I left Bear with you? Evie loves him."

Before she could answer, Bear went back to the rear window and growled softly.

Myka followed and glanced outside. "Do you have workmen out there?"

"No, and last night's guests have already checked out, so it can't be one of them. My guess is that Bear's heard what I've been hearing on and off all day, a crunch through the leaves, then nothing."

"It could be Tony. Did you call Will?"

"The first time I did, but he didn't find anyone. I can't keep calling him—our police department is stretched really thin. Usually there's just Will and one other officer on duty."

"Okay. Let's take this one step at a time,"

Myka said, her thoughts racing. "Where's Evie right now?"

"She's with Grandma Medeiros. She promised Evie the doll she's been wanting in exchange for help picking out Christmas presents for her grandnieces, so I couldn't say no."

"Okay, I'm going to phone Joshua." Myka made the call, and, following Joshua's suggestions, she checked to make sure the back doors were locked, then locked the front entrance, as well. "He'll be here shortly. In the meantime, let's have a cup of tea. Have you got any herbal blends—something not loaded with caffeine?"

"Sure."

Myka knew she had to distract Betty, whose hands were shaking. "I'm glad that you're finally letting Daniel and Grandma get to know Evie better."

"Evie wanted that doll so badly, Myka, and there was no way I could afford it, even at cost. I'm hoping for good winter business, and I'm already getting reservations, but the inn is still running in the red."

"Daniel would have found a way to give Evie the doll," Myka said with a smile, then seeing Betty's puzzled look, added, "don't you get it?"

"Get what?"

"Daniel's crazy about you!"

"*Me?* You're nuts. He's always nice, but I've never given him any reason—"

"He didn't need one—the attraction's been there since high school. Seeing you move back into town just brought those feelings to the surface."

Betty shook her head. "You're not talking about Daniel—what you've just described is you and Josh."

"I was Tanner's girl in high school. Joshua was just the cute guy next door."

"And now Tanner's gone," she said in a gentle voice. "My brother and I were close, and there's one thing I know for sure. He would have never wanted you to spend the rest of your life alone."

"I'm not alone."

"I think you can do better than your sheep and the dog."

Myka laughed. "I've got plenty of friends and family watching out for me." Hearing a vehicle pull up and seeing Bear by the front window, tail wagging, she knew it was Joshua. Myka went to let him in.

Several seconds later he joined them in the lobby. "Are you two okay?"

"Yes, but we need your help," Myka said, and explained.

"I'll go check around the outside of the building and see if anyone's hanging around." He brought a flashlight out of his jacket pocket. "Lock the door behind me. I'll be back in a few minutes."

"Joshua, be careful. If it is Tony, he's big and mean. He'll hit you for no reason at all," Betty said in a whisper-thin voice.

Myka felt her stomach clench as she heard the pain laced through her words.

Joshua gave Betty a tight-lipped smile. "It takes a lot to bring me down. I'll be fine."

As he walked out, Myka said, "He's a good person to have on your side. Believe that."

"Tony's incredibly strong, Myka. Don't underestimate him."

"I won't, but I think you're underestimating Joshua."

Betty looked at Myka and smiled. "You may be right."

JOSHUA STUDIED THE TRACKS with his flashlight. They'd been left by a man about his own height, at least judging by his shoe size.

He was a chain smoker, too. A half-dozen cigarette butts lay scattered on the ground. From all indications, he'd stood there for a while, watching the inn through the evergreens. With the lights on inside, he'd had a clear view of the dining room and sunroom. From that position, he could have also kept an eye on the vehicles pulling up front.

Hidden in the long shadows of twilight, Joshua made his way to the entrance. His gut told him that danger was still close by.

Inside the lobby moments later, he told them what he'd found. "You need to get blinds or curtains back there, Betty, so he can't see inside at night."

"I'll find something tomorrow. I don't have guests at the moment, so right now I'm going to lock up, get my daughter and head home. We'll have all the privacy we need there. Mr. Harrington, our neighbor, keeps an eye on us. He played college football at UNM and he's still in good shape. I don't think anyone, including Tony, would take on a guy who's six foot six and close to three hundred pounds."

"Don't leave—not yet," Joshua said, standing to one side of the window and looking out into the street. "Let me call Will. He can escort you home."

"Do you think Tony's out there some-where?" she asked, her voice unsteady.

"I haven't seen anyone, but something feels wrong."

"I'm going to get Evie right now. She's at Grandma Medeiros's house," Betty said, getting her purse.

"If someone's really after you, you're better off waiting for Will," Joshua said. "I'll go get Evie and bring her home."

"I'm not sure.... Evie doesn't know you very well."

"She knows me," Myka said. "I'll go with Joshua and leave Bear with you."

Joshua called Will, then took Myka aside. "You should stay with Betty."

Myka shook her head. "You heard her. We don't want to frighten Evie, so this is the best way."

"If Myka goes with you, I'm okay with this plan," Betty said, then looked directly at Myka. "Just be careful what you say to Evie. She loves her father. I've never given her any reason not to. A child her age doesn't need to deal with the ugly reality."

"Don't worry. I won't mention Tony. She'll have her new doll, too, so she'll probably be distracted."

Several minutes later, Will showed up and Betty let him in. He strode into the room, then pulled Joshua aside.

"What did you see out there?" he asked in a voice only Joshua could hear.

"Just footprints and fresh cigarette butts," Joshua said, telling Will that whoever had been hiding in the trees could see right inside the inn.

"I'll take Betty home and ask Jake Harrington to stay with her," Will said. "Bring Evie as soon as you can. Once we know everyone's safe, I'll look for Tony around town. I'm going to run his name against MVD and see if he owns a vehicle. If not, I'll process the plates on anything I don't recognize."

"All right. Myka and I will get going right now," Josh said.

"No, not yet. Betty and I should leave first. Call me if you notice anyone tailing us."

"Consider it done," Joshua said.

"Check in with me the second you have Evie. Otherwise I'll assume you've run into trouble."

"Got it."

Five minutes later, Joshua walked to his truck with Myka. They waited until Will pulled out, then followed at a distance. "I'm

glad you let Betty keep the dog with her tonight," he said. "Bear will be a great deter-
rent."

Joshua tailed Betty and Will for a half
mile, giving them plenty of room and making sure no one followed them. At long last,
giving Will the all clear with a flash of his
high beams, he turned away and headed to
the Medeiroses' place.

"Tony's a sick creep, so be careful if you
run into him. He roughed up Betty a few
times," Myka said.

"Really? I bet Will never found out. He'd
have gone after him with both fists."

"Betty kept it a secret. She didn't want to
see her brother in jail for murder. I didn't find
out until recently, and now it's over and done
with, I guess."

"Well, Tony was always trouble, even back
in high school, but he never picked a fight he
couldn't win." His gut was telling him that it
was no different now. The dirtbag had something up his sleeve.

"Did you two ever face off?"

"No, he left me alone. He'd seen me take on
a few tough guys and hold my own. I think
he knew if he leaned on me I wouldn't back
down."

Bad scenarios crowded his mind, and he speeded up. The way he saw it, the only leverage Tony had was Evie, and if he tried to take the kid, Daniel wouldn't be able to stop him. Of course Daniel would try, but the best he'd be able to do was slow Tony down. The sooner they got Evie home, the better off everyone would be.

The Medeiroses' residence was across an alley behind the store. As Joshua parked, they both saw that although the market was closed, the Medeiroses' kitchen was brightly lit. A radio tune drifted toward them as they crossed the alley.

They'd only just gone around the corner of the house when Joshua heard a loud crash, followed by another.

"Stay here," he told Myka, and shot forward.

The kitchen door was wide-open, the wood splintered by the latch. On the floor, beside a tipped over chair, Daniel lay on his back, trying to ward off Tony's punches.

Joshua dove straight for Tony, grabbing his head like it was a fumbled football, wrestling him off his friend and knocking the big man into the refrigerator with a crash.

Joshua jumped to his feet, fists up as Tony

lunged at him from a crouch. Joshua raised his knee, catching Tony in the forehead, and both of them bounced backward from the impact.

Joshua hit the kitchen table hard but recaptured his balance quickly.

Tony rose to full height and took a step forward, crouching like a boxer, ready to jab and weave. "You're mine now, you…"

Myka appeared behind Tony and struck him hard on the back of his head with a skillet. Tony sank to his knees, stunned and feebly reaching for his head with both hands.

"Stay down!" Joshua ordered, stepping up.

He glanced at Myka. "I told you to stay outside." Her gaze was still fastened on Tony and she held on to the skillet with both hands, ready to swing it again if necessary.

"I don't do as I'm told," she answered predictably.

As the kitchen door swung open, Grandma entered, leading with the barrel of a shotgun. "We done here?" she asked. Noticing Daniel on his knees, the front of his shirt ripped open, she aimed the shotgun at Tony. "If you move another inch…" she said, her voice shaking.

"Grandma, it's okay," Daniel said.

"I'll watch him now, ma'am," Joshua said, reaching for the shotgun. "Facedown on the floor, Tony, hands away from your body," he snapped. "Try anything, and you'll leave here in two plastic bags."

Tony eased himself to the floor.

"Where's Evie?" Myka asked Grandma.

"She's okay. We're playing 'hide and seek.' This animal came to the door and tried to push his way in, but Daniel held him off while Evie and I got away."

Daniel was on his feet now, tending his bloody nose with a hand towel. Grandma came over to take a look. "You should get yourself checked out at the hospital, Daniel."

"I'm fine. Just cuts and bruises," he muttered.

"You done good, as Grampa Medeiros used to say," Joshua said.

Grandma rolled her eyes. "Get cleaned up, Daniel. I called the police while you were in here destroying my kitchen, but it seems Will was already on his way."

Joshua nodded. "I didn't call when he expected."

"Show me where Evie is, Grandma," Myka said, looking toward the living room. "She's probably scared to death right now."

Grandma shook her head. "I told her we were playing a grown-up game that was like cops and robbers. She wanted to believe it, so..." Grandma shrugged. "It was the best I could do off the cuff."

"Uh, Myka, I think you can leave the frying pan behind," Joshua said.

FIVE MINUTES LATER, Will came into the kitchen, pistol in hand. "Give me the shotgun, Joshua," he ordered, placing his weapon back into the holster.

"Gladly," Joshua said. "It's not loaded," he added, looking over at Daniel, who shrugged.

"Roll over, moron," Will ordered, tapping Tony's foot with his boot. "But stay down."

Tony's eyes fastened on Will's badge. "Hey, Solis, a man has a right to see his daughter," he growled. "I asked to see her, but they wouldn't let me in. Then that one attacked me," he said, pointing to Daniel.

Will gestured to the splintered door and the imprint of a boot on the trim. "Evidence indicates it was the other way around. Breaking and entering, assault and attempted kidnaping are serious offences. Better find a lawyer. You're under arrest."

"You'll never get any of those charges to stick."

"You're on parole with a record for violent behavior. They'll stick," Will said.

Tony twisted away and reached inside his boot. A second later, he brought out a knife.

In a lightning fast move, Joshua stomped down hard on Tony's hand.

Something snapped and Tony howled.

"Looks like I'll be adding assault with a deadly weapon on a police officer to the charges," Will said, kicking the knife away.

"He broke my fingers," Tony said, then looked at Joshua. "You'll pay for this. I'll find you."

"Not where you're going," Will said. "Don't make any travel plans for the next ten years— assuming you survive prison."

Will jerked Tony to his feet, hauled him to the police cruiser in handcuffs and placed him in the backseat. Then he read him his rights.

With the prisoner secure, Will turned to Joshua and gave him a brief nod.

Joshua nodded back, acknowledging the gesture in silence. No words were needed.

CHAPTER SEVENTEEN

THE FOLLOWING DAY, Myka sat in her office, Bear by her feet. Taking a break, she leaned back and rubbed her eyes. The company was doing better than anyone had expected—including her.

Robyn knocked lightly, then came in. "Reps from two regional retailers have accepted our invitation to come take a look at our products and facility. How did you make out?"

Myka smiled slowly. "I went directly to Grabel and Sons."

Robyn's eyes grew big. "They've got stores in a half-dozen major cities!"

"I know, and it took me a while to work up the courage to call them. I did my homework first, found out everything I could about their regional buyer, then took my shot."

"And?"

"Well, at first I got the runaround. I figured I'd eventually reach some upper level secretary and be politely kissed off. Then, a little while ago, I got an email from their buyer. He's coming to take our tour."

"We did it, Myka. We've got some heavy hitters interested!"

"I know. We'll give the reps a tour of Independence, focusing on our recovery—thanks to HMI—then come back here. I see this as an all-day event. They'll be able to watch our wool processing, the spinners at work and our wood carvers' basement toy shop. We'll conclude with a display of all our merchandise."

"This could be a huge break," Robyn said.

"We'll have to get things perfectly organized, and I mean down to the last detail," Myka said.

She reached into her desk drawer and popped an antacid in her mouth.

Robyn shook her head. "Myka, you've been putting in longer hours than anyone else. If you keep pushing yourself, you're going to be a wreck by the end of the year. You really need some downtime, girl."

Robyn turned her head at the sound of a closing door just down the hall. "Joshua, I need your help here," she called out.

Joshua came up to Myka's open office door. "What's going on?" he asked.

"Myka needs to get away for a few hours to unwind. Any suggestions on how to pry her out from behind that desk?" Robyn asked.

"I have one," Joshua responded immediately. "Myka, how about taking off with me today? I'm making a list of what's needed to convert the Brooks Mansion into a public museum. The rear living quarters will also be preserved as a historical site. Would you like to come with me and walk through the place?"

"I'd love it!" Myka said.

"I went by the bank yesterday and the renovation you did there turned out great," Robyn said. "That enormous wagon wheel at the front and the open wooden porch and sidewalk look wonderful. There's even a hitching rail," she added, looking at Myka.

He smiled. "The building's facade needed some flair. Now it's a fusion of old frontier and modern Southwest. I like the way it came together."

"Can't wait to see it," Myka said. "Let's go. This'll give Bear a chance to get some fresh air."

When they reached Main Street, Myka noted that most of the storefronts had been fixed up, even the buildings that were still

unoccupied. The center of town looked alive
again. She saw doorways and window trim
painted a vibrant shade of Southwest blue that
was said to drive evil away.

"What are those kids doing?" Myka asked,
seeing three high schoolers in front of the
bank. One student was filming and another
read from cue cards that were held up by a
third teen.

Joshua had no answer, so they waited until
the one with the script yelled cut before going
to ask.

"It's our telecommunications project," the
girl explained. "We're filming the town's
comeback. Aren't you two the founders of
HMI, the company that took over the old
plant building? We'd love to film there, too.
Would that be okay?"

"Call the office or stop by and ask for
Robyn Jenner. Whatever she says goes."
Myka handed the girl one of their business
cards.

Deciding to enter the Brooks Mansion
through the older Territorial-style residence
on Second Avenue, they circled the block.
Soon they entered the gated compound and
stepped onto the full-length veranda facing
Second Street.

"I like this older section of the mansion best," Joshua said. "It'll need to be repainted, have some cracks fixed, and the electrical systems will need to be updated, but all that can be done easily and without changing its character."

"I was only inside this building once, and that was way back when, but I remember it as if it were yesterday. The doorways are arched, and there are beautiful wooden columns throughout. There's also a special *banco*— a window seat—that faces the courtyard. It was such a cozy spot!"

"All that's still there. As a kid, I'd walk by here often and daydream about all the cool things I'd do to the place if it were mine."

"Like what?"

"Keep in mind that I was a kid and I'd never been inside at all," he said and grinned. "My plans were to take full advantage of the thick walls and turn it into one super fortress—with a TV and game room," he added, laughing. "Come on. Let's go in and I'll show you around."

Bear followed them in, content to keep pace as they toured the house.

Joshua pointed out his favorite areas, like the massive central fireplace in the *sala,* decorated with inlaid Spanish tile and stenciled floral designs near the mantel.

He called her attention to the hand-carved posts and trim around the windows. "The floors here are either wood plank or brick throughout and they're in remarkably good shape. The tile roof has held up well, too, so there's been very little water damage."

"That's because we've had practically no rainfall—as in drought conditions," she said with a smile.

"Dad wrote to me about that," he answered, smiling back.

She stopped by a large square indentation in the thick adobe wall. "I wonder what was here? It looks like a *nicho,* but this could hold an entire collection of statues, not just one."

"The hand-painted decorations around the sides don't fit with a *nicho* either. They're mostly Indian fetishes, like what you'd see in Anasazi sites."

She studied them carefully. "What an odd thing this is. Maybe he had a TV here, but with the thick walls reception couldn't have been great. He certainly didn't have cable or one of those dishes."

"There's another one of these strange *nichos* in a back room. The one there was framed with wood and the interior has Indian corn motifs. I have a feeling these were originally meant to hold something specific—maybe a small safe—then Brooks changed his mind."

"He certainly took the word *eccentric* to new levels," Myka said.

"That's why I think Dad was right, and the will's hidden here. Silas would have wanted to keep a close eye on it," he said. "I've looked around and I haven't found anything, but frankly I've been focused on the architecture."

"Perfectly understandable."

Joshua smiled. "There are so many odd structural details in this house. It's almost as if he'd been deliberately trying to misdirect anyone searching for the real hiding place."

"That might explain those massive *nichos,* or come to think of it, maybe those were just his version of bookshelves."

"It would certainly fit Brooks's odd way of thinking," he said. "Let's keep looking around. Maybe something that seems out of place will catch your eye. Hiding places could be almost anywhere, and four eyes are better than two. If we don't find anything here, we can go check out the building on the other side of the passageway."

Bear remained by Myka's side as they went from room to room. The house was eclectic and beautiful in a classic New Mexico style, with Mr. Vega's painting of the Cross of the Martyrs the focal point of a small private chapel. The furniture that remained was comprised of heavy, hand-painted pieces that looked to be in nearly perfect shape.

"This *trastero* is gorgeous," she said, standing by an armoire. "Look at the beautiful colors around each painted-angel panel on the doors."

"Some of the finest pieces of colonial furniture were crafted with religious themes," he said.

The rear portion of the house held four bedrooms, the last three having been added on, one after the other, over the years. The most interesting part was that there were no hallways. The rooms' only access points were through the passage doors of the previous bedroom.

"I've been told that this part of the house was his favorite because it's impossible to gain access to it without going through the carved wooden door leading to the first bedroom. The dead bolts and metal locks would have taken several gun blasts to dislodge. In the meantime, Brooks could have retreated to the second bedroom, giving the intruder yet another door to break down."

"It's sad that he spent so much of his life living in fear," Myka said as they turned back and entered Silas's home office, just off the *sala*.

Myka turned in a circle, admiring the decor. "Imagine having this as your office! Those big dark *trasteros* and the heavy wood plank flooring make it all look so regal." She ran her hand over one of the intricately carved wooden posts that supported the ceiling.

"It's a blend of New Mexican style architecture and early European. Again, nothing really fits."

"Yeah, it does," Myka said. "The house is a bit like a crazy quilt that comes together despite itself. At least there's nothing really modern in here that would jar you—well, except for the wiring and plumbing, I suppose."

"Despite its history and eclectic design, this place really gets under my skin. I love it," Joshua said.

Myka traced the grooved, carved section

on one of the posts with her fingertips. "I wonder how old this is. Do you know?"

He ran his hand over the matching post on his side of the room. "I'm not sure, but judging from what I learned about wood carving from my dad, this level of craftsmanship could take weeks. All of this was done with hand tools—it's old-school artistry."

He was brushing a dusty cobweb from the curves when he suddenly jerked his hand back.

"You okay?"

"The center gave," he said, shaking the stubborn web from his fingertips.

She tapped the post beside her. "This one's solid wood—no give at all."

He knocked right above the spot where he'd felt something. It sounded solid there, too, but as he moved downward and continued tapping, the sound changed subtly.

Joshua got down on one knee for a closer look. "There's a cut in one of the grooves." He brought out his pocket knife and tried to force the section open, but nothing happened.

"Press in instead," she said.

He did as she suggested, and an eight-inch curved section of wood fell onto his hand.

"It's spring-loaded and shaped like an *E,* or maybe the number 3," he said.

"It's hollowed out. Anything inside?" she asked, her heart suddenly beating overtime.

"Yeah," he said and reached in. "There's a carved stone fetish and old folded papers." He brought out the fetish first and studied it. "It's Lynx. My dad told me once that he's the guardian of secrets. Smart of old Silas, putting a hiding place below eye level."

Next, Joshua pulled out the paperwork, which had been scrunched into a groove. "These are so dry and fragile I'm afraid to handle them," he said, gently placing them on the nearest table.

The papers had been folded then rolled up tightly. After a few minutes on the table, they began to unfurl slightly on their own. He pulled his leather gloves from his pocket, pressed one end lightly and tried to read a few lines.

Myka came up behind him. "I recognize the town seal. The document's been notarized. Maybe it's the will," she said, trying to stay calm but not quite succeeding.

He peered inside the roll, angling for a better look. "I think the top ones are deeds to various properties." Very gingerly, he moved the sheets aside, using only one finger. "I can't see it all, but I think the bottom one's a will—maybe *the* will. It's dated five years ago."

"We've got it!"

Myka jumped into his arms and he twirled her around while Bear barked.

"We did it—you and me!" she said.

"We're one heckuva team," he said. "Maybe fate's telling us something." Tilting her chin upward, he took her mouth slowly and thoroughly.

His kiss tantalized her, enveloping her in a warmth that left her tingling. She didn't want it to stop, but she pulled back and said, "We better go." Then she stepped out of his embrace.

Every day that passed took him closer to a destiny that didn't include her. The knowledge cut deeply. Trying not to let him see what was on her mind, she did her best to focus on the papers. "We have to find someone who can help us figure out how to flatten and read these documents without damaging them."

He brushed his knuckles over her cheek. "We don't have to rush off, Myka. Stay here with me a little longer." His voice was deep, his words seductive, and the fire in his eyes inescapable.

"No," she whispered, taking another step back. The more tempting the warmth of the fire, the easier it was to get burned. "You're going to be leaving too soon as it is. Let's not do anything we'll regret."

"Like walking away?" he pressed, holding her gaze. "I love you, Myka, haven't you figured that out by now?"

"Yes, and that's part of the problem, isn't it?" She swallowed hard. If things had only been different, she would have stepped back into his arms and told him how she felt, too, but she couldn't change what was.

Myka turned away quickly and headed to the door. When it came time for him to leave, as she'd always known he would, her heart would break into a thousand pieces. The closer they were, the worse it would be.

Her instinct for self-preservation urged her to go, but if she was doing the right thing, why did it hurt so much?

Afraid she'd change her mind and move into his arms again, she hurried outside, back to the real world and away from what could never be.

CHAPTER EIGHTEEN

BY THE END of the week, the mayor and the town attorney established the authenticity of the documents and presented a right-of-way offer to the railroad. A deal was reached quickly and it was only a matter of time before rail service would be restored.

The timing was perfect. The buyers from the major retailers would be touring the town and HMI.

Myka was in her office taking care of last-minute details when Joshua came in. He was wearing a bolo tie, leather jacket and polished Dan Post Western boots.

"Wow, you're going to be a hit with the buyers," Robyn said, following him into Myka's office.

"Talk about false praise. You were behind me when you said that," Josh said.

"Exactly," Robyn answered, grinning as she gave him a wink.

Myka burst out laughing. "Just what I needed. Sexual harassment in *my* office."

"Feel free to harass, either of you," Joshua said with a grin. "I'm easy."

Myka laughed. "Okay, guys. Are we ready?"

"As we'll ever be," Robyn said. "The Blue Spruce will be putting up the clients who choose to stay overnight, and HMI will cover their expenses. I personally helped Betty hang the new tapestries and place the rugs so they catch the light. Liza will be their tour guide here at the plant. She'll take them through the wool processing sections, the woodworking areas and the special craft rooms. Sophie has also arranged for her nieces to model some of the clothing made with our wool."

Myka gave Joshua and Robyn a shaky smile. "I don't know about you guys, but I'm scared to death. So much is riding on today! We can make it without those big retailers— we have so far—but this could mean reaching a whole new world of potential customers— those who shop at brick-and-mortar stores."

"Just relax and show them what Handmade in Independence is all about," Joshua said.

"I was thinking…IVA's motto used to be Luxury—American style. Ours could be

Handcrafted with American Know-How. What do you think?"

"Hey, I like that!" Robyn said.

"See?" Joshua said. "The right ideas come when you need them, so don't panic. Just be yourselves."

"Aren't they scheduled to arrive soon?" Robyn asked.

"Within a half hour. Once they're here, we'll start the tour with Main Street."

"Walking around is a good idea. It's nice outside today," Joshua said.

"No, it's not just a stroll. I wanted a more captive audience, so I've arranged for us to use Mr. Granger's restored limo. He'll be driving. We'll give them a tour of the town and the vicinity, too, maybe even show them *Churro* sheep firsthand."

Joshua grinned. "Wait—Mr. Granger? He still has the stretch limo he restored when we were in high school?"

Myka laughed. "Yeah, and it looks brand-new. He loves that car. I figured it might impress, at least a bit."

As they walked out onto the front steps, Myka's phone rang. The second she heard Mr. Granger's voice, she knew it was bad news.

"Myka, I can't get Cleopatra to start," he

said, referring to his enormous 1966 Cadillac Fleetwood limousine. "The problem's somewhere in the fuel system, probably the carburetor. She turns over but just won't start."

"How long before you can get her to work?" Myka asked, her heart beating overtime.

"I'm not sure. Maybe an hour, or maybe not till tomorrow if I have to take the thing apart."

"Mr. Granger, you've *got* to get that car running!" As she spoke, she saw Robyn's eyes widening. Joshua's face remained impassive.

"So much for impressing them," Myka said after hanging up. "And look, our guests are early!" She gestured to the cars pulling up at the curb.

Leading the group was Jane Jonas of Grabel and Sons. To her right was Lourdes Martel with Vintage Lane, one of the largest online stores for specialty goods. Coming up behind her was Emily Reichert of Traditional Southwest, a high-end specialty outlet headquartered in Scottsdale.

"I've got an idea," Joshua said. "Take them over to the Blue Spruce for breakfast or coffee and pastry. Whatever. Keep them busy and entertained. I'll handle the rest."

"What are you going to do?" Myka asked.

"Trust me."

Before she could answer, he jogged across the parking lot to his truck.

"Smile on, Robyn. It's showtime," Myka whispered.

Even without advance notice, Betty had set out a beautiful spread on the banquet table, with help from Sophie's pastry shop.

After being treated to everything from Southwestern omelets with spicy green chile to freshly baked fry bread with lots of honey, the buyers were in a remarkably good mood. Myka encouraged them to take their time over Mabel's special coffee, all the while stealing glances at the clock and hoping for a miracle.

Forty minutes later, Joshua walked in wearing a cowboy hat, a tan shearling leather jacket with rollback cuffs, jeans and boots.

"Ladies, your transportation has arrived," he announced.

With a wave of his hand, he opened the door and invited them outside. Waiting at the curb was a horse-drawn hitch wagon replete with hay bale seating in the back and Western print fleece blankets to ward off any chill. The two horses were sturdy gray Percherons, and the woman holding the reins was Katie McCoy, owner of the feed store.

One of the buyers smiled broadly. "How terrific! I was raised in a small town, and we used to have hay rides every fall. And those horses—they sure beat the old John Deere tractor that used to pull our wagon."

Seeing the happy faces, Myka wanted to give Joshua a big hug, but there'd be time for that later.

"We'd like you to look at Independence through our eyes. This is a town with a strong Western tradition. We took a hit when our largest employer closed down, and we could have given up, but that's not who we are. Now we're coming back, stronger than ever," Myka said.

As they toured the town, Myka could feel the buyers opening their hearts to the strength of Independence's dream. They stopped by her parents' house, and Myka showed them the *Churro* sheep that had started them all on the road to becoming HMI. Naturally, the flock came right up to the fence to be petted.

By the time they returned to the plant, the second stage was already underway. Myka and Robyn led the buyers upstairs, taking the freight elevator.

"This is your *freight* elevator?" Jane Jonas asked.

"I wanted you to see it because it captures the spirit of who we are. Our company is all about the freedom to dream, and our products represent Rio Grande traditions and good old American know-how," she said, the heartfelt speech coming naturally.

Next, they entered the woodworking shop and watched the toys being made. As the different steps in the process were demonstrated, Myka heard their guests' low, appreciative comments. Afterward, they continued on to the wool processing area. Each step was explained and demonstrated to the delight of their visitors. Finally, the finished projects were displayed in a fashion show.

Myka sighed. Today was about standing out and showing the buyers that HMI's passion was a gift meant to be shared. As she watched their faces, she knew they'd succeeded.

"See? I told you it would work out," Joshua said quietly, coming up behind her.

"You saved the day with the wagon. I couldn't have pulled it off without you, Joshua," she whispered back.

He took her hand and gave it a squeeze. "You could have, but it's nice to be needed."

"This community needs you," she said, "and so do I."

"I know," he said, then grinned.

ROBYN HAD FILMED most of the tour, and each of the buyers was given a DVD to take back to her corporate office. By the time they'd all left, Myka was beyond exhausted.

"We made it through the tour without more mishaps. That's a win!" Myka said. "Everyone was incredible today."

"Just today?" Joshua responded.

She laughed. "Okay, you're all awesome every day."

"We knew that," Robyn joked. "Now I'm off to soak my feet, and after that, I've got a dinner date with J.R."

"Have fun!" Myka said as Robyn left, then she checked her watch. "I need to go home and take care of Bear. If you don't have plans tonight, why don't you come over for dinner?"

"You've had a long day—you sure you want to cook?" he asked. "I could pick up something at Shorty's Burgers."

"No, tonight I want something special, not

just an ordinary dinner. I wanted to fix Dad's special pancakes."

"The ones with the chocolate chips?"

"Yeah! You remember?"

"Sure I do. We rode in the buckboard to Miller's Pond and had a pancake breakfast there."

"Miller's Pond is just a muddy swamp these days, but when I saw you pull up in that horse cart, it reminded me of our 4-H club outing. I've been craving those pancakes all day."

"You're on."

AFTER DINNER, they sat outside on Myka's back porch. The weather was in the fifties, and as a breeze blew past them, she shivered.

Joshua put his arm around her shoulders and drew her against him.

She didn't resist. It felt wonderful to lean into him, to enjoy that steadfast warmth and feel his strong body there, sheltering hers.

"You're right where you belong," he murmured, tightening his hold slightly.

She sighed happily. "At this very moment, everything's just perfect." This was romance—two souls connecting, the warmth, the gentleness, the utter thrill that came from...rightness. "I'm glad you came back home, Joshua."

"I think it was meant to be," he said.

"When I first started down this road, hoping to help Independence get back on its feet, I had no idea how difficult things could get. Reaching a goal, something that calls to you but doesn't come with directions, takes everything you've got—including a friend who'll stand by you every step of the way." She looked up at him and smiled. "I never could have gone this far without you."

"You may not realize it, but you helped me, too. When I came home, life had kicked me in the gut, and I was still reeling from the blow. Helping you forced me to focus on something positive. I owe you a thanks," he said, then kissed her gently.

"Feel free to thank me as often as you'd like." Myka smiled.

He eased his hold and held her gaze. "I'd love to do just that, but there's something I need to tell you, and I've been putting it off too long."

She held her breath. Something told her that this perfect day was about to come to an abrupt end.

"I got an interview request from an established and prestigious architectural firm in Santa Fe. They've received a special grant to restore an old section of the city filled with historical buildings. I don't know the details, but it sounds like a terrific opportunity and I could really make a name for myself there. Mind you, I'll be competing with some of the area's top architects," he said.

"You'll knock 'em dead," she said, trying to muster up some genuine enthusiasm. He'd helped her, and she had to do the same for him by not standing in his way.

"It's not an easy decision for me, Myka. What we have—"

"You can't let anyone, or anything, stand in the way of your dreams, Joshua," she said softly. "This is exactly what you've wanted and you'll never forgive yourself if you don't see it through. What-ifs can haunt you for the rest of your life."

"I'm not so sure. My dad gave up his dream and never looked back. From everything I've learned about him, I think he died a happy man."

"Yes, but your father traded one dream for an even greater one."

He nodded thoughtfully. "Maybe so. Of

course this may all be moot. I may not get
the job."

"You owe it to yourself to give it your best
shot. This is exactly the kind of work you
love. I can see it in your eyes and hear it in
your voice," she said, and saw him nod. "Go
for it. Santa Fe isn't that far."

Despite her attempt to be positive, she
knew that if he took the job, life would pull
them apart a little at a time and soon there
would be nothing more to hold on to. Even if
he gave up on his dream and stayed, he might
regret missing this opportunity. That in itself
could pull them apart. Either way, the choice
had to be his.

"You have to follow your heart." She silently prayed it would lead him back home
for good.

ALTHOUGH MYKA LEFT for work early the
next morning, Joshua's truck was already
gone when she pulled out of her driveway.
Not wanting to dwell on things, she drove to
HMI right away.

Myka walked quickly down the hall toward
her office, the dog at her side. "Why does everything have to be so complicated, Bear?"

He gave her a panting grin.

"Yeah, maybe that's it. We take life too seriously." She patted his massive head. "At least you won't be leaving anytime soon."

As Myka stepped into her office, she saw Robyn already there, waiting. "What's up? You're sure here early," Myka said.

"I've been trying to reach you for the past half hour, but all I got was your voice mail," Robyn said. "I was about to leave you a note." Now that their big day had passed, Robyn was back to wearing jeans, a wool sweater and boots.

Myka reached for her cell phone. "Oops. I forgot to turn it on." Once she had service, she searched for any messages from Joshua. There were none.

"I got here at seven and when I checked my email, I saw that one of the buyers had already placed an order." She showed Myka a printout of the message. "Grabel and Sons, no less."

Myka looked at the numbers and let out a whoop. "We did it!"

"Yes, but this is a huge order. We'll have to step up production. What we have in inventory won't cover this. The only good thing is that they asked for three separate delivery dates."

"Our people will come through. We'll make it."

As they spoke, Myka's computer and Robyn's cell phone dinged at the same time, signifying incoming email.

"Another order," Myka said, sitting at her desk. "Smaller than Grabel's, but that's good. They're testing the waters. If sales reach their projections, the next order will be bigger."

"Myka, it's only eight o'clock," Robyn said. "Do you realize what this means? They must have made up their minds and set the purchase orders before they even got home."

"We nailed it!" Myka gave Robyn a high five. "Let's call a special meeting and get everyone together. Filling these two orders will require some overtime."

"It'll be just like old times, when IVA was here. Remember when we had rush orders come in?"

"No, Robyn, it will never be like that. What we have to offer the world isn't mass production. We'll craft each piece with care and attention to detail because we love what we do. If we ever lose sight of that, we'll lose a lot more than just some orders. Once demand levels out, we'll resume a less hectic schedule."

"Good point," Robyn said after a beat. "That's what makes you a good leader, Myka."

"What does?"

"Your ability to stay on target. And Joshua's your other half. Do you realize that? You dream it, but he's the practical one who takes care of the nuts and bolts and finds a way to help you make it real. Like with the wool, remember? We almost ran out. Business was coming to a standstill, but he found a supplier for us. You two blend together like…peanut butter and jelly."

"Joshua's got his own dreams to make real," she said, then gave Robyn the latest news.

"I don't get it," Robyn said after a moment. "I thought he was happy renovating the old buildings around town. With these new orders, we could easily offer him a full-time job helping run HMI."

Myka shook her head. "It's not that easy. Joshua grew up knowing a lot of people looked down on him and his father, so he always had something to prove. That still drives him. Owning the biggest house on the block—not just renovating someone else's—is his idea of coming out on top. It's his way of proving to himself that he's a man worthy of respect—one who earned his success through hard work and determination, that he's achieved the American Dream." Realizing her eyes were welling with tears, she turned away.

"Myka, are you okay?"

"Oh, sure." Her words didn't hold conviction and Robyn realized it almost instantly.

"You're in love with him!"

"Yeah, and that means not standing in his way. He has a right to pursue the career he loves," Myka said. "You should have seen him at the Brooks Mansion. It's the kind of place he's always dreamed of owning. Renovating a place like that and making it his own—that's his definition of success."

"Then why don't you ask the mayor if he'll sell it to Josh at a reasonable price? Maybe Josh could agree to make the Main Street building available to the town, and that way everyone would come out ahead. Josh is being paid a pittance for the work he's done in Independence," Robyn said. "Think about it, Myka. That could be the incentive Josh needs to stick around."

She shook her head. "I'd like him to stay because he sees Independence as his home.

Otherwise, he'll never really be happy here," she said.

Before Robyn could respond, Myka's phone rang. She answered it and listened to the caller before saying, "We'd be thrilled to become your supplier."

Myka smiled as she looked back at Robyn and held up three fingers. The third buyer had come through.

AFTER A SUCCESSFUL company meeting, Myka went home for lunch. Truth was, she was curious to see if Josh had returned, but he wasn't home when she pulled up.

After eating a sandwich, she was ready to go back to work. Myka stepped out onto the porch with Bear just as Joshua drove down the street.

As he parked at the curb and climbed out, she hurried across the lawn to meet him.

"I'm glad you're back," she said, and told him about the new orders. "You never did tell us what salary you'd find acceptable, but with all this new business, we can offer you a full-time consulting job. Quote me a number you think is fair, now that you're in demand, and make it competitive with what the city pays you."

He gave her a reasonable figure.

"Done," she said and shook his hand.

"That's only if I stay, okay? Otherwise, we'll keep things as they stand."

"Fair enough," she said. "So how did the interview go?"

Although she'd tried to sound casual, she scarcely breathed as she waited for his reply.

"I think it'll be a great job, but I'm not sure it's for me," he said, looking at his feet.

"Really?" she asked. Realizing how hopeful she'd sounded, she cleared her throat and tried again. "What was wrong with it?"

Myka checked her mailbox and pulled out the envelopes inside, trying to avoid looking at him. Her feelings showed too easily on her face. She would have starved as a professional poker player.

"It turns out that they're doing more renovation than restoration. At least three-quarters of the work will be converting a large number of the houses into office buildings. They'll lose the essence of what they once were. I don't find that as satisfying as restoring a place like the Brooks Mansion. That kind of work requires a special hand." He paused. "I could turn the building facing Main into an office without any major alterations."

"Take that to the mayor. The building is

just sitting there. It's a liability to the town because they still have to pay taxes on it. Talk to him and see what happens. If anyone could do the job, it would be you."

He captured her eyes and held them. "You know, you have a very special gift. You make others want to believe." He reached into his jacket pocket. "Which reminds me—I bought you a present. When I was in Santa Fe I saw a pen-paperweight combination that made me think of you."

She opened the box carefully. The paperweight bottom was fashioned out of hand-blown glass. In its center was a pen and below it, the inscription Dreams and Courage Are Inseparable Companions. Without Both, Neither Is Possible.

"I love it," she said and sighed softly as he leaned over and kissed her. For one wonderful moment, she felt protected and valued… even loved. It was so easy to lose herself in his warmth, to forget everything except him.

A heartbeat later the loud ringing of Myka's home phone shattered the moment. Joshua's cell phone also started to beep. It was a bad sign and they both knew it. After exchanging a quick look, Joshua reached into his pocket and Myka ran inside, Bear at her heels.

Myka grabbed the living-room phone, and as she answered it, Robyn's high-pitched voice confirmed her worst fears.

"Myka, get back to the office as soon as you can. There's a fire. When I powered up the new computer and laser printer, lights flickered and sparks shot out of the outlet. Smoke started curling up, and that terrible electrical smell was everywhere. I ran to the breakers and shut the power off but it was too late."

"I'll be there in five," Myka said, her mouth dry, her heart pounding.

Joshua rushed in. "That was Will. He saw smoke pouring out of HMI's windows so he called the fire department. They've arrived but haven't been able to account for everyone yet."

For a moment, she couldn't move or even breathe. Scenes from the day of Tanner's accident replayed in her head.

"Let's go!" Joshua said, grabbing her hand and pulling her toward the door.

Reality broke through as she realized the confused dog was blocking the way. "Stay, Bear!" she ordered, slipping around him. Myka locked the front door and raced out toward Joshua's truck.

SMOKE WAS ESCAPING from two downstairs windows when they arrived. One belonged to Robyn's office, the other the inventory stockroom.

Although Myka hadn't been at the plant the day Tanner died, she'd pictured the scene over and over again. As she stared at the smoke, the flashing lights of the fire department and the cluster of people watching from the street, she began to tremble.

Joshua took her hand as they walked toward the crowd. Holding on to him made it easier for her to fight the panic swelling inside her. She tried to swallow, but her mouth was parched.

Will saw them, and as he approached, Myka tried to read his expression.

"Is everyone…" She found herself unable to complete the sentence.

"They're all out, and nobody's hurt," Will said instantly as if he'd read her mind. "The windows have been opened to vent the smoke, and an exhaust fan will be set up once it's verified that the fire is completely extinguished. It's a brick-and-steel building, so my guess is that we're okay now. We got lucky."

"Except for our work!" She stared at the gray smoke flowing from the windows. "It looks like most of that smoke is coming from our main storage area—all our supplies and outgoing merchandise are in there!"

Joshua placed his arm around her. "One thing at a time."

Robyn, her face smudged with smoke and wearing a fireman's coat over her wet clothing, came rushing up. "Myka, I'm so sorry! I'm not sure why the electrical sockets in my office started to spark. Then the sprinklers came on, spraying water everywhere. I ran out of the office, and as I passed the storeroom, I saw flames shooting out from a wall socket. It looked a lot worse than in my office. I used the fire extinguisher, but the smoke got too thick and I had to leave."

"It's okay. You did what you could," Myka said, her voice shaky.

"The storeroom's a complete disaster. Boxes filled with merchandise are completely soaked. And the wool…" Her voice broke. "The bulk of it was inside vacuum-sealed bags, but a fireman said a lot of those boxes are covered in water and soot. I'm sure some of them must have picked up that horrible smell." She brushed away a tear with the back of her hand, leaving a sooty trail in its wake. "It's all my fault."

"Robyn, it was an accident," Myka said

firmly. "The important thing is that everyone made it out okay."

"At least nothing reached the toy room or the woodworking shop. Their sprinklers never came on."

"That's good, but we'll have to get those sprinklers tested ASAP," Myka said, hoping she could go inside soon. Facts were easier to deal with than the fear that came from not knowing the extent of the disaster awaiting them.

Sophie and Betty showed up with blankets. They set up a table outside the building and got busy serving hot coffee and homemade doughnuts to the firemen and those who'd remained.

The determination and resourcefulness of the people didn't surprise her. This was what Independence was all about. Yet seeing them try to bolster each other's courage made her heart feel leaden. She'd talked the workers and townspeople into opening HMI, they'd all worked so hard—and now this.

"We'll be allowed back inside soon, then we'll see what we can repackage and save," Liza said, coming up to Myka. "Once we get the water mopped up, we'll know how much—if any—of our electrical system can be turned on. If we have to, we'll use the emergency lighting."

Nearly two hours later, Myka entered the building, Joshua and Will by her side. Fire department volunteers, using portable lights, were busy vacuuming water from the floors.

"Myka, are you sure you're up to this?" Will asked, leading the way through the open doors of the small foyer.

"I need to know exactly what we're facing, then I'll figure out a way to fix this. Everyone's counting on me, and I can't let them down." Her voice shook, but she refused to fall apart.

Joshua gave her an encouraging smile. "Let's see what we're dealing with, then we'll know what the options are."

"I need to confirm the origin of the fire," Will said.

"Then we're headed to the same place." As Myka walked, the soles of her boots splashed through water deep enough to float a pencil, despite the enormous wet-dry vac roaring nearby. The only lighting came from battery-powered emergency lamps mounted high on the walls, but they were enough to illuminate a scene that almost made her ill. Water continued to drip off the metal shelves, which held labeled cardboard boxes ready for shipping. These were completely soaked and blackened, especially the ones on the top that had received the brunt of the spray. The smell of burnt wool was everywhere.

This was even worse than she'd imagined. Barring a miracle, most of the merchandise in this room would have to be discarded.

"It's okay. We'll see this through," Joshua said, staying right by her side.

She fought to stay focused. "I'll have to contact the buyers as soon as possible. I'll ask for an extension...maybe offer them a discount for their patience," she said, choking back a sob and trying to force herself to think clearly. She had a job to do.

"You're not in this alone. Here come the others," Joshua whispered. "Buck up. Together, we'll find a way to get through this."

She took an unsteady breath and swallowed hard. She wouldn't fall apart now... that was for later, when she was alone and no one could see her cry.

CHAPTER NINETEEN

MYKA STOOD IN FRONT of the women who'd stayed late to help clean up. As she looked into their moist, dirty faces, she was surprised to see courage mirrored there along with exhaustion.

"Power is back on except for the faulty circuit, so we'll have light and heat. That's one win," Myka said.

"Will we survive this?" someone asked in a tired voice.

"I think so, but we're going to have to dig in and work harder than ever. Although some of our merchandise has been damaged beyond repair, not everything's a loss. We'll need to sweet-talk the dry cleaners in town so they'll give us a reduced price, but whatever can be cleaned and repackaged will be salvaged and sold at a discount. That's our starting point."

"My cousin owns the cleaners," a voice

piped in from the back. "She'll help—I'm sure of it."

"We'll have to sort through everything and salvage as much as possible," Myka said. "We were due to receive a new shipment of wool first thing tomorrow, but we'll need to keep that well away from this mess and process it as soon as possible. While our spinners handle that, the rest of us will focus on cleanup."

"I have an idea," Fran said. "Students from my granddaughter's high school class have been trying to get permission to film inside HMI. Robyn, you haven't said no, but you haven't returned their call yet."

"I got sidetracked," Robyn replied.

"So here's what I was thinking," Fran continued. "Let's give the kids the access they need to film and in return, we'll ask that they help with the cleanup."

"Great idea! Robyn, get on that as soon as possible," Myka said. "If any of you are willing to give up some sleep tonight, I can sure use your help here."

"We'll stay as long as we're needed. This is our company, too," Liza said, and everyone nodded.

"Good. Let's get busy," Myka said.

THEY WORKED UNTIL four in the morning, sorting the items that could be restored and resold from the merchandise that was ruined. The only construction company in town had donated big heaters and fans to help dry out the storeroom and other places that had been thoroughly soaked.

The volunteer fire department had been called away a few hours after putting out the fire, but they'd loaned HMI one of their big wet-dry vacs to help with the cleanup. By then, things were pretty dry, except for the merchandise and the tops of the shelves, which would have to be wiped down by hand.

Joshua made a point of checking the walls, and fortunately, water hadn't infiltrated them. They were made of brick and stone and were protected at floor level by impermeable tile baseboards. There was little risk of mold, though that would have to be monitored. The smoke damage wasn't as bad as they'd first feared, since the spray mist had literally washed most of that out of the air.

After less than three hours of sleep, Joshua returned to work and joined others just arriving. It was seven in the morning. He could see the strain on Myka's face, but she was a woman to be reckoned with. Though exhausted, she continued to push herself.

"Time to relax, Myka. We're insured," he said. "It turns out the fire was caused by faulty switches on that new circuit. It was a manufacturing defect, and the supplier is already putting out a recall. We'll be compensated, eventually."

"I need some more coffee," she said, looking at her empty HMI mug.

Robyn, who'd been worried about Myka, came over. "I'll continue checking the contents of the shipping and storage boxes. Take a break."

"There are plenty of people here now," Joshua said, looking out into the hall. Some were the sons and daughters of the craftspeople who made up HMI, others were townspeople who just wanted to help. "Let's go get that coffee."

Joshua and Myka walked upstairs to her office. Everything there looked amazingly normal. No damage had touched the second floor except for the lingering scent of smoke. All the electronics had been plugged into surge protectors.

"We can still meet the majority of our small orders by pulling items we'd planned to sell online, but I'll need to negotiate new shipping deadlines and offer our major customers special discounts in return for any delays." She sat down at her desk and stared at the phone.

"What's worrying you?" Joshua asked, switching on the coffeemaker.

"What if our three new vendors cancel, or worse, decide not to reorder? Our company's reputation will take a huge hit," she said. In a barely audible voice, she added, "When you have no track record to speak of, first impressions are everything. If we drop the ball now, how can we ever have that future you keep talking about?"

She was staring down at her hands. One was clenched into a tight fist, and the other held her pen in a death grip.

Joshua understood what she was going through. She was fighting for a dream she could see slipping through her fingers. Losing his company had knocked Joshua to his knees, and he'd move heaven and earth to spare her that heartbreak and help her keep going.

"Show them they'll come out ahead. Make them see that second best isn't good enough for HMI, so the delay is there to ensure quality. The discount proves you put customers ahead of profits. You'll be surprised how far straight talk will take you."

Myka took a slow, deep breath, then made that first call.

Joshua sat down and tried to look busy with his smartphone, curious but not wanting to make her self-conscious. She was pushing her fears back and doing what had to be done. That was Myka in a nutshell, and he was crazy about her.

When she looked up, apparently on hold, she reached out for him. He smiled and gave her hand a light squeeze.

Ten minutes later she hung up and jumped out of her chair and into his arms. "We did it! Grabel and Sons accepted the discount and even increased the follow-up order they initially gave us! Apparently, upper management had already decided we're somebody they want to deal with on a regular basis. We can still provide them with products for this holiday season, which was their biggest concern."

He twirled her around, stopped, and taking advantage of the moment, kissed her. The softness of her lips and the slight coffee taste on her tongue drove him crazy. His blood racing, he tightened his hold. She was as strong as the mountains, yet in his arms she was both vulnerable and soft. He was crazy about her, and maybe he always had been.

Robyn stepped into the office, stopped short and smiled. "Finally, something good. Way to go, guys!"

He eased his hold on Myka immediately and stepped back. "Lousy timing, Robyn," he grumbled.

She laughed. "I've got some good news, so maybe that'll make it better. The high school kids are here. They've split up, and half of them are helping with the cleanup and restoration while the others film our 'rebirth.' They'll be here for about a week, so heads-up. Cameras will be everywhere, so don't get caught off guard."

"Thanks for the warning," Myka said with a grin. "That video is going to mean lots of free publicity for HMI and you can't beat that."

"The counselors at the high school have asked us to consider offering some business internships come spring, not only to their distributive education classes, but also to the art students. It turns out quite a few of the kids are interested in traditional Rio Grande crafts. I think we should go ahead and say yes."

"I think so, too, but one thing at a time. We need to become fully operational again, play catch up and meet our deadlines."

"Of course." She smiled. "I also spoke to the buyer for Traditional Southwest. She said that she trusts us to give her quality merchandise and the delay won't be a problem."

"So Lou Martel of Vintage Lane will be the last call," Myka said, and told her about Grabel and Sons.

"That's great!" Robyn replied.

"It's a start," Myka said, "but we still have a long, hard road ahead."

BY THE END of the next day, all the distributors had accepted new deadlines along with the discounts. HMI's bottom line had taken a hit, but it was one they could weather, especially because they'd been insured. A claim had already been filed, along with extensive photo evidence of the damage, courtesy of the high school students.

Joshua came into her office about three-thirty, just as she was backing up the day's bookkeeping entries. "Everything's working out, isn't it?"

"You bet," she said, updating him on the latest news. Instead of elation, though, Myka saw something else in his expression and a chill ran up her spine. "What's wrong?"

He remained standing, hands clasped behind his back. "I wanted to tell you that the Santa Fe firm I interviewed with has narrowed their selection to five candidates. I made the first cut."

"Sounds great." Her heart sank, but she was determined not to show it.

"Yeah, the projects will be challenging and they pay well, but I'm not so sure I want the job anymore. I'm already doing the kind of work I love. When I look at the restoration projects I designed, I feel like I'm part of this town."

"You are!" Myka said.

"But once those projects have been completed, then what? There isn't enough business here for someone in my profession, not until I make a name for myself."

"Maybe," she said, growing quiet because she didn't want to pressure him. She straightened the folders on her desk and avoided looking at him.

Silence stretched out between them.

"Have you made any plans for Thanksgiving?" he asked at last.

Myka glanced at the calendar. "Ohmigosh. That's *tomorrow*."

"I'll take that as a no."

"I've been so busy here, I just put everything else on hold." She took a breath. "Come over tomorrow and we'll watch some football and have Thanksgiving dinner at my place. What do you say?" She stopped, her eyes widening. "That is, providing I can find a turkey or ham at this late hour."

"The menu won't matter, but we really should celebrate. We both have a lot to be thankful for."

"Okay, then let's get going." She grabbed her purse, called Bear, who'd been sleeping on his bed in the corner, and headed to the door. "If there's one turkey left in this town, we'll find it."

"If all else fails, we can celebrate with turkey TV dinners."

"No, I'm not settling," she said, sticking out her chin. "We're going to find a way to celebrate with a traditional meal worthy of Norman Rockwell."

MYKA AND JOSH visited all the grocery stores within thirty miles of Independence, but there were no turkeys or hams to be had. Out of desperation, she called the local restaurants that would be open for Thanksgiving, but all were booked.

"Sally's Diner in Painted Canyon was almost sure they could find two stools by the counter for us—eventually," she said, putting the phone back into her jacket pocket.

"You were right to turn them down. I'd rather defrost the hamburgers in my freezer and cook them out on the grill. That's really our best option now—short of ambushing a wild turkey, that is," Joshua said.

She looked out the window at the sky. "Come on, please? What's one more miracle?" she asked softly.

Joshua smiled, then glanced back at the dog in the rearview mirror. He was sitting up on the bench seat. "Think Bear can scare up a rabbit for us?"

"No way. He's no hunter. He'd turn vegan if he had to be on his own."

"So that's that."

"We have one shot left," she said, suddenly getting an idea. "Mind you, our chances aren't good, but it's worth a try. Let's go talk to Betty."

They arrived back in town after sundown.

As they pulled up in front of the inn, Betty was just coming down the steps.

"Hey, guys!" she greeted. "I'd invite you in, but I just locked up. I won't have any more guests until Friday, and this weekend we're booked completely."

These days, Betty looked like a new woman. Her smile was brighter, and there was a spring in her step. "That's great news. But I need a favor for tomorrow."

"Name it and it's yours," she said instantly.

"Better wait until you hear," Myka warned with a smile.

"After what you two have done for me, I'll help however I can."

"Remember last fall when you said Will had bagged a wild turkey? You froze it, but you also said that if times were good, you were having ham this year because it's Evie's favorite."

"Which is why tomorrow, Will, Sophie, Evie, Daniel, Grandma and I are having a huge spiral ham. If you haven't made plans…"

Joshua spoke first. "We have, but the problem is we both forgot about the turkey. We're planning a traditional meal—down to the football games. I got this new TV…"

She laughed. "I hear you. Plus it'll be particularly good for both of you to get away from everyone and breathe," she said. "Follow me home and I'll give you the turkey, but it'll be frozen solid. You'll need to put it in a water bath pronto."

"We'll figure it out," Myka said. "And Betty, thanks so much!"

"It should be just the right size for the two of you, but I wouldn't mention that in front of Will. He was so proud, you would have thought it was a five-hundred-pound bird."

THEY WERE ON their way back to Myka's with the turkey a short while later. "If you've really got a new TV, maybe we should put this bird in your sink overnight. I'll bring dessert and fix dinner at your place tomorrow."

"You gonna make one of those pecan pies your mother used to bring over?"

"Yeah, I've got all her recipes and everything I need in the cupboard. I've also got potatoes we can boil up and mash. We'll make it work," she said as he pulled into her driveway.

He reached over and gave her hand a squeeze. "I think that should be our motto."

She laughed. "I'll see you tomorrow. And don't forget to dress up for dinner—cowboy style. Your best boots, jeans and maybe that leather vest."

"I like the way you think." He leaned over and gave her a quick kiss.

As he drew back, his gaze stayed on hers a moment, and Myka sensed that he was troubled.

"Something else is on your mind. What is it?"

He shook his head. "I'm not ready to talk about it yet," he said.

"Then when?"

"I'll let you know."

ONCE HE WAS back home, Joshua watched through the window as Myka fed the sheep then hurried back into her house. If he took the job in Santa Fe, he'd be leaving a piece of his heart behind.

Joshua expelled his breath in a hiss as he looked around the house. It had been emptied of clutter and rearranged to suit his needs, but it was still far from the kind of home he'd envisioned for himself. Yet he was happy here and there was a lot to be said for that.

Adam Nez had switched dreams and never looked back. Maybe it was time for him to take a good long look at himself and figure out what he really wanted. He was no longer the same man who'd left for college bent on taking the world by storm.

Hearing a knock on the door, he went to answer it and found Daniel waiting there.

"Saw your truck and figured you might like company," he said, holding up a six-pack.

"Come in. Any friend bearing brews is welcome. Want a glass to go with those?"

"You're kidding, right?"

Joshua walked over to the fireplace and stacked kindling to build a fire while Dan went to the kitchen for a bottle opener.

"The one thing about Dad's place is that the heating system's not that efficient. Without a wood fire, the place gets cold," Joshua said. "He'd intended to put in a wood pellet insert once he got too old to chop wood."

Daniel nodded, silently handing Josh an opened bottle.

He didn't disturb the silence that fell between them as he lit the fire. It was clear that something was troubling Daniel.

"I don't know how I got roped into this," he said at long last, taking a swallow of beer.

"What's up?" Joshua stepped back from the hearth.

"You know Betty and I are friends, right?"

"Yeah," he said, then grinned. "You here to ask me to be your best man?" He held up the bottle in a mock toast.

Daniel choked but still clinked bottles with him. "Man, we're nowhere near that, not yet. I came to talk about *you*."

"And Betty?" Josh stared at him. "You want *me* to ask her out?"

"Will you shut up for a second and just listen, bro? I'm here 'cause I promised Betty I'd talk to you." He took a breath. "She's worried about Myka, and maybe she's onto something. Is it true you interviewed for a job earlier this week?"

Joshua raised his eyebrows. "How did you—" He smiled and nodded once. "I get it. I remember seeing Grandma at the gas station and she commented on my suit and tie. I never told her where I was going, but I guess I didn't need to."

"Nothing stays secret around here," Daniel said. "Here's the thing. I've known you for a long time, and these past few months you've been happier than I can ever remember. So why are you still hunting for a job elsewhere? Myka needs you here."

Joshua shook his head. "She can handle the company without me. It's her dream," he said. "Being an architect is part of who I am. Work here, though satisfying, will be far from steady."

"Is nothing else important to you right now?"

"What do you mean?"

"Are you in love with Myka?"

"Yeah, and she knows it."

"So you've told her?" Dan asked.

"Once."

"Maybe she needs to be reminded."

"Maybe," Joshua said, unconvinced. "But if I relocate, the most I could give her is a long-distance relationship." He paused, added a log to the fire, then continued. "Myka knew I'd leave someday and she's not interested in anything permanent. She's never asked me to stay."

"I hear you, but women are really strange about stuff like this. They reason things out differently. Perhaps she's been hinting and you haven't been listening close enough. Or maybe she's waiting for you to say something more."

"I doubt that. You know Myka—she speaks her mind."

"In business, yes, but this is personal. You're walking onto emotional territory, and when that happens, all the rules go out the window," he said. "You need to think hard about what you're doing or not doing. You could end up blowing everything."

Joshua sighed. "I'll see how things go tomorrow."

"You don't really want to leave town—leave Myka—do you?"

"You ask too many questions," Joshua said, but he grinned to soften his words. "Now get going with the rest of that beer before you get roped into helping me clean this place. Myka's fixing Thanksgiving dinner, but we're eating here."

"Your new TV wouldn't have anything to do with that, would it?" he asked, pointing.

"Yeah, but sharing dinner was her idea."

"Likely story," Dan said, heading to the door.

"Have a good holiday," Joshua said.

"Grandma Medeiros and I will be joining Betty and her family, so I've got what I want. Figure out what *you* want before it passes you by. A guy's got to grab what he can before it's out of reach."

As Daniel walked off, Joshua considered what his friend had said. There'd been a time in his life when he'd wanted it all—but his definition of "all" had changed.

After straightening out the den, which didn't take long because he'd already gone through the place twice, he decided to take a break. Trying to sort out his thinking, he lay back in the easy chair and watched the football recap for the current season. He took a long swallow of the cold one in his hand and put his boots up on the hassock.

He'd left town to become an architect and pursue his goals. He'd wanted to create a legacy—something that would continue long after him. He'd imagined becoming a twenty-first-century Native American Frank Lloyd Wright, at least.

Then that chapter of his life had ended and he'd been forced to return home with his tail between his legs. Despite that debacle, he'd turned things around and had ended up achieving what he'd wanted, though admittedly, in a way he'd never expected.

He pictured the facelift he'd given Main Street, and the other buildings being renovated with his stamp on them. He'd left to find a legacy, but maybe it had been here all along.

CHAPTER TWENTY

BY THE FOLLOWING AFTERNOON, the turkey was still frozen solid. Myka stood at Joshua's sink, staring down at it. She tapped it with her knuckles and it felt as hard as a cinder block. Clearly, things were moving a lot slower than they'd planned.

"Guess we should have thawed it in hot water," he commented.

"It's too late for that," she said and sighed. "The good news is that we now have a Christmas turkey."

"We could try to microwave it for a while, or heat up some oil in a kettle and fry it on the grill out back," he suggested.

She laughed. "No, I don't want to set fire to your house. I've had enough smoke and flames to last me a lifetime. Let me browse through your refrigerator for ideas."

"Good luck. At least we've still got dressing, mashed potatoes, salad and pies. How about a vegetarian Thanksgiving?"

"Hold on," she said, looking inside his fridge. "I just found a packet of turkey hot dogs."

"Yeah, I picked those up by mistake. I had a craving for a good old-fashioned grilled hot dog. Then I realized I'd bought something for the calorie counters. In my book, turkey dogs are one step above soy burgers."

"Well, at least we'll have turkey represented on our plates. Let's go back to my place to eat, then come here to watch the game and have dessert. What do you say?"

"Sure. But why eat at your place?"

"If we can't have a turkey bird, I want to use my great-grandmother's china. What's actually on the plate won't matter as much then—the china will make all the difference. Mind you, it's not expensive or fancy. The bottom says, Made in Hungary so I don't know how or where she got them. But Grandma valued them. She brought the entire set from Maine as part of her trousseau."

"I never saw you as the type of person who needs a formal setting."

"I'm not, but I do like having those plates around. They've traveled more than I have. Can you imagine all the places they've seen?"

"Is that what you want to do someday—travel?"

"I think I would," she said. "There was a time when even the thought of leaving home terrified me. I didn't like change of any kind. Things seemed perfect just the way they were."

"And now?"

"I'm thinking I might like going off on an adventure every once in a while. I can handle it."

"You've met a lot of challenges over at HMI. That builds confidence."

"It does," she said.

"HMI has taught me a lot, too. I'm still waiting to hear about that Santa Fe job, but if I don't get the position, I'm going to take it as a sign that this is where I belong. I have some great options here in Independence and people I love. Between my new salary at HMI and what I make working for the town, I'd have enough to open my own architectural firm. It's bound to be rough going, so before I commit to that, there's something I need to know."

He took a deep breath, thinking of Daniel's advice. The first time he'd said he loved her, it had come so naturally, right from the heart. Why was it so hard to say now? "Myka, I—"

At that precise minute Bear put his front paws up on the counter and made a grab at the frozen turkey in the sink.

"No!" Myka yelled. "You thief!" Laughing, she pulled the dog down by his collar. "Go outside," she ordered, opening the back door.

The dog looked over his shoulder with the equivalent of an apology, then slunk outside.

"Sorry, Josh, I didn't mean to interrupt, but I think I know what you were trying to say."

"You do?" he asked, almost relieved.

"You want to follow your own dream, but you need to know if you'll have support from the people around you," she said. "The answer is yes, of course you will. We're on your side no matter what happens."

She looked at the clock. "Right now, we better get on the move if we're going to have Thanksgiving dinner before the game starts."

He'd intended to tell her how he felt and take his chances, but the moment had passed. Besides, she could have preempted him on purpose, not wanting to ruin the day. She loved him, but maybe it was more like the deep affection one felt for a close friend.

"Okay, let's work on that awesome Thanksgiving experience."

"One of a kind," she said.

THEY GRILLED THE hot dogs outside on Myka's back patio, ate using the china, then returned to Joshua's house to watch the football game.

"This wasn't exactly a traditional Thanksgiving, but I don't think I've ever had more fun," Myka said, sitting next to Josh on his couch and eating a slice of pecan pie practically smothered in whipped cream.

"Me, neither," he said.

As the team captains met on the fifty-yard line for the coin toss, Myka walked over to her tote bag, resting on the floor in the corner. She put on her favorite NFL team's ball cap, then looked up. "Now I'm ready. Get this game underway!"

She was the perfect woman for him. He couldn't just let her go. Without a second thought, Joshua wrapped his arms around her, pulling her against him. "I love you, Myka," he said, then lowered his mouth to hers, kissing her deeply.

As he drew back to take a breath, she nuzzled against him.

"I love you, too, Joshua, just as you are—no demands, no expectations," she whispered.

He looked into her eyes. Was this her way of being careful with her heart?

"We all make demands—even if they're unspoken," he said.

"There are certain commitments that can't be asked for or rushed. They're freely given—or not." She met his gaze and smiled. "It's a perfect day and we're together. Let's be grateful for that."

The television crowd roared in preparation for the kickoff.

"Okay, I take it back—one demand." She grinned impishly. "No more sweet talk until halftime."

THE NEXT EIGHT DAYS went by quickly. Josh had finished the remaining restoration plans for all the buildings he'd been assigned to evaluate, including both structures on the Brooks estate.

He sat in the reception area outside of Mayor Allen's office, waiting. It had been two months since he'd first interviewed for the Santa Fe position, but he'd broken through the pack. It was now between him and one other architect.

That possibility had brought him to the mayor's office today. He needed to know if he still had viable options here in Independence, job opportunities that would allow him to turn down the Santa Fe position, assuming it was offered to him. If he was going to start a relationship with Myka, he wanted to be able to "provide for her," in the words of his father's generation.

After a few minutes, Phil invited Joshua into his office, and Joshua laid it on the line. He needed to know what his chances were of finding permanent work here in town—as an architect.

"The town needs you and your skills, Joshua," he said. "Remember the documentary the local high school students made? They posted it on the internet this past weekend and titled it *The Little Town That Could*. It went viral, and the largest paper in New Mexico is coming by tonight to cover our rebirth and the lighting of our tree. So are two of the local TV network affiliates. We're on the map again!" he said proudly. "Robyn's passing the news along to Myka as we speak."

"That's wonderful," Josh said, although he couldn't see how that would create jobs for him.

"The buzz has started. I've been getting

phone calls all morning. With our low tax rate, available properties, trained work force and low cost of living, several companies have approached my office about relocating here. The fact that rail service will be reinstated soon is icing on the cake," he said.

Joshua smiled. "That's great news for the town...."

"And for you, too. The bottom line is that more of the buildings here will have to be renovated to fit in with the historical theme of the town. New housing will also be needed to accommodate additional families. I expect most, if not all, of the former IVA buildings will be converted to suit new employers. You could be a part of all that."

Yet the mayor had still not made him a firm offer. "I'll keep it in mind before I consider any out-of-town positions," Josh said, a little disappointed.

"Call me before you actually accept any jobs outside of Independence. Maybe I can come up with something on my own. Right now, I've got to get going. Old Bobby Miller's bringing in a fifteen-foot blue spruce for the tree lighting."

"He still has the tree farm?"

"Yes. Personally, I don't know how he

makes ends meet, but I was told his business is growing, too, pardon the pun. A lot of the merchants in town and over in Painted Canyon have ordered trees." Mayor Allen stood. "I'll see you again this evening, right? And bring Myka."

"I will," Joshua said and shook his hand.

Joshua walked outside, and squaring his shoulders, looked down the street toward HMI. What he wanted most was right here. It was time to step up.

MYKA STARED AT ROBYN. "Really? *Viral?*"

"The first day they put it up, it got a huge number of hits, and by the end of the week, it had skyrocketed. Let me show you," she said, moving the computer mouse.

Hearing a knock on the door, Myka glanced past Robyn and saw Mayor Allen standing there.

"Myka, I need a few minutes of your time," he said.

"I'll get back to my desk and show you that video later," Robyn said, standing. "I'm trying to set up web seminars on wool processing. I listed some possibilities on the website to gauge the level of interest and got a terrific response."

As Robyn left, Myka waved at Mayor Allen. "Please, sit down. Can I offer you some coffee or maybe tea?"

"Coffee," he said with a nod. "I'm here because I need to do a little brainstorming with you. It's about Joshua Nez."

"I'm listening," she said, going to the pot in the corner and pouring two cups.

JOSHUA STOPPED BY the Medeiros Market and found Daniel carrying three cases of canned soda from the storeroom.

"You need a hand?" he asked.

"Yeah, as a matter of fact," Daniel said. "Wanna grab the top case?"

After they'd restocked the shelves, Daniel looked up at Josh. "Come on, bro, you've earned a cream soda. It's on the house." He led the way to the break area in the back.

Moments later, Daniel handed Joshua a can from the small fridge and joined him at the table. "So how are things going?"

Joshua told Daniel the latest about the job in Santa Fe, then added, "I've decided to pull my application. I don't want to walk away and risk losing Myka."

"If that's the only reason you're going to pass on that big job, don't," Grandma said, coming into the room with a platter of cookies covered in powdered sugar. She held out the plate, and each man took a cookie instantly. "Stay because you love her, not because you're afraid to lose her. That might seem like the right answer now, but ten or twenty years down the pike, you may feel differently."

"I've thought long and hard about this, Grandma. The truth is that nothing means as much to me as Myka," Joshua said. "I've made my decision and that's why I'm off to Painted Canyon, but I needed to ask you two something first. Who's going to set out the luminarias tonight?" Josh had always loved this particular Southwestern tradition. Paper sacks were weighed down by sand and turned into Christmas lanterns with a votive candle. Each year, they were placed in a circle around the tree for the town's tree-lighting ceremony.

"That's Walt Driscoll's job," Daniel said and pointed to an elderly man placing bundles of paper sacks into his shopping cart. "There he is now."

"I've got to run. Catch you later," Joshua said.

IT WAS PAST SUNDOWN on the first weekend in December. Tonight their town would officially welcome the Christmas season. Joshua finished getting dressed and glanced at his image in the mirror. He was wearing his lucky bolo tie—the one his dad had given him before he'd left for college. On the slide, crafted out of inlaid turquoise, was a bear, the best of allies when facing uncertain times.

He took a deep breath. No matter how things turned out, the course of his life would change forever.

He took the white box from the dresser and placed it in his pocket. It was cold out tonight, in the high thirties, so he wore his black leather jacket. No chill ever penetrated that, and tonight he wanted no distractions.

He was on his way to the door when he heard a loud knock, the sound of several voices, then one above the others telling everyone to shush.

Back in his teens, he would have suspected a group of ticked off parents at the door, but those days were long gone. Maybe carolers? Nah, not tonight, they'd be at the town square.

He opened the door and found a small crowd. Along with Myka, Mayor Allen, Will, Robyn, Betty and Daniel were faces he quickly recognized as town council members.

"What's going on? Is the party at my house tonight?" he joked.

Myka smiled, shook her head, but didn't answer.

"We've come to the unanimous decision that the town of Independence needs you," the mayor said. "Please hear us out."

"Well, then, come inside," he said, inviting them into his living room. "I don't have enough chairs, but I can brew some coffee. Anyone?" he asked, looking at the faces around him.

"No, let's get right down to business. If you'll take the position of town architect, we'll give you the salary and benefits equal to that of our highest paid town employee," he said, looking back at Will, who rolled his eyes.

Joshua bit back a smile and nodded, considering it.

"I know that's still not much—sorry, Will—so we're ready to lease you the Brooks Mansion for a dollar a year for the next five years. You can set up your own business office there, too, if you'd like. At the end of the lease, you'll be free to buy the place from the town at market value or continue leasing. We'll also structure your work contract with us so you can be free to accept private architectural or consulting jobs, too, as long as they don't interfere with your projects for us."

"That's an incredibly generous offer," Joshua said, looking around and seeing everyone nodding their heads, except Will, of course, whose face was completely unreadable.

Only one problem remained. Staying, to him, meant a future with Myka. He needed to show her what was in his heart and see how she felt about a serious commitment. If she pulled back, he'd have his answer and wouldn't stick around.

Seeing Joshua hesitate, Mayor Allen quickly added, "We know there are a few loose ends in the package, so feel free to give us your answer later. We just wanted to put this on the table so you knew where you stood with our community."

Joshua saw the mayor glance at Daniel, who nodded. That one look spoke volumes. Somehow, word was out that he intended to talk to Myka tonight. Maybe Mr. Driscoll had given Grandma the details. Keeping a secret in Independence was impossible.

"Come on, people, stick to the schedule. We need to get back for the lighting of the tree," Robyn said. "There's a network TV crew and reporters coming in from Albuquerque to film this event!"

Myka remained behind with Joshua as the others hurried to their vehicles. "Is it just me, Joshua, or are people acting really peculiar tonight?" Myka asked. "I'm not talking about the offer. I think that's terrific."

"It is, but we'll talk about that later," he said. "Let's get over to the town square."

"Why the hurry? The tree ceremony doesn't start for another forty minutes. The luminarias will have to be lit first."

"That's exactly why we have to get there early. Come on, you can ride with me," he said, urging her outside.

"Oh, you want to help light the luminarias?"

"Yeah, I was hoping you would, too. Walt Driscoll's back is giving him some trouble, so I offered to help him put the candles out."

"Sure. It'll help us get into the Christmas spirit."

THEY ARRIVED AT the town square less than ten minutes later. To Myka's surprise, almost everyone was already there, but the crowd was standing back. "Why isn't anyone helping Mr.

Driscoll? What's the matter with everyone?" Myka paused. "Wait a minute. Why is everyone looking at *us?*"

"Maybe they're trying to figure out what my answer to the mayor will be," he said, thinking fast.

"Yeah, that must be it. Come on. I'll help you light the luminarias. I've always liked that part."

"I know," he said with a smile. "I remember how you'd get our entire neighborhood to line the streets with them every Christmas Eve."

"We still light the town square on the twenty-fourth. These luminarias are just to remind everyone that our traditions are a blend of old and new."

As they approached the small paper sacks, Myka saw the TV crew up ahead. "Our town's in the spotlight," she said. "We've come such a long way!"

As the mayor announced the beginning of the festivities, Joshua moved off and returned a moment later, a box of votive candles in his hand. "Come on. We'll start in front of the tree and work our way around."

Moments later, Myka took the candle Joshua gave her and went to the sack closest to her. As she reached in, she saw a white box atop the layer of sand within.

"Oh, someone's left—" She saw Joshua smile.

"Look inside the box," Joshua suggested.

It was too large to hold a ring. Excited and curious, she did as he'd asked. Nestled in a bed of cotton was a gold heart-shaped locket.

"Open it, then you'll see what's in my heart," Joshua whispered, coming closer.

Scarcely breathing, she opened the locket with trembling fingers. Inside was the drawing of a ring—a carved band with an inscription that read Everlasting.

"Those will be made for us, matching wedding bands...if you say yes." Joshua went down on one knee. "Will you be my bride?"

Tears filled her eyes. "Yes," she whispered past the lump at her throat. "Yes, yes, yes!"

As Joshua helped her fasten the locket around her neck, their friends began lighting the luminarias. The tree lights came on minutes later, and pinpoints of light danced in the darkness. The townspeople began to sing "Silent Night."

Joshua pulled her gently into his arms. "We belong to each other now," he whispered. "Merry Christmas, Myka."

She rested her head against his chest and listened to the steady beat of his heart. "Merry Christmas, Joshua."

* * * * *

REQUEST YOUR FREE BOOKS!

2 FREE INSPIRATIONAL NOVELS
PLUS 2
FREE
MYSTERY GIFTS

Love Inspired®

YES! Please send me 2 FREE Love Inspired® novels and my 2 FREE mystery gifts (gifts are worth about $10). After receiving them, if I don't wish to receive any more books, I can return the shipping statement marked "cancel." if I don't cancel, I will receive 6 brand-new novels every month and be billed just $4.74 per book in the U.S. or $5.24 per book in Canada. That's a savings of at least 21% off the cover price. It's quite a bargain! Shipping and handling is just 50¢ per book in the U.S. and 75¢ per book in Canada.* I understand that accepting the 2 free books and gifts places me under no obligation to buy anything. I can always return a shipment and cancel at any time. Even if I never buy another book, the two free books and gifts are mine to keep forever.

105/305 IDN F49N

Name _____ (PLEASE PRINT) _____

Address _____ Apt. # _____

City _____ State/Prov. _____ Zip/Postal Code _____

Signature (if under 18, a parent or guardian must sign) _____

Mail to the **Harlequin® Reader Service:**
IN U.S.A.: P.O. Box 1867, Buffalo, NY 14240-1867
IN CANADA: P.O. Box 609, Fort Erie, Ontario L2A 5X3

**Are you a subscriber to Love Inspired books
and want to receive the larger-print edition?
Call 1-800-873-8635 or visit www.ReaderService.com.**

* Terms and prices subject to change without notice. Prices do not include applicable taxes. Sales tax applicable in N.Y. Canadian residents will be charged applicable taxes. Offer not valid in Quebec. This offer is limited to one order per household. Not valid for current subscribers to Love Inspired books. All orders subject to credit approval. Credit or debit balances in a customer's account(s) may be offset by any other outstanding balance owed by or to the customer. Please allow 4 to 6 weeks for delivery. Offer available while quantities last.

Your Privacy—The Harlequin® Reader Service is committed to protecting your privacy. Our Privacy Policy is available online at www.ReaderService.com or upon request from the Harlequin Reader Service.
We make a portion of our mailing list available to reputable third parties that offer products we believe may interest you. If you prefer that we not exchange your name with third parties, or if you wish to clarify or modify your communication preferences, please visit us at www.ReaderService.com/consumerchoice or write to us at Harlequin Reader Service Preference Service, P.O. Box 9062, Buffalo, NY 14269. Include your complete name and address.

LIDIR13R

REQUEST YOUR FREE BOOKS!

2 FREE INSPIRATIONAL NOVELS
PLUS 2
FREE
MYSTERY GIFTS

Love Inspired

HISTORICAL
INSPIRATIONAL HISTORICAL ROMANCE

YES! Please send me 2 FREE Love Inspired® Historical novels and my 2 FREE mystery gifts (gifts are worth about $10). After receiving them, if I don't wish to receive any more books, I can return the shipping statement marked "cancel." If I don't cancel, I will receive 4 brand-new novels every month and be billed just $4.74 per book in the U.S. or $5.24 per book in Canada. That's a savings of at least 21% off the cover price. It's quite a bargain! Shipping and handling is just 50¢ per book in the U.S. and 75¢ per book in Canada.* I understand that accepting the 2 free books and gifts places me under no obligation to buy anything. I can always return a shipment and cancel at any time. Even if I never buy another book, the two free books and gifts are mine to keep forever.

102/302 IDN F5CY

Name	(PLEASE PRINT)

Address	Apt. #

City	State/Prov.	Zip/Postal Code

Signature (if under 18, a parent or guardian must sign)

Mail to the **Harlequin® Reader Service:**
IN U.S.A.: P.O. Box 1867, Buffalo, NY 14240-1867
IN CANADA: P.O. Box 609, Fort Erie, Ontario L2A 5X3

Want to try two free books from another series?
Call 1-800-873-8635 or visit www.ReaderService.com.

* Terms and prices subject to change without notice. Prices do not include applicable taxes. Sales tax applicable in N.Y. Canadian residents will be charged applicable taxes. Offer not valid in Quebec. This offer is limited to one order per household. Not valid for current subscribers to Love Inspired Historical books. All orders subject to credit approval. Credit or debit balances in a customer's account(s) may be offset by any other outstanding balance owed by or to the customer. Please allow 4 to 6 weeks for delivery. Offer available while quantities last.

Your Privacy—The Harlequin® Reader Service is committed to protecting your privacy. Our Privacy Policy is available online at www.ReaderService.com or upon request from the Harlequin Reader Service.

We make a portion of our mailing list available to reputable third parties that offer products we believe may interest you. If you prefer that we not exchange your name with third parties, or if you wish to clarify or modify your communication preferences, please visit us at www.ReaderService.com/consumerchoice or write to us at Harlequin Reader Service Preference Service, P.O. Box 9062, Buffalo, NY 14269. Include your complete name and address.

LIHDIR13R

REQUEST YOUR FREE BOOKS!

2 FREE CHRISTIAN NOVELS
PLUS 2
FREE
MYSTERY GIFTS

HEARTSONG
PRESENTS

YES! Please send me 2 Free Heartsong Presents novels and my 2 FREE mystery gifts (gifts are worth about $10). After receiving them, if I don't wish to receive any more books I can return the shipping statement marked "cancel." If I don't cancel, I will receive 4 brand-new novels every month and be billed just $4.24 per book in the U.S. and $5.24 per book in Canada. That's a savings of at least 20% off the cover price. It's quite a bargain! Shipping and handling is just 50¢ per book in the U.S. and 75¢ per book in Canada.* I understand that accepting the 2 free books and gifts places me under no obligation to buy anything. I can always return a shipment and cancel at any time. Even if I never buy another book, the two free books and gifts are mine to keep forever.

159/359 HDN FVYK

Name _____ (PLEASE PRINT)

Address _____ Apt. #

City _____ State _____ Zip

Signature (if under 18, a parent or guardian must sign)

Mail to the **Harlequin® Reader Service:**
IN U.S.A.: P.O. Box 1867, Buffalo, NY 14240-1867

* Terms and prices subject to change without notice. Prices do not include applicable taxes. Sales tax applicable in N.Y. This offer is limited to one order per household. Not valid for current subscribers to Heartsong Presents books. All orders subject to credit approval. Credit or debit balances in a customer's account(s) may be offset by any other outstanding balance owed by or to the customer. Please allow 4 to 6 weeks for delivery. Offer available while quantities last. Offer valid only in the U.S.

HSPDIR13

ReaderService.com

Manage your account online!

- Review your order history
- Manage your payments
- Update your address

> *We've designed*
> *the Harlequin® Reader Service*
> *website just for you.*

Enjoy all the features!

- Reader excerpts from any series
- Respond to mailings and special monthly offers
- Discover new series available to you
- Browse the Bonus Bucks catalog
- Share your feedback

Visit us at:
ReaderService.com